THE WAY BACK TO YOU

Bianca Lee Sharp

Published by Bianca Lee Sharp

ISBN: 978-1-7643866-0-9

Editing and cover design by The Sharp Edit

To my girls,
Never be afraid to step out of your comfort
zone and chase those dreams xx

CONTENTS

BIANCA LEE SHARP

ONE

Chelsea

The toaster jammed, again.

Chelsea Carter smacked the side of the ancient thing with her hand, swearing softly under her breath as her youngest daughter, Olivia, sang loudly and off-key to a cartoon in the living room. The smell of burnt bread drifted through the kitchen, and somewhere down the hallway, her husband's electric razor buzzed, setting the soundtrack of yet another forgettable weekday morning.

"Mum! Lucy changed the channel again!" Chelsea heard her youngest daughter, Olivia, call from the living room.

Chelsea closed her eyes for three seconds. Breathe in, breathe out. She sighed, then yelled back, "Come on, girls, sort it out and pick something you both like, please!"

Chelsea heard footsteps before the negotiations on what to watch began. She turned her attention back to the over-cooked toast; she considered for a moment if she could scrape off the burnt parts to make it acceptable for the two small critics who still hadn't decided on a cartoon to watch. Chelsea sighed as she put two fresh pieces of bread into the toaster and dropped the burnt pieces onto her own plate. It wasn't worth the argument, trying to convince the girls that they wouldn't die because their toast was slightly darker than they expected. Chelsea barely tasted her own breakfast these days. Between school lunches, lost school hats, and trying to get out the door to make it to school on time, mornings had become more of a survival sport.

Ryan walked into the kitchen as she was buttering her toast, already dressed and ready for work, wearing an expression that Chelsea had been seeing more of lately. The one where it looked like he wanted to be anywhere but here. Her husband was a good-looking guy, ageing gracefully. He had sandy blonde hair that was always maintained and styled. He took pride in his appearance, sometimes more than she did, always maintaining a clean-shaven look and dressing well. This was something Chelsea was drawn to from the moment they met. Perhaps because she was always sporting the hot mess kind of vibe, or maybe it was because he was entirely different to the type she went for in the past. One downside to his good looks was that Ryan often caught the attention of other women when they were out. Even more so if he happened to be dressed in his scrubs at work. A hot young doctor was a dream for some women.

"Have you seen my new scrubs?" He asked, without looking at her, as he picked out a banana from the fruit bowl on the kitchen bench.

"No, I washed them so they should be hanging up in the wardrobe." She replied.

He paused just long enough to let the silence stretch, then he picked up his coffee travel mug and car keys from the bench. As he walked past, he leaned in slightly to brush a kiss on Chelsea's cheek, so light it was barely there, before saying goodbye to the girls and leaving out the front door.

Chelsea stared at the spot where he'd stood, long after the sound of the front door closing echoed through the house. Their whole marriage felt like that lately. Like trying to remember the shape of something or someone that used to be there. There was once a time when they hated leaving each other, when every kiss goodbye would leave them wanting more, eager to get back to each other at the end of the day. Chelsea couldn't remember when it stopped feeling like that and when it just became routine. She couldn't remember when they stopped being them.

Chelsea had met Ryan not long after she had finished high school. She was still figuring out what she wanted to do with her life at the time, but had been accepted into university to study for a teaching degree. That was until a tall blonde guy swept her off her feet. At a house party, of all places. So maybe it wasn't the most romantic setting, but when Ryan and his friends entered the party thrown by some other guys who were a couple of years older than Chelsea, she was instantly drawn to them. Chelsea's one and only boyfriend before Ryan was a guy she had gone to high school with. When she met Ryan that night at the party, she was still very much in the depths of her high school sweetheart heartbreak, but Ryan gave her attention. And as a fresh nineteen-year-old who had just had her heart ripped out, some attention and fun was exactly what she needed. So, they partied the night away together, and then they never really left each other's side again. Ryan had grown up a few towns over and was a couple of years older than Chelsea, so they had never crossed paths before. In the early days of their relationship, they had to balance the honeymoon stage with Ryan's busy schedule as he was two years into medical school. This meant they had to take turns visiting each other when their schedules lined up. All the while, Chelsea was working towards going to university herself and figuring out what her life goals looked like. It was something that was supposed to be a rebound for her. A bit of fun to get over her heartbreak. But as always, life doesn't care for plans, and before they knew it, their relationship was forced to become very serious, very quickly.

The pop of the toaster brought Chelsea back to the present as she thanked God that the toast was up to the standard of the girls. She glanced at the clock as she buttered the toast.

8:23 am.

"Girls! Shoes on, please! Now!" she shouted, while flinging the buttered toast onto the plates for the girls to eat on the drive to school. She shoved her burnt toast into her mouth as she grabbed the plates, school bags, keys and phone on her way to the front door.

Chelsea had dreamt of being a mum for as long as she could remember. She was always the kid who would pester her friends to play mums and dads, and then quickly announce that she was the mum. She knew it was what she wanted most in life, and although having children at a young age had been difficult, being a mum had always come naturally to her. These chaotic school mornings were usually a breeze for her. But lately, she had started counting the minutes until they were over. She had started feeling overwhelmed with her life, but she was struggling to figure out what had changed.

The drive to school from their house wasn't very long, but as usual, it was filled with Taylor Swift and a whole lot of bickering. It seemed that Chelsea wasn't the only one feeling overwhelmed by the mundane weekday tasks. After walking the girls to their classrooms, since kiss-and-drop was still a dream Olivia had made clear would not be a reality anytime soon, Chelsea got back into the car and sat in silence for a minute. She should have driven straight to the gym, as she usually does after school drop-off, or made a start on her never-ending to-do list, but instead, she just sat with herself and her thoughts for the first time in what felt like forever. Very quickly, her thoughts drifted to her husband and their relationship. They had always been solid. Sure, they may not have always had the overwhelming spark that people seem to chase, but Ryan had always been consistent. They had always been honest with each other and had pretty good communication when it came to their feelings, so what was going on now had Chelsea baffled. How did they get here? Was this just a rough patch, or was this something more? Before she could continue her thoughts, her phone buzzed in the centre console of her car.

Facetime call from: Emily ♥ Old School Crew

Chelsea stared at the screen and smiled for the first time that morning —Emily Matthews, her ride-or-die from high school, her person, and her confidant. There was a group of them who, despite all going off in different directions, had managed to stay close all these years later. Chelsea loved all her girls, but she and Emily had always had a bond that ran deeper. More like a sister relationship. They had met on the first day of high school after Emily and her family moved to the town. Emily sat next to Chelsea in the first lesson of the day. When they were ten minutes into the lesson, a Justin Bieber ringtone came blaring from Emily's school bag. Instantly, they clicked over their Bieber fever, and before long, they had formed their group of girlfriends. Chelsea and Emily's parents got along well, so eventually their families began spending time together on weekends, which meant the girls spent even more time together. Although both girls had moved from their hometown and no longer lived close by, they made sure to speak most days and catch up in person whenever they could.

Chelsea answered the video call. "You're calling before 9 am, so either you're pregnant or engaged." She said sarcastically as her best friend's face filled the screen.

Emily laughed. "Bingo. Option B. I said yes last night." She said, holding up her left hand that was now sporting a huge diamond.

Chelsea's eyes widened, and she almost had to physically close her mouth, which was hanging open. "Wait...Dean proposed? Like Dean Dean?"

"Sure did," Emily confirmed, her voice and face oozing with happiness. "And before you start freaking out, the engagement party is next weekend, and you have to come. We're doing it back home."

Chelsea tensed. "Back in Somerdale?"

"Yep. Dean's parents are hosting. You can bring the kids. It'll be like a big high school reunion, even Jake is back in town for it."

Chelsea felt herself holding her breath. Emily kept talking, but Chelsea didn't hear a thing.

Jake.

The name hit her like a skipped heartbeat.

"Sorry, let's circle back to that. Did you say Jake's going?" She asked, trying to sound breezy.

"Yeah," Emily said casually, but not casually enough. "He is back in town helping his dad for a bit, and obviously Dean wants his best friend there, and so do I. So don't worry, it won't be weird. Unless it is. In which case, I'll keep the champagne flowing." She said with a smirk.

Chelsea managed a laugh, though her mind was already drifting, not to Jake as he was now, but to the boy he'd been. The first boy for Chelsea. The one who made her believe in always.

The boy she had first loved. The boy she had planned to spend her life with. The one who had broken her heart.

"I'll come," she said finally. "It'll be fun to see everyone and a good excuse to see mum and dad as well."

Emily squealed, "Yay, I am so happy! I will text you the details, and we can get planning."

Chelsea smiled, "Can't wait, and hey Em?" She continued, "I am very happy for you and Hotshots."

Emily laughed, "Thanks, Chels, love you."

As Chelsea ended the call, she stared out into the empty parking lot, something heavy stirring in her chest. She tried to tell herself it was just nerves about going back to her hometown for the first time in years.

But she knew deep down that it had more to do with the fact that she would have to see the boy who had broken her heart for the first time in over a decade.

~

The rest of the day went by in a blur, like always. Chelsea's usual mornings consisted of heading to the gym after the school run, picking up a coffee from her favourite cafe, before heading home to pick up their beloved family dog, a black Labrador named Crumpet (obviously named by their 4-year-old at the time), to go for a walk along the beach.

They lived in a coastal town in the northern end of Australia, Port Mac, which meant the beach was always just down the road.

Not long after he and Chelsea had met, Ryan was offered a job at a hospital in Port Mac. It would mean his foot would be in the door when it came to him finishing medical school and applying for internships. They both were madly in love and couldn't stand the thought of being hours away from each other, so Chelsea packed up her life and moved to be with him. A year later, they were surprised to find out they were expecting their first child, Lucy. She arrived on her due date, born wide-eyed and peaceful. She slept and ate like a dream, completely throwing them into a false sense of reality. A few years later, their parenting got put to the test when Olivia came flying into the world. She was nearly two weeks overdue when she was forced out. Despite not wanting to come out, once labour started, it escalated very quickly and dramatically. Chelsea had always thought her entrance into the world was just a taste of her personality that was to come. While her sister was quiet, observant, and felt things deeply, Olivia was loud, wild, and so stubborn.

Because of the nature of Ryan's job and the unpredictability of his shifts, Chelsea had always been the stay-at-home parent. It was important to her that the girls had stability in those early years, and her decision to stay home provided that. But now that both girls were in school, going back to work was something Chelsea had been thinking more and more about. When Chelsea and Ryan moved before having the girls, Chelsea tried to keep up her university studies mostly online. However, once Lucy was born, she deferred the course with the hope of returning once she was out of the depths of the newborn bubble. That was eight years ago now, and she had never gone back.

Chelsea's thoughts started to wander to Emily and Dean's engagement party as she walked along the beach with Crumpet and a takeaway coffee. To going back home to Somerdale.

It shamed Chelsea to say that she had hardly returned to that town since she had packed up and left with Ryan all those years ago. Her parents and younger sister, Chloe, still lived in Somerdale, but Ryan and Chelsea had a decent-sized house, so her family often came to stay with them to spend time with Lucy and Olivia. Because of that, there hadn't been much of a need to go back to Somerdale. And if she was being completely honest, she was scared to go back. Scared to have to face everything she had left behind. It felt like that place was tainted with pain and heartbreak.

After a long walk along the beach with Crumpet, Chelsea returned home slightly sun-kissed and sandy to continue her to-do list for the day. She admired her beautiful weatherboard coastal home as she pulled into the driveway, Crumpet puffing in her ear from the backseat. They had done well for themselves despite being thrust into parenthood so early. Ryan had landed a job at the local hospital while he was finishing medical school to support them financially, while Chelsea was off work with their baby. He then secured his internship at the Port Mac hospital, where he had already been working, and once his internship was up, they went on to offer him a spot in their residency program, which is where he is now. His next step is to apply for surgical training to pursue his goal of becoming a paediatric surgeon. With all of this study and training came very long hours, which meant Chelsea had put her dreams and career on pause so that she could hold down the fort at home and raise the kids. Although this seemed depressing now that she realised that she was thirty and still didn't know what she wanted to do, it wasn't all that bad. She was able to spend every day with her two girls, time she would never be able to get back. She smiled at that thought as she got out of the car and headed toward the front door with Crumpet following close behind.

~

Later that evening, Chelsea placed her plate of dinner on the dining table across from the girls as she listened to them talk over each other about their days at school. She watched them speak with such animation about regular things like who they played with at lunchtime and who was the star of the day. Lucy had really lost her baby face now that she was nine. She had her straight, blonde hair cut to her shoulders, which made her blue eyes really pop. She was a spitting image of Chelsea. Olivia, on the other hand, had the same facial features as Ryan, but with long, dark hair. Her curls were impossible to tame, but her wild hair matched her personality perfectly. Chelsea was lost, admiring her beautiful, yet completely different girls, as she heard Ryan come through the front door from work.

Lucy and Olivia squealed in sync, "Daddy's home!"

Ryan made his way into the dining room, kissing both girls hello before bringing his dinner plate to join them at the table. Dinner times always involved Lucy and Olivia talking over each other, with hardly any eating or adult conversation. Once they finished dinner, Chelsea and Ryan would always split up, with one tidying the kitchen and any other leftover mess, while the other tackled the fun job of getting the girls bathed and ready for bed. One job they had always been good at was working together as a team in parenting.

Tonight, Chelsea had drawn the card of cleaning up after dinner and found herself zoned out, scraping the plates and stacking the dishwasher. The kids were upstairs with Ryan, finishing off their book together after a shower. The house had a heavy, post-chaos stillness to it. The kind where you could hear every creak of the house and the birds outside singing before settling down for the night.

Ryan came back into the kitchen a short time later and headed to the fridge to get a can of Coke Zero before sitting down at the kitchen island bench.

"The girls are in bed; they convinced me to leave their lamps on so they can read a few more books to each other," Ryan said as he cracked open the can.

Chelsea nodded as she turned around to wipe down the stone island bench. They remained in silence for a while before Chelsea finally spoke. "I'm thinking of going back to Somerdale next weekend," she said, throwing the dishcloth back into the sink, "Emily's engagement party."

Silence. Then a small, pointed laugh.

"To Dean? That guy with the terrible tattoos?"

Chelsea let out a quick laugh, "Yep, that's the one. Apparently, he has grown up, and she seemed really happy on the phone earlier."

Ryan took a sip of his drink. "So, is it just you going, or do you want us all to go? Because you know I am really busy with work at the moment and studying for this surgical training exam."

"I know, so maybe I will just take the kids back. It will be a good excuse for them to see mum and dad, plus I have hardly been back since we left, so it will be good for the girls to see where I grew up." Chelsea said as she flicked the kettle on and leaned back against the bench facing Ryan.

Ryan nodded, "The girls would like to see your mum and dad. Who else is going to the party?" He asked as he took another sip.

Chelsea shrugged, "A bunch of people, I assume, a lot of the high school crowd. Em mentioned Jake."

Ryan leaned back in his chair and crossed his arms across his chest, "*Jake* Jake?"

She gave him a long look. "Yes, that Jake."

A long pause stretched between them, an almost buzz in the air with all the unspoken things in the air.

Ryan rubbed his jaw, "Yeah, okay. I mean, of course I want you to go and celebrate your best friend, it's just you have barely mentioned that town in years and now you are packing up for a high school reunion."

"It's not a reunion," she said. "It's a party. A weekend. And maybe I want to feel like a person again for five minutes. Not a mum, taxi driver, or... your housemate."

His expression didn't change, but something behind his eyes flickered. "You could have just told me that you needed a break."

She exhaled. "I didn't think I had to ask permission."

He stood, walking over to put the empty can into the recycling bin. "You don't. Of course you don't. We aren't those people. I want you to go and have fun." He said, giving her a small smile. "I am going to go take a shower."

As he left the room, Chelsea leaned against the island bench, pressing her fingers to her temples.

It wasn't a fight. Not really. They didn't fight often, but it felt like another stretch of distance had lain quietly between them, adding to the long road they'd already been walking in opposite directions.

Chelsea turned back around to make her cup of tea.

Somerdale.

Jake.

Everything she used to be.

She whispered to herself like a confession:

"I need this."

TWO

Jake

J ake Callahan had never intended to stay this long.

He was only supposed to be helping his dad recover from surgery for a few weeks before he got back on a flight, out of this town. His dad owned the Brewery in Somerdale, so when he called and said he needed to have surgery on his knee, Jake flew across the country to help run the brewery while he recovered from his surgery. But six weeks quickly turned into ten. The town had a way of pulling you in. Not with excitement, but with that quiet, heavy comfort you forgot you had missed. He had missed the town, but he couldn't seem to escape the memories that came with being back.

He sat on the back steps of his father's house, beer in hand, the sharp scent of freshly cut grass mixed with salt, thick in the air. The crickets were loud, but not as loud as his thoughts that were currently racing around his head.

His best mate Dean had texted him earlier that night:

Engagement party next weekend, brother. You better show up. And yeah....Chelsea's coming.

Jake hadn't responded yet.

He'd read the message once. Then again.

Then he stared at it, as if it might change the longer he looked at it.

Chelsea Quinn.

He hadn't seen her since they were eighteen.

Twelve years ago.

Twelve years since he'd last spoken to her.

Twelve years since he'd last kissed her.

Jake was young when he first saw Chelsea on their first day of high school. He had not been very interested in girls before, but when he saw her across the hall that day, he quickly became very interested. She caught his attention straight away in the way she was so effortlessly beautiful. She quite literally lit up every room she entered without trying, and Jake found himself wanting to be around her all the time. Thankfully, that happened for him as they formed a friendship group consisting of his guy friends and her girl friends. He was content for the first few years of high school just being friends, but somewhere along the way, their relationship shifted. They never really had other relationships, as if they both knew they would eventually end up together. To be honest, Chelsea had never seemed that interested in the guys at their school, despite the effort they put in to win her attention. Until one night, when Chelsea and Jake were hanging out with their friends, they blurred the lines of their friendship by sharing a kiss. And things were never the same after that. They were that couple. The couple who were obsessed with each other. The couple whose relationship everyone looked up to. Until they weren't anymore.

The night they'd said goodbye had never really left him, no matter how hard he tried to forget it. It was the night of the graduation party. They had graduated from high school and had been celebrating at a classmate's house. Chelsea had worn his blue hoodie, and no makeup, eyes red from crying, and still she'd looked like home. They'd promised to stay in touch, calls, letters, and visits. Promised it wasn't forever. But life, as it tends to do, got messy. Fast.

He'd heard that she got married not long after that. Two kids. A tidy little life. Sometimes he would search her name on social media and then close the app before hitting enter. He had removed her from his social media accounts pretty quickly after he left. Not because they hated each other, but because she wasn't someone he could just be friends with. He knew that if he reached out to her, he would more than likely run straight back to her, unable to stay away. So, he forced himself to stay away, let her live her life in peace. He didn't think he had a right to know her or be in her life. He had left her. Broken her heart. And his own. He didn't think he deserved to be able to check in on her.

Jake took a long sip of his beer and rested his elbows on his knees.

He wasn't the same guy she knew back then. He'd done the travelling thing. Travelled all over the world, lived in different countries, had flings with random girls. But none of it had stuck. He was back here now, surrounded by memories, trying not to feel like a failure for circling back to square one with not much to show for the past decade.

"You think she'll show?" Dean's voice called from across the yard, cutting through his thoughts.

Jake looked up. His best mate stood leaning against the fence, smug as hell, holding a beer of his own. They had become instant best friends on their first day of primary school. Dean asked him if he wanted to be his best friend within the first five minutes of entering the classroom, and it was as easy as that. They had been virtually inseparable all through school until Jake decided to take off travelling after graduation. Dean had met up with him in a few countries, but for the vast majority of it, Jake had been on his own. Fighting to figure out where he belonged.

"She said yes," Dean answered himself with a shrug. "Em is stoked. Chelsea's bringing the kids too."

Jake ran a hand through his hair.

"Is that a problem?" Dean asked, making his way over to sit next to him on the step.

Jake shook his head. "Not a problem. Just…. a surprise."

Dean took a sip, grinning. "You ever going to get over her?"

God, he was still such a shit stirrer. Dean had always been the one to say whatever he was thinking. To be honest, when Jake thought back to high school, he was surprised that Dean was the first one of them to get married. He was always the one with a different girl every week, unable to settle down, and, honestly, never treated the girls very well. It shocked him when Dean said he was seeing Emily. Emily had always been the girl of their group who didn't put up with shit, so the two of them together was a shock to everyone. But it turned out they worked perfectly together.

"I don't know what you are talking about. I haven't spoken to her in years, man."

Dean smirked. "Yeah, sure. You can try to convince me all you like, but I know you have been pinning over that girl since the day you left. Hell, since the first day of high school."

"She's married. She has kids. She is happy." Jake said, almost to himself.

Dean took another long swig of his beer. "Maybe. Maybe not. Hard to lose the kind of love that you two had for each other. Either way, it will be fun having the whole crew back together. Just get out of your head and get ready to celebrate me." Dean nudged him with his shoulder.

"And Emily, you idiot."

Dean laughed.

The silence stretched between them as Jake got lost in his own thoughts again, while he sipped his now-warm beer.

It was just being back home that was digging up all these past feelings.

Right?

THREE
Chelsea

The road into Somerdale hadn't changed much.

The same narrow lanes curving along the coastline. Surrounded by lush greenery on one side, and white sprawling sand and turquoise water on the other. The same small-town signs, welcoming her back like she'd only popped out for the weekend and not disappeared for years.

As they got closer to town, Chelsea rolled down the window slightly, letting the wind ruffle through her hair as she drove. The air smelled salty and fresh. Familiar and comforting.

In the backseat, Lucy was deep into her book, and Olivia was fast asleep, one shoe off, softly snoring. Chelsea smiled in the review mirror at her daughters, envious of their innocence and not having a care in the world.

A couple of minutes later, the GPS in her white SUV chirped:

"You have arrived at your destination."

Olivia woke up as Chelsea pulled into the driveway of her parents' house. The house looked almost the same as it always had, minus the fresh coat of paint and the new garden her mum had worked hard to bring to life. Chelsea couldn't remember the last time she was here for longer than a couple of hours. She had avoided it big time, too many ghosts for one place.

Chelsea and the girls had hardly gotten out of the car when they heard the front screen door creak open.

"Oh my god, you're actually here!" Chloe, Chelsea's younger sister, squealed as she flew down the front steps, barefoot, arms outstretched.

Chelsea barely had time to process what was happening before she was pulled into a hug that smelled like vanilla perfume and nostalgia.

"Look at you!" Chloe said, holding her at arm's length. "Still hot, still stressed. Still the normal Chels." She said with a wink.

Chelsea laughed. "Watch out, I am running on caffeine and spite. Don't get too close."

Chloe grinned before looking behind Chelsea to see that Lucy and Olivia were standing, watching the sisters' reunion. "There's my girls!" She said, pushing past Chelsea to get to the girls.

Chelsea watched as they all joined in a group hug. She smiled to herself; the girls loved their aunt. The thought hit her with a stab of guilt that she hadn't made more of an effort to come back home. She and Chloe were only a few years apart, so they had their ups and downs growing up. One minute, they would be in a full-on fight over one sister wearing the other's clothes, and the next, they would be the best of friends. As they came out of their teenage years, they became closer with fewer fights, but most of their conversations these days were over text or FaceTime, unless Chloe came to stay for a weekend. In person now, Chloe looked... happy. Her highlighted hair was cut shorter than usual, and her skin looked extra tan after a summer of sun, paired with her green workout clothes. Her sister was always the fun, carefree one, and somehow, Chelsea always felt younger when she was around her.

Chloe interrupted her thoughts. "Come on, let's go find Grandma, I heard she has filled the freezer with ice cream!" She said as she held one of the girls' hands in each of hers and went inside the house.

Chelsea grabbed their bags out of the car and followed the noise through the house to the kitchen, which was tucked at the back of the house, looking out over the back deck area.

"Darling! I cannot believe you are here." Chelsea's mum made her way to her and pulled her in for a hug. Although her mum wouldn't have meant to make her feel guilty with that comment, Chelsea couldn't help but feel it. She was starting to wish she hadn't spent so much time staying away from Somerdale.

Chelsea found herself melting slightly into her mum's arms. She had not realised how much she needed a hug from her mum.

They spent the next half an hour catching up with Chelsea's parents, which really meant they just spent the next half an hour listening to Olivia and Lucy talking over the top of each other to fill everyone in on every second of their lives since they last saw them. Finally, Chelsea's parents decided to take the girls down to the beach to give her some time to unpack and settle in.

Once they had left, Chelsea made her way to her childhood bedroom, which was no longer filled with posters of Justin Bieber and polaroids of her and her friends. Now, the bright-coloured bed had been replaced with a neutral bedspread, and the walls were white and empty, apart from the family pictures framed on the walls. Her mum had set up the spare room for the girls to sleep in, although Chelsea wasn't sure it was necessary, seeing as most of the time they ended up in her bed anyway.

"So, how does it feel being back here?" Chelsea jumped, not realising her sister had joined her and was standing behind her in the doorway.

"God, you scared the crap out of me," Chelsea said, trying to slow her heart rate down, "I don't really know yet. It's definitely weird."

"Yeah, I bet, I can't even remember the last time you stayed here," Chloe said whilst plonking herself down on the crisp bed.

"Me either," Chelsea mumbled as she unpacked her weekender bag.

"So, what's the goss? Why isn't Ryan here?"

This was typical Chloe, always straight to the point. She was never the type to sugarcoat anything. She was younger than Chelsea by a few years, but she was fierce, a little wild, and Chelsea knew never to mess with her.

Chelsea felt her face redden, "Oh, you know, he is super busy at work, trying to get into this surgical rotation. It didn't make sense for him to take the time off."

"Mhm, sure. Not even to celebrate his wife's best friend's engagement." Chloe said as she inspected her nails.

Chelsea spun around with her hands on her hips, giving her sister a pointed look.

"Okay, okay, got it. We aren't talking about Ryan right now. But just so you know, you are going to have to talk about it at some point."

Chelsea sighed and fell onto the bed next to her sister. Somehow, her sister always knew what was going on with her, sometimes before she even did it. It was kind of weird, come to think of it.

"Changing the subject. I can't believe Emily managed to tie down Dean. He was always known as the biggest player at school, even to us younger girls." Chloe said as she sat up and leaned on her elbow, facing Chelsea.

Chelsea laughed. "I know, right? I knew they spent a lot of time together, but I think Em didn't let on how serious they were to save any judgment."

Dean had always been a part of their wider friendship group, along with Jake and a few other boys. But no one ever took Dean seriously. He was always the jokester, getting himself into trouble and walking around the school oozing the bad boy vibe. His cocky personality won him over countless girls during high school, but never any of the girls in their friendship group, much to his disappointment. The only thing he ever got from them was a nickname, Hotshots. But Chelsea guessed she had been so removed from this life; she didn't really know him anymore. He must have changed enough for Emily to agree to marry him.

"I take it you know Jake will be at the party tomorrow night," Chloe said, the casual bomb-drop.

"Yep, Em gave me the heads up," she paused, "How do you know he is?"

Chloe shrugged, "Well, I just assumed since it's his best mate who has gotten engaged," she paused to lie back down, "and since I saw him at his dad's brewery the other day and he asked about you."

Chelsea's eyes widened. "He did?"

Chloe rolled back over to look at her sister, "God, you are difficult sometimes. Of course he did. That boy was in love with you. It doesn't just...evaporate."

Chelsea didn't answer. She just stared at the ceiling, her stomach fluttering. An old familiar ache. Not quite nerves, or regret. Something far more complicated.

She glanced around her bedroom. Although it looked different now, being back in this space, in this town, was like stepping into a version of herself she hadn't worn in years.

The girl who believed in big love.

The girl who had plans.

The girl who'd stood on the front steps of this house, tears streaming down her face while Jake promised they'd find each other again someday.

The girl who was buried somewhere under years of nappies, school runs, and a marriage that felt more like a contract than a connection.

Chelsea cleared her throat. "It's just a party," she said, mostly to herself. "It's not like anything's going to happen; besides, I'm married. And I love Ryan."

"I never said you didn't." Chloe said as she stood up, she paused as she got to the door, "I'm glad you are home, Chels. I have a feeling we will have fun this weekend." She said with a smirk before leaving the room.

Chelsea grabbed a pillow from behind her and put it over her face as she groaned.

I don't know if I am ready for this, she thought to herself.

FOUR
Chelsea

T he day of the party started like any other.

Except it wasn't.

Chelsea had helped Emily all morning, getting the final jobs done before coming back to her parents' house to start getting ready. The party was being held at Dean's parents' house, and Chelsea had felt on edge the whole time she was there, helping Emily with the finishing touches. Emily had assured her that Dean and Jake were busy getting all the alcohol from the brewery, but it didn't stop her from anxiously checking every time she heard a car door or another voice.

Her parents and sister were coming to the party and had decided that, depending on how Chelsea felt, her parents would bring the girls home after a bit to put them to bed, while Chelsea would stay and have fun at the party with her friends.

Now she was in her old bedroom, curling her golden blonde hair in loose waves and pretending her hands weren't shaking. Emily had told her it was "just a casual backyard thing," with a few fairy lights, drinks, and some good music —nothing fancy.

But Chelsea still tried on three different outfits before settling on her trusty black mini-halter dress, which hugged her curves perfectly. She had worked hard to get fit after having the girls, and although her body had definitely changed, she was proud of her body and what it had achieved.

Chloe had helped her pick out the outfit and told her she looked hot before smacking her on the ass. Which gave her a nice confidence boost since she was starting to feel more nervous the closer they got to the time of the party.

Chelsea finished off her hair and touched up her makeup, which was not much. She hardly ever wore makeup these days, partly because she would start and then be interrupted every five seconds, and partly because she had no idea what she was doing. While other girls were watching YouTube makeup tutorials and keeping up with the latest trends, Chelsea was watching the Wiggles.

Chelsea was putting on her gold jewellery when her sister entered the room wearing a flowing, floral dress.

"Sheesh, Emily is going to be mad you are upstaging her."

Chelsea rolled her eyes. "I am not."

"Uh-huh." Chloe plopped onto the bed. "You're nervous."

"I am not."

"You are."

Chelsea finished putting her earring in and turned to face her sister. "Ok, fine. Maybe a little. It's just…weird. I haven't seen him in a decade, Chlo. Or anyone really."

"You also haven't smiled like this in a while."

"Is it that obvious?"

Chloe stood up and smoothed her dress. "He was a big deal. Of course, it's going to feel weird. But this is your home and your best friend too. You're allowed to show up."

Those words landed somewhere deep as she watched her sister walk out of the room.

She was allowed to show up.

~

Finally, after quickly downing a glass of champagne to ease her nerves, they arrived at Dean's parents' house. The house was the same as the rest of the houses in Somerdale, except Dean's parents had completely renovated it. As Chelsea walked around the side of the house, she admired the new timber deck that wrapped around the entirety of the house. As they entered the backyard, she noticed they also spared no cost on the landscaping. The backyard was already buzzing with familiar faces. Fairy lights glowed overhead as the sun began to set and the air cooled slowly after a warm tropical day. The sound of laughter drifted above the sound of a 2000s playlist, and the scent of a barbecue wafted through the air.

It could have been any party from a decade ago, except this time, she had two kids in tow and a marriage quietly cracking beneath her skin. She had briefly chatted with Ryan this morning when he got home from his night shift and had called to check in on her and the girls. Even though they were only a few hours away from each other, it felt like they were on opposite sides of the world.

In her high school friends' messenger group, they had all messaged earlier, saying how excited they were to be reunited today and had sent through their outfits to get the others' approval. Proof that not much had changed since high school, despite the distance and time.

As they entered the party, Chelsea's mum and dad took Lucy and Olivia over to where other children were chasing bubbles and shouting about hide-and-seek. Chelsea glanced around, nerves settling under her ribs like static. There were lots of familiar faces, but she was realising quickly how removed she had become from this town and the people. She needed a drink, now.

"Champagne?" Emily offered, appearing with two glasses and Dean by her side. Emily looked radiant in her simple white short dress. Her brown hair was straight and had been styled into a half-updo. Her makeup was more than Chelsea had on, but you could still see her freckles poking through. Dean had also scrubbed up nicely, dressed in tan chino-style shorts and a white linen shirt. They matched perfectly and had come a long way from the one-sided flirty friendship they had all those years ago.

"Yes, please," Chelsea said, gratefully taking one of the glasses. "Hotshots! Congratulations. I can't believe you convinced my bestie to marry you." Chelsea said as she leaned in to give Dean a one-armed hug.

Dean laughed and hugged her back, "I'm never going to get away from that nickname, am I? Thanks, though, Chels, but no one is more surprised that I convinced her than me."

Chelsea stood back and took a long sip of her drink as Emily and Dean looked at each other lovingly. Chelsea made a mental note to corner Emily later to grill her on not telling her how serious she and Dean were. She could see the love flowing between them; it was clear they were obsessed with each other. Another pang of guilt hit her. She was beginning to realise that, without realising, she had even distanced herself from Emily.

Emily leant in and gave Dean a quick kiss, "Ok, you can go and mingle now, we are going to go and find the girls."

Emily grabbed Chelsea's hand and led her over to where two girls were standing over by the bar. Brooke and Mel. The other half of the foursome. The four of them were inseparable in high school. They had all gone to different primary schools, so the first week of high school, they formed their little group. People floated in and out of the group over the years, but the four of them remained solid. Mel had gone to university straight out of high school and was now a nurse working in the Somerdale hospital. She was married to a mechanic in town whom she had met on a dating app, and they had a two-year-old son. Brooke was a teacher at a local school in town and had her fair share of relationships over the years, but had yet to find the right one. They had both never left Somerdale, unlike Emily and Chelsea, so their in-person catch-ups all together were very rare.

"Oh my god, are my eyes playing tricks on me?" Mel shrieked as they walked over to them. "Chelsea Quinn. In the flesh!"

Chelsea and Emily were quickly pulled into a group hug, full of squealing and jumping around.

When they broke apart, they looked around to see that they had people watching their reunion. They all cracked up laughing. It straight away felt like no time had passed.

For a moment, Chelsea forgot about the ache in her chest. About Ryan. About Jake. She just laughed. Told stories. Let herself be known.

Chloe kept popping in, but since she still lived in the town, she knew many of the guests, so she fluttered around the party socialising like the social butterfly she was. She kept tossing Chelsea knowing glances now and then. Chelsea dodged each one with a long sip of her drink.

Around dusk, when the fairy lights began to glow against the dark sky, and the music seemed to have grown louder, the kids started to tire. Olivia rubbed her eyes and yawned whilst dancing, determined not to go home, but Lucy declared she was "bored of grown-up parties."

"We are going to take the girls home for some ice cream before bed, darling." Chelsea's mum said to her as she gathered the girls' things. While her dad tried to coax Olivia off the dance floor.

Chelsea hesitated for a moment, feeling slightly guilty that she was staying at the party and not going home with the girls.

"Don't worry, they are fine. Stay and have fun." Her mum said, reading her thoughts.

"Okay," she said, kissing the top of her daughters' heads. "Be good for grandma and grandad, and I will see you in the morning."

"Love you, Mumma!" Olivia called out as Lucy tucked herself under her grandad's arm.

Chelsea walked the girls and her parents out to the car, sneaking in another kiss before she waved them off.

As she watched them drive away, she stood on the porch alone for a second, feeling slightly buzzed thanks to Emily making sure her champagne glass was never empty. She took a moment to catch her breath and sort through her thoughts before she turned back towards the yard and the growing party.

She froze.

Across the space, standing by the bar with Dean, stood Jake.

Somehow, she hadn't seen him that night yet. She had been distracted by her friends or Lucy and Olivia, so their paths hadn't crossed. But there he was. It was like the crowd on the dancefloor had parted, giving her the perfect view of him.

His body was turned slightly away, smiling at something Dean said. His brown hair was slightly shorter now, but still had the signature shagginess to it; his jawline was sharper, and his top lip was now sporting a moustache. He was wearing a white linen shirt similar to Dean's, except he had the first couple of buttons undone and the sleeves rolled up, revealing some black ink on his arms that was definitely new. But the smile? That was still the same.

And then, as if he felt her looking at him, he turned his head slightly, and their eyes locked across the yard.

Just for a second.

Just long enough to knock the air from her lungs.

He didn't wave or smile. Neither did she.

They just held each other's gaze.

As if the last decade hadn't happened, memories and feelings swarmed her body. She swallowed hard as her body began to feel warm from the weight of his gaze on her again. She needed to look away and catch her breath, but she couldn't bring herself to break eye contact first.

Fortunately, or unfortunately, Chelsea wasn't sure yet, the moment was broken when Emily came up to her holding yet another glass of champagne. "There you are. Ok, girls are gone, now we can dance."

Chelsea turned to Emily and forced a laugh, grabbing her best friend's hand in one of her hands and taking the glass with the other, before following her back towards the party.

Her heart thudding with the ache of everything she hadn't let herself feel. Not yet. Not fully.

But maybe soon.

FIVE
Jake

Jake stood by the bar, nursing a beer that had gone warm while Dean rambled on about honeymoon options, Bali maybe, Greece, something about beachfront cocktails and swim-up rooms.

He nodded along, only half listening.

The party around them had swelled – fairy lights tangled in tree branches, warm summer air, old friends laughing like time hadn't passed at all. But Jake felt every minute of the almost twelve years he'd been away. He wasn't sure if he fit in here any-more. Everyone around him had moved on with their lives, built families, homes and careers. And he was just...lost.

And then something around him shifted.

He couldn't explain why he turned, a flicker in his chest, a hitch in the noise, some sixth sense he hadn't used in years. But some-thing made him turn and look up.

And there she was.

Chelsea Quinn.

Through the perfectly parted crowd, standing on the porch like something out of a dream, he didn't know he still had.

Her hair was longer now, but still the golden colour it had always been with the natural highlights from the Australian sun. Her body different, stronger maybe, softer somehow. But her face? Her eyes?

The same.

For a second, just one sharp, endless second, the years disappeared. He was eighteen again, standing on her parents' front porch. Her face pressed into his chest. Tears staining his jumper and his heart. Her hand slipping from his like she was already halfway gone.

She didn't smile. Neither did he.

But she didn't look away.

Not until Emily slipped a glass into her hand and tugged her toward the crowd, and she turned, laughing like she hadn't just lost her breath, like he felt he had.

Dean said something, but Jake didn't catch it.

"Sorry – what?"

"I asked if you were gonna say something to her or if you are just going to keep staring at her like a total freak," Dean said, grinning over the rim of his drink.

Jake looked away, forcing a shrug. "It's been a long time."

"Not that long, apparently," Dean muttered. "You look like you just saw a ghost, man."

Jake didn't answer; he just took a long swig from his warm beer.

Because maybe he had just seen a ghost.

Chelsea wasn't someone you just *got over*. She was someone you had to learn to live without. Like phantom pain. Sometimes dull, sometimes sharp, but always there. Always just beneath the surface.

He had spent years running away from the feeling. Literally travelling to the furthest parts of the world to try and get away from the pain.

And now here she was.

Not in a memory. Or a dream.

In the same backyard again. Breathing in the same air. Laughing just meters away. Forcing him to stop running away.

Jake finished off his beer and signalled to Dean it was time for another.

He wasn't ready yet.

~

Jake drifted through the conversations there, but not really there. A pat on the back here, a few beers there. He laughed at stories he barely heard, smiled at people he barely remembered. All the while, his eyes kept flicking toward her. In that first moment when he saw her across the yard, he had been in shock. He hadn't been able to drag his eyes away from hers. But now that the shock of seeing her had somewhat settled, when his gaze did flick towards her, he could really appreciate how good she looked. He had seen a few pictures here and there of her over the years, but a photo couldn't compare to the real thing. Her tanned legs were somehow even longer than he remembered, the black dress she was wearing hugged her figure perfectly, and he could tell her blue eyes still sparkled from here.

Jake swore under his breath as he dragged his gaze from her yet again. If he didn't control himself, she was going to think he was an absolute freak who couldn't stop staring at her.

If he were honest, it was kind of annoying. His body was failing him completely as he tried to remain cool, calm, and collected. It's like his eyes had a mind of their own and couldn't help but keep track of her. It was something he had always done when they were together, never able to take his eyes off her, no matter where they were. But it seemed weirder now since they weren't anything anymore.

She moved through the crowd with effortless grace, the same way she had in high school, like the sun just slightly bent itself in her direction. She'd always been magnetic without trying. She still was.

He didn't mean to follow her.

Not exactly.

But as he said, his body was failing him, and when he stepped away to grab another drink, she was suddenly there at the make-shift bar, alone for the first time in what felt like hours. Her golden blonde hair was tucked behind one ear, head tilted as she studied the label on a wine bottle as if it held more answers than just the alcohol content.

He hovered for half a breath too long. Wondering if this was a stupid idea. But before he could decide, as if she sensed him before she saw him, she slowly turned.

For a second time that night, their eyes locked.

No noise. No crowd. Just the two of them and everything they hadn't said in over a decade.

"Hey," he said, low and careful.

She didn't flinch, but something flashed across her face. "Hey."

His throat felt tight. "Didn't think you'd come."

"I couldn't miss it; Em is my best friend."

He nodded. "Still, it's been a while."

Chelsea glanced at her drink, Jake watched as her throat bobbed, "Almost 12 years."

He smiled, faintly. "But who's counting, hey?"

She finally looked at him fully, eyes wide and slightly glossy but still unreadable. "Apparently, we both are."

He had so many questions he wanted to ask: How've you been? Do you still run your fingers through your hair when you're nervous? Do you ever think about our last summer together? But instead, all he said was:

"You look good."

"So do you," she said, her voice soft. "You grew into that face I see." She said playfully, but Jake could hear the slight tremble in her voice. She was nervous.

Jake huffed a laugh. "Took a while."

Chelsea smiled, her eyes searching his face. He wondered if she was doing the same thing he was. Was she searching his face, desperately trying to commit his face to memory? Trying to gauge how she felt about him? Did she hate him? Was she finding it hard to breathe being around him again?

A beat passed. The hum of the music filled the silence, but between them something heavier pulsed, waiting to be unpacked.

Chelsea finally stepped back, blinking quickly as if she were trying to blink back her emotions, wine in hand. "Well...I guess I'll see you around?"

He nodded once quickly, slightly panicking that she was about to walk away, and he wouldn't get the chance to speak to her again. "Yeah."

But as she turned to leave, Jake reached out, not quite touching her, just enough to make her pause.

"Hey," he said again, quieter now. "I'm really glad you came."

She met his eyes, and for a flicker of a second, she smiled. Not a full one, just enough to crack something open in his chest. God, what he would do to have her flash one of her full Chelsea smiles at him again. He couldn't stop his eyes from flicking to her mouth as she spoke.

"Me too." She took a deep breath before she finally turned and walked away.

Leaving him standing there with his heart pounding and every regret he'd buried deep, clawing its way to the surface. Being close to her, breathing the same air again, brought back every single memory he had tried so hard to forget.

SIX

High School: Second Year
Jake

*T*he music from Dean's stereo rattled the walls of the garage, the bass thumping while their circle of friends passed around bags of chips and sipped at cans of soft drink. It was their usual Saturday night, all hanging out after the boys had played a game of football. It was usually at Dean's house because his parents worked weekends, so the group of them would have the freedom to be loud.

They were now in their second year of high school, and their group had pretty much remained the same since the first week of high school, give or take a few additions. Jake looked around the group. Dean, his best mate, was beside him, and Billy was next to him, who had Tom in a headlock on the other side of him. On the other side of Tom sat Brooke, who was rolling her eyes at the boys' roughhousing. Jake's eyes flicked to Dean, who then had Emily sitting beside him. Dean was trying to flirt with her, but Emily was quick to put him in his place, scrunching her nose up at something he said. Beside her sat Mel. Beside her and directly across from Jake sat Chelsea. Jake tried to join conversations with the boys, but he couldn't help having his whole attention on Chelsea. Her golden blonde hair was draped over *her shoulder, making her blue eyes pop. She was naturally stunning, and he didn't even think she realised. Jake couldn't help the grin spread across his face as he watched her throw her head back and laugh at something Emily had said to Dean. He had no idea what was said, but he couldn't take his eyes off of her long enough to find out.*

Jake had always been good friends with all of the girls in their group, but something about Chelsea had always felt like more. Although nothing had ever happened between them, something about her felt more to him than just a friend. While the other boys would flirt with girls or try to convince them to kiss them, Jake had always found excuses as to why he wasn't interested. But the older they got, the more he realised that the truth was that he only wanted to kiss one girl.

Dean stood up, mentioning something about sparklers. The rest of the crew jumped up to follow him outside, but Jake took his time as he watched Chelsea finish off her drink before shivering as she stood up. She was in denim shorts and a tank top. It had been a warm day, but now that the sun had set, it had started to cool down. Jake was wearing his football jacket but had his favourite blue hoodie tucked beside him.

"Here," he said as he threw the hoodie to Chelsea.

She caught the hoodie and opened it up to look at what he threw her. "Your favourite jumper? You sure about that?"

Jake shrugged, suddenly feeling very nervous. "You'll probably look better in it. And besides, I can see you shivering from here."

Chelsea grinned. "Thanks, Jakey. I am freezing."

He watched as she pulled the hoodie over her head. He instantly realised he was right; she looked a lot better in it than he did. The silence stretched for a minute before Jake broke it.

"So... fun night."

Chelsea smirked, "You mean watching Dean try to flirt with Emily? Yeah. Totally fun."

They both laughed. The sound of her laugh warmed Jake's whole body, and he felt his skin flush. Chelsea cocked her head slightly and just looked at him. Jake's heart skittered in his chest, and before he could stop himself, he was walking towards hers.

"You've got, uh…" He reached forward, hesitating, then brushed his thumb over her cheek. "Dorito dust. Right there…Got it."

He heard her breath hitch. 'Smooth, Jake. Real smooth." But her voice was barely a whisper.

He should have dropped his hand, but he didn't pull back. He was so close to her. And she was looking up at him like he was the only person in the world.

Before he could think or talk himself out of it, he leaned in and kissed her.

It wasn't perfect. Their noses bumped, and they both laughed against each other's mouths. But then her arms slipped around his waist, and he brought his hands up to cup her jaw, and the kiss deepened into something that stole every thought from his head.

When they finally pulled apart, both a little breathless, Chelsea stared up at him, a look of lust and surprise on her face.

Jake grinned, feeling proud of himself and nervous all at once. "Guess that's one way to shut Dean up about who I like."

He noticed Chelsea's cheeks turn pink as she grinned back at him.

Jake dropped his hands before intwining one with hers as they walked out to meet their friends.

He should have been embarrassed holding a girl's hand. Most of the other guys would be. But this felt like the most normal thing in the world.

SEVEN

Chelsea

Chelsea stepped away from the bar, wine in hand, heart in her throat.

She didn't let herself look back. Fighting every fibre in her body that was screaming at her to turn around and walk straight back to Jake. She was feeling such a mix of emotions. She had imagined plenty of times over the years what she would say if she were ever faced with him again. In her mind, she would be strong and tell him everything she didn't get to when she was eighteen. How angry she was at him for leaving her. How angry she was at him for never reaching out. For leaving her in this town with everyone giving her the pity looks because she was the sad girl whose boyfriend had left her. But the second she was in front of him again, that all went out the window. All the anger she had felt through her heartbreak dissipated as soon as his eyes landed on her.

The hum of the party returned around her as she walked away. Laughter, music, someone shouting out a drink order. But everything felt a little…. muffled. Like she was underwater, moving in slow motion, while everyone else danced on the surface.

She found Emily near the fire pit, surrounded by a circle of friends, spinning a dramatic retelling of the proposal. Chelsea slipped back into the circle beside Brooke, smiled in the right places, even toasting when everyone else did.

But her mind was focused on other things.

Jake's voice was still echoing in her ears.

"I'm glad you came."

"Me too."

God. Why had she said that? She could have given him more than that, surely.

She could still feel the warmth of his eyes on her, like sunlight filtered through time. He looked older, yes. Stronger, perhaps a bit rougher around the edges. But there was still that same Jake underneath. The one who used to scribble her notes or lyrics in the margins of his notebooks. The one who knew exactly how she liked her toast, how she hated thunderstorms, how she loved deeply and quietly.

The one she'd never really let go of.

Chelsea got up from the group and walked towards the back fence, away from the lights and music, swirling her wine. The grass was cold under her bare feet, grounding her, but it still didn't feel like enough.

What was she doing?

She was a mum.

She was married now.

Ryan knew Jake existed, sure, but he didn't really know him. He didn't know what Jake had meant. Not what he still might mean. He had always just thought Jake had been her high school boyfriend. Nothing serious. Nothing real. And she had never corrected him.

Chelsea closed her eyes and took a deep breath.

A soft voice behind her pulled her from her thoughts.

"Chels," Brooke said as she walked up beside her, "Are you okay?"

Chelsea hooked her arm through her friend's arm. "Yeah, I am okay, just taking a minute."

Brooke nodded. "I saw you talking to Jake before."

Chelsea pursed her lips. "Yep, seems to be bringing up a lot of memories and feelings seeing him again."

"Yeah, I bet." She continued, "You guys were the biggest love story of our high school. I can't imagine what it's like seeing him again. But I guess love stories don't always go the way we think they will. And now look, you are married with two kids." She squeezed Chelsea's arm. "A happy ending, right?"

Chelsea forced a smile. "Right."

"Come on, let's go get a refill," Brooke said, letting go of her arm.

"You go; I'll be there in a sec."

Brooke gave her arm one last squeeze before walking back to join the party.

Chelsea sighed. This was supposed to be a simple weekend. A party. A trip home. A break from the noise.

Not a time machine.

She drained the rest of her wine.

She wouldn't go looking for Jake. That was the rule she would make for herself. She would go back and enjoy celebrating with her best friends.

But that didn't stop her from secretly hoping he would come looking for her.

~

Sometime later, the firepit had burned down to a lazy glow, chairs mostly empty except for a few stragglers. Half-filled glasses were abandoned on tables, and the music had been switched to a sleepy playlist.

Chelsea had offered to help Emily and Dean tidy up, but she was mostly wandering around, picking up plastic cups and pretending to be useful. When she turned around the corner of the house to go to the bin, Jake was there, stacking plates onto a tray. His sleeves were rolled up, and he had the same slight scowl on his face that he had always had when he was doing something with his hands.

He looked up at the sound of her footsteps, eyes catching hers in the dim light.

"Didn't think you were still here." She said, voice low and unsteady as she slowly walked towards him.

He gave a half-smile. "I'm helping Dean. But he disappeared about twenty minutes ago, so now I'm helping no one."

Chelsea laughed softly and leaned against the table, still holding a bundle of napkins. "Want a hand?"

He hesitated, his eyes searching her face, then nodded. "Sure. You still good at stacking cups like a champion?"

She smirked. "Some skills stay with us forever."

They worked in silence for a minute, the rhythm oddly comfortable. Their shoulders brushed once as they reached for the same plate. Neither of them pulling away straight away.

"So, how's your mum and dad going?" Jake asked, keeping his head down, focused on the plates in front of him.

"Good. Enjoying being retired. Gives them more time to come and visit us. To travel."

Jake nodded as he kept working.

"How about your dad? How's the brewery?" Chelsea asked, scared to let the silence swallow them.

Jake let out a sigh as he looked up at her. "He is okay. He had to have surgery a few months ago, but of course, he hasn't listened to the doctor about taking it easy." He placed both hands on the table and shook his head. "Honestly, he is driving me nuts. He is physically fine now, but I think I might go insane being this close to him again."

Chelsea couldn't help but laugh at that. Growing up, Jake and his dad had sometimes clashed, especially when they were together for a long period of time and didn't have their own space.

They were very similar and both very stubborn, so she could imagine they would be driving each other crazy now.

They fell into another comfortable silence as they continued to clean up. Chelsea was racking her brain on what would be appropriate to talk about with someone you had loved so much, but who had broken your heart. She didn't think this was the time or place to really hash out all those old feelings.

Thankfully, Jake broke the silence first. "That was weird earlier."

Chelsea glanced at him. "What was?"

He didn't look at her. "Seeing you. All at once like that."

She let out a slow breath. "Yeah. It was."

Another pause. Not heavy, just real. Both of them just figuring out how to be around each other again. It was a weird feeling for Chelsea. Being around someone who once knew her better than anyone but now really didn't know her at all. Not this version of her anyway.

He looked over at her then. "You happy?" he asked quietly.

She blinked. The question landed harder than he probably meant it to. She wasn't sure how to answer it.

"I have two beautiful daughters," she said carefully. "I have a lot of things I am grateful for."

Jake nodded, lost in thought for a beat. "But are you happy?"

Chelsea looked down at the napkins in her hands, which were now crumpled.

"I don't know, sometimes I am," she said honestly.

And then she looked at him, really looked, and added, "Are you?"

He held her gaze, something in his jaw tightening. "Sometimes."

The air between them crackled, soft and electric. Chelsea could feel tears threatening to pool in her eyes. She quickly blinked them away before she shifted to face him, placing the crumpled napkins down on the table. "We were kids, Jake."

"I know."

"We had no idea what we were doing or what the real world was like. We made promises we couldn't keep."

He smiled, a little sadly. "We did okay, though."

She nodded. "We did."

He looked like he wanted to say more, and as much as she had things she had been holding onto for years, she didn't want to make Emily and Dean's night about her and her past heartbreak. The sound of a bottle clinking loudly against the bin behind them broke the moment, causing them both to flinch.

Jake stepped back slightly. "I guess I should go. See if Dean needs any more help."

Chelsea nodded. "Yeah. I should go too."

"Night, Chels," he said gently.

Everyone called her that, but it still struck a different chord when he did. It always had.

"Night, Jake."

She stood there long after he walked away, holding a tray of dirty dishes.

Her chest a little tighter.

Her hands a little colder.

Her heart not quite sure what came next.

The backyard was almost unrecognisable now. Half-packed away tables, empty chairs scattered throughout the yard. They had left the fairy lights in the trees for another day, so they were gently swaying in the breeze now.

Jake sat on the edge of the deck, draining the last inch of his beer. It had long gone flat and warm, but he barely noticed.

Dean tossed a rubbish bag into the bin and walked over to him, clapping his hands together. "Well, that's that. Party of the year if I do say so myself."

Jake smirked. "Big call, buddy. There was a beer pong party in 2012 that still takes the rank, I think."

In high school, when football season was over, their favourite thing to do was throw house parties. Calling it a party could be a bit of a stretch, though. Mostly, they just used it as an excuse for their whole group —the girls and the boys —to get together. Sometimes these parties turned out to be huge, and other times it was just their core group. But it never really mattered. They would set up beer pong tournaments, where the rules were constantly changing, and they would play all night before all crashing in whoever's house they were at that night, like a huge slumber party. The particular party Jake was talking about now had been one of the last ones they had before they had graduated high school. It had been one of the big parties with most of their year level there, but by the end, only their crew remained. They all ended up jumping into the pool at Emily's parents' house, fully clothed, to finish off the night. Nothing in particular happened, but they had all agreed the morning after that it was one of the best.

Dean laughed and leaned against the deck beside him. "Yeah, but nobody cried at that one."

Jake glanced at Dean. "Who cried tonight?"

Dean gave him a knowing look. "Don't play dumb with me. You looked like you were holding your breath half the night. You gonna talk about it or keep pretending Chelsea Quinn doesn't still haunt you?"

Jake looked back over the yard. "I didn't think she would actually show up."

"But you had hoped," Dean said quietly.

Jake didn't answer. He didn't have to. Dean knew him better than he knew himself and had always had a way of knowing what he was thinking without needing to say a word. It was kind of weird now that Jake thought about it.

Dean nudged his leg. "It's been over ten years, man."

"I know exactly how long it's been."

Dean studied him for a second, "You think she is happy?"

Jake sighed and rubbed his hand over his jaw. "She's married with two kids. She has built a whole life."

"That doesn't answer my question."

Jake didn't say anything again. He didn't know how to answer the question when Chelsea herself couldn't even answer the question. She physically looked like herself. But there was something written on her face that he couldn't quite place. It was exactly what he had been thinking about before Dean had joined him.

Dean stood up and stretched. "Well. I am going to go find my hot fiancé and take her to bed before I start giving you unsolicited advice like an old man. But for what it's worth..." He paused. "Sometimes life gives you another shot, and it's not about fixing the past. It's about facing it. He clapped his hand on Jake's back. "You have spent the past decade running away from your feelings. I think it's time to face them, man."

Jake stared at the empty firepit, long after Dean had walked away and the embers had gone. Dean was right. He had spent the past decade running away from his life. And his feelings. Nothing had helped him get over Chelsea, and he had tried. He tried dating, but it never stuck. It always seemed forced, and despite his best efforts, he found himself comparing his feelings to those he had with Chelsea. It wasn't fair to the women he tried to date, so before it could get serious, he would end it. But if tonight showed him anything, it was that the past had a funny way of always catching up with him, no matter how much he tried to run.

He didn't believe in fate. Not really.

But tonight?

He wasn't so sure now. Jake shook his head and sighed at the thought that he could have blown his only chance to talk to her tonight.

NINE
Chelsea

The kettle whistled, sharp and shrill in the sleepy kitchen.

Chelsea reached to switch it off before it woke the entire house. She was wearing a tank top, but the morning light filtered through the curtains, the summer air already warming up her skin.

Chelsea looked around the familiar kitchen. Her mum's floral coffee mugs still sat in the same cupboard. The same cookie jar. The same humming fridge. Come to think of it, surely the refrigerator needed to be replaced by now.

Everything was familiar.

Everything except her. She was far from the same girl who once stood in this kitchen.

She stirred her coffee absentmindedly, barefoot on the old tiles. Somewhere down the hallway, she could hear the girls giggling, probably deciding who was going to sneak in and wake up Grandma and Grandad. For once, there was no bickering, so Chelsea wasn't in a rush to interrupt them. She also imagined that her parents weren't going to complain that their grandchildren, who they don't see very often, were waking them up this early. Chelsea laughed at the thought of how different it would have been if it were her waking her parents up early back in the day. Funny how grandchildren magically made all the rules disappear.

Her phone pinged on the bench, pulling her from her thoughts.

Chelsea glanced at the message from Emily confirming their coffee plans for later this morning. Chelsea fired off a response quickly, letting her know that she would be ready when she picked her up shortly, before scrolling through to the next unread message.

Ryan had texted her late last night when he had woken, ready for night shift:

Hope the girls were okay and the party was fun. Send pics tomorrow. X

Chelsea hadn't replied yet, so she quickly sent off some pictures of the girls at the party and said she would see him later that night when they got home, before placing her phone back down on the kitchen bench.

She sat down at the wooden kitchen table and drew her legs up towards her chest, holding her mug of coffee, steam curling around her face, and let herself breathe for the first time since seeing Jake.

It was a fun night celebrating and catching up with the girls, but God, it had felt like the longest night in history.

Even after she'd gone to bed after the dishes and the goodbyes and the "we need to do this more often" promises from Mel and Brooke, she couldn't sleep. Her brain just kept torturing her by replaying the night over and over again.

"Are you happy?"

"Sometimes."

That answer had dug under her skin and was buried deep.

Jake hadn't pushed her to answer. He just…looked. Like he always used to. Like he could see her even when she was trying to hide. Most other people would take her words at face value, but not Jake. He could always see straight through her words.

She'd spent so long trying not to think about him. Trying not to compare or to wonder.

And now?

Now she didn't know what to do with the ache that had come rushing back. Like it had just been waiting for a crack in her armour.

"Mum!" Lucy called out from the lounge room, slicing through her thoughts, "Where's the remote?"

Chelsea smiled softly and stood, carrying her coffee. "Coming!"

But as she passed the hallway mirror, she caught her reflection and hesitated. Her long golden hair was messy, and she looked like sleep had barely touched her face. But behind her eyes, she saw something raw. Something she was scared to explore.

She wasn't that eighteen-year-old girl anymore. But last night had proved something she hadn't wanted to admit:

That girl still lived inside of her.

And she still had the same feelings.

~

Chelsea spent the next hour or so cuddled up on the couch with her coffee and a daughter curled up on each side, watching morning cartoons. She quickly jumped in the shower and got herself dressed before Emily was due to pick her up.

Chelsea wiped toast crumbs off the kitchen bench and shouted a quick "Be good!" to the girls as her mum ushered them into the backyard with snacks and their bathers ready for a swim.

Emily pulled up a few minutes later, wearing oversized sunglasses and a messy bun, waving from the driver's seat like they hadn't just danced under the fairy lights and drank a ridiculous amount of champagne the night before.

Chelsea climbed in, greeting her with a smile and a groan. "I swear my head's still pounding. Why are hangovers so much worse once you have kids?"

Emily passed her a takeaway coffee like a gift from the gods. "Double shot. You're welcome."

They drove in comfortable silence for a while, the roads still quiet, a slow Sunday morning in the sleepy town.

Chelsea glanced out the window as the town flashed past her. The bakery, football oval, and the same old surf shop that hadn't really changed since year ten.

It was like time here hadn't moved at all.

"So," Emily finally said, flicking on her indicator. "How are you doing? Like... really?"

Chelsea took a long sip of her coffee. "I'm okay."

Emily gave her a look over her sunglasses. "Try again, sister."

Chelsea sighed. "I don't know. It was a lot. Seeing everyone. Being back here after so long."

"Seeing *Jake*," Emily gently corrected.

Chelsea leaned her head against the window. "That too."

They pulled into a little café near the water. Their old spot. The same tables, with bright, coloured, mismatched chairs. Chelsea couldn't believe it was still here and that it still looked the same.

They ordered their favourite muffins and sat out on the deck, the ocean glittering in front of them. For a moment, they just sat and listened to the waves, watching a few people walk up and down the beach.

Finally, Emily spoke. "I saw the way he looked at you last night."

Chelsea didn't answer. She had felt the weight of his gaze most of the night.

"I know you've got a whole life now, and I'm not saying anything has to happen. But you should be honest with yourself, Chels. If you've still got feelings – "

"It's not that simple, Em."

"I know," Emily said softly. "But that doesn't make it any less real."

Chelsea picked at the edge of her muffin. "I can't just blow up my life because of a few looks and a heart that never completely moved on."

Emily reached across the table, covering her hand. "No one's asking you to blow anything up. But you deserve to *feel.* You've been holding your breath for years."

Emily continued, "I love Ryan, and I love that he has given you two gorgeous girls, but I think you need to be honest with yourself, and him. I haven't seen you truly smile or laugh in God knows how long unless it is at something Lucy or Liv have done."

Chelsea's eyes burned, but she blinked it away.

"I don't even know what I want."

"Yes, you do," Emily said. "You are just scared to say it out loud."

Chelsea didn't respond.

She didn't have to.

The silence between them said enough.

~

An hour later, after Chelsea had managed to change the conversation topic by asking about the wedding, the girls had said their goodbyes, and Emily had headed off to Dean's parents' house to finish with the rest of the clean-up. Chelsea had told her she didn't need a ride home because she wanted to go for a walk along the beach. Emily had been reluctant to leave her on her own, but a phone call from Dean asking where she was was enough for her to give in and go.

The wind had picked up slightly by the time Chelsea had made it down the wooden steps to the sand. She kicked off her shoes and let her feet sink into the cool sand grains, breathing in the salty air and silence. The beach stretched wide, lined with palm trees, their fronds leaning over the clean, white sand. The beach was mostly empty now on the warm Sunday morning, except for a few kids with buckets down near the tide line and a jogger in the distance.

The ocean was calm today. Turquoise blue and slow, like it had nowhere to be. She didn't mean to walk far. But her legs carried her down the shoreline, each step feeling like all the tension in her body was falling away. The café, the party, Emily's voice, it all slowly faded, replaced by the steady sound of the waves.

This beach had been *their* beach once.

She and Jake used to walk here after school, after fights, after everything. No matter how messy things got, they always ended up here. Together and barefoot. Nights down here watching the stars with the sound of waves in the background, telling each other everything and anything. This is where they truly knew each other. Where their friendship and relationship were built.

It's funny how your body manages to remember all of the feelings and memories, even when your mind has tried everything to forget them.

Chelsea was rounding a cluster of rocks when she saw him.

Jake.

Hands in his pockets. Shoes hooked by two fingers. Head down. He wore his cap backwards, just how Chelsea had always liked it, despite it not doing anything for sun safety against the Australian UV.

He hadn't noticed her yet.

Her instinct was to turn around, to let him have this moment. The worry and stress etching his face made her think he needed it just as much as she did.

But then he looked up.

And paused.

Just like at the party, it felt like the space between them folded in for a second. Almost like a soft kind of gravity pulling at things between them that hadn't been named in years.

Chelsea swallowed hard and took a few steps forward, half a smile tugging at her mouth. "We really need to stop running into each other like this."

Jake returned the smile, but it didn't quite reach his eyes. "You say that like we haven't been doing this since we were fifteen."

She came closer. "You still walk this beach?"

"Sometimes. When I am back home." He glanced around. "Guess I still half-hoped I'd find something here."

Chelsea didn't ask what he was hoping he would find. She didn't need to because she was starting to think she was hoping for the same thing.

Chelsea turned to join him. They walked side by side for a while, words not needed. Just the footsteps in the sand, soft and still in sync. Again, like their bodies remembered things, they had both tried to forget.

Chelsea eventually broke the silence, settling on small talk. "So, you travelled?"

"Yeah, I did. For a bit, anyway. I worked more than I expected, but you know, life experience and all that." He said playfully, but Chelsea got the impression that there was more to that.

"What about you? Did you go out and see the world like you had dreamt of?" Jake asked as he looked at Chelsea while they walked.

Chelsea sighed, "Well, I guess if visiting other places around Australia counts as the world, then I guess so." She replied as she finally met his eyes.

Jake's brow furrowed as he studied her face. He had a look on her face that she couldn't quite read. Concern, sympathy, maybe even guilt. She waved him off.

"I could have, but life had other plans. One day, the world won't know what's hit it." She said, playfully nudging him with her shoulder, trying to lighten the mood slightly. She didn't need him to feel bad for her. She was blessed to have lived the life she has lived so far. She had no regrets about that.

Jake softly smiled as he looked out over the water. They continued to walk in a comfortable silence, both gazing out at the water.

This time, it was Jake who broke the silence. "You always did like walking things off. Whenever we had an argument or something big was happening, I knew I could find you here."

"Still do," she said with a shrug. "Especially things I don't know how to talk about."

"Like us?"

Chelsea stopped walking.

He didn't say it to be cruel. He said it cautiously, like someone cracking open the window in the middle of a storm.

She looked at him, really looked, at the tiredness behind his cobalt eyes, the hope that hadn't quite died. She had so many things she could say to him, so much anger that had built up after he had left her all those years ago. She had speeches rehearsed in her mind for when she was faced with him again. So that he could understand the pain she went through after he left. Understand that she didn't leave the house for weeks. Or that her family had to remind her to eat or shower. How she had turned into a shell of herself. How she had to rebuild herself and her life so that she could survive without him. But now, standing here with him, she realised all of that anger had disappeared somewhere along the line. Chelsea didn't hate him; she never truly did. She just needed to accept that he was a big part of her life, and she couldn't erase that. She hoped that seeing him now would be enough for her to do that and move on with her life.

"Yes," she said quietly. "Like us." They continued walking, slower now.

Jake nodded like he agreed.

The waves rolled in and out beside them, slowly edging closer with each roll.

Jake stopped walking and turned to look at her. Then he asked, "Would it be okay if we talked? Really talked. Before you leave."

Chelsea hesitated, heart tight and stomach doing flips. "Yeah," she said eventually. "I think we should."

~

They sat on an old palm tree that she assumed had been a casualty in one of the tropical storms that had rolled through the town recently. The wind had softened, a slight breeze brushing against them as they gazed out at the ocean.

Jake rested his elbows on his knees, turning a flat, white and smooth pebble over in his hands.

Chelsea watched his fingers move, more comfortable than she expected to be sitting in the quiet beside him.

"Do you remember," he said, without looking up, "when we thought we'd leave this town and never come back?"

Chelsea smiled faintly. "I do remember saying that. Loudly. A lot."

Jake chuckled, the sound hitting her hard somewhere deep. "You were so sure there was a better life out there somewhere."

"There was," she said softly. "And then there wasn't."

Jake glanced over at her now. "Do you regret it?"

"Moving away?"

Jake shrugged, "All of it."

Chelsea took a moment before responding. "No. I don't think so. Because that would mean I would regret the girls. Which I don't. I don't think I even regret marrying Ryan. We were...right for a time."

Jake nodded. "Right until you weren't."

"Exactly."

A pause settled between them, not quite comfortable.

He turned the pebble in his hand again. "I came back for you, you know. I cut my trip short and came back."

Chelsea looked at him, too shocked to speak for a moment. "I didn't know that."

"I figured. I didn't tell anyone. Not even Dean." He let out a breath. "I thought maybe we'd reconnect. It was stupid in hindsight. That I thought you would be here waiting for me. That I thought I could tell you I was stupid for thinking we had to go and live our lives separately. That we could chase all our dreams together. But then I heard you'd moved, and then you were married. Then...kids."

"I did wait for a bit. The weeks after you left were...dark. I was scared," Chelsea admitted. "I think I ran. I ran to the first person who made me feel like I could start over, and then...things just happened so quickly after that."

He nodded again, like he understood more than he wanted to.

"I used to wonder," she added quietly. "If I'd called you. If you'd stayed. If we'd made it work. If I had just waited longer for you to come back. God, if you'd asked me to wait, I probably would have."

Jake smiled, but it was full of sadness. "I would never have asked you to wait for me. As much as I may have wanted to."

Chelsea fidgeted with her wedding rings. "I couldn't wait any longer. I had to believe that there was more out there for me."

"We were kids," Jake murmured.

"I know. But what we felt was more than some adults ever feel in their lives." She knew that now.

They sat with that for a moment. Both watching the waves rolling in, steady and slow.

Chelsea turned to face him. "Why didn't you ever reach out?"

Jake didn't answer right away. "I didn't want to be the guy chasing someone who had chosen someone else." He took a deep breath. "I didn't want to show up and tell you I was wrong when you had moved on and created a life with someone else. I also didn't think I could live with myself if I did reach out and you changed up your life for me," he exhaled before continuing, "I guess I let my ego get in the way."

Chelsea swallowed. "Except I didn't move on. Not really. And I'm beginning to think maybe I didn't choose myself either, back then."

He looked at her. "Are you now?"

The question hung in the air between them like a cloud of smoke.

"I'm trying," she said truthfully. "Coming here, it's the first time I've really thought about what I want. Not what's expected from me. Not what's safe."

Jake's eyes searched hers. "So, what do you want, Chelsea?"

She opened her mouth and then closed it again.

Then said, "I'm working on figuring that out."

And he nodded, like he could live with that. Like he'd wait a little longer to ask again.

They sat in silence for a while, both of them staring straight ahead, hearts quietly thudding with the weight of everything between the past, present, and what might still be.

TEN

Jake

Chelsea sighed beside him "I guess I should head back," she said finally, tucking a strand of her hair behind her ear, avoiding his eyes but not making a move to leave yet.

"Yeah," he said, nodding. "Of course." But he also didn't make a move to get up purely because he selfishly wanted to keep the conversation going, so he didn't have to leave her yet.

"Did you finish your teaching degree?" Jake asked, as he watched her.

Chelsea shook her head and turned to look at him. "I tried. But studying a degree with a newborn just wasn't possible. Especially because Ryan was finishing medical school and heading into an internship. Our families weren't exactly around the corner," she shrugged. "So, it made sense for me to put a pause on that."

Jake watched her as she spoke. She didn't seem sad or disappointed that she had put her dreams and career on hold so that someone else could chase theirs. But that was Chelsea. She had always put other people well above herself, sometimes to her own detriment. But that didn't stop Jake from feeling disappointed for her. Not necessarily because she wasn't a teacher, he wasn't sure that was ever her true passion, but more so because it was becoming clear to him that she hadn't thought about herself for years.

As if Chelsea could read the disappointment on his face, she quickly added, "Don't feel bad for me. I did what was best for my family. I am okay with that."

Jake swallowed hard. "I don't feel bad for you, Chels. You always did the right thing. But it does suck that you haven't been able to chase your dreams as well."

Chelsea smiled at him. "It does, but I also did get a dream of mine. The girls." She paused before continuing, "What about you? Did you get to chase all of your dreams?"

Jake huffed a laugh as he lifted his hat to push his hair back before placing the cap back on, backwards, of course. "I didn't really know what my dreams were. I thought I did, but I was wrong."

Chelsea cocked her head as she studied him. He must admit that was a pretty cryptic way of saying his main dream was sitting right next to him. But he didn't want to completely embarrass himself when that dream of his was now married and totally unavailable.

As much as Jake wanted to stay sitting there with Chelsea until the sun had set, he knew he had to let her get back. He stood slowly, brushing the sand from the back of his jeans. "Come on, we'd better head back before that afternoon rain hits," he said, pointing towards the grey storm clouds rolling in across the ocean.

Chelsea rose beside him, eyes soft but unreadable.

They didn't say anything straight away.

For a second, it felt like old times, after a long walk, where they had talked and talked, Jake would pull her in for a hug, where he would feel her melt into him slightly. God, he craved that feeling so badly. He had spent most of a decade chasing that feeling wherever he could. But no matter how far he searched, he had never been able to catch it.

But this wasn't old times. He wanted to say something, to reach for her hand, to pull her in for a hug, to ask her if there was still space in her life for him. But he didn't. She'd just given him more honesty than he deserved. That had to be enough.

For now.

They lingered a moment too long.

She looked up at him then, and for a second, Jake wondered if she'd lean in. If he should. If the weight of the past decade would collapse in on itself, and he would kiss her for the boy who never stopped loving the girl in a blue oversized hoodie and a messy bun. But he couldn't cross that line. She was married. And lost.

Just before she could step back, Jake reached forward and pulled her into a hug. He couldn't help himself. The magnetic pull between them was too much to ignore, and he could tell she needed it just as much as he did. He felt her stiffen for only a second, out of shock, before he felt her snake her arms around his waist. He cradled the back of her head with one hand, the other arm firmly around her shoulders. Holding her against his chest, where she had always fit so perfectly.

He could feel her melting into the hug as she had always done. He wondered if she could feel his heart hammering away in his chest.

He didn't care. He was so far beyond caring. All that mattered right now was this moment. This feeling. He was beginning to realise how ridiculous it was of him to be searching the world for a way to replicate this feeling. There was nothing in this world that could compare to it.

After what felt like forever but was probably only a minute or so, Chelsea slowly let go and stepped back. Jake instantly missed the warmth of her body against his.

She smiled, "Thank you," she said.

"For what?"

"For remembering me. And us. Like that."

Jake felt something in his chest crack. An ache settling in his chest. "Impossible not to."

She didn't answer that. She just nodded and turned, walking

slowly back across the sand, arms folded against the breeze.

Jake watched her go until she was a silhouette in the sunlight. He remembered watching her walk away like this so many times in high school, feeling giddy after spending the afternoon with her. Counting down the minutes until he would see her again. Or texting her before she had even disappeared. But now, under the hot sun and impending storm clouds, he felt a mix of emotions. He felt grateful that they were able to spend time together. That she felt comfortable enough to let her walls down slightly. But he also felt sad. Sad for her, but also for himself. He had built the story in his head that she was happily married and better off without him. But that woman was not the happy Chelsea he remembered.

He exhaled, bent down to pick up the pebble he'd dropped, and slipped it into his pocket.

She may not know what she wants yet.

But he knew what he wanted.

And he wasn't sure he could walk away again. Not until she told him or showed him that there was nothing more between them.

ELEVEN
Chelsea

Chelsea eased the screen door open and stepped inside her childhood home. The late-afternoon sun was still clinging to her skin despite the storm that was now rolling through. Laughter floated from the living room from the girls who were curled up playing a game with her dad, who was most likely making the rules up as he went.

She slipped quietly into the kitchen and poured herself a glass of water, needing a minute before she could rejoin the version of life she'd pressed pause on earlier this morning.

The beach walk with Jake still lingered, soft and electric. The hug. The way his hands had held her strong, like muscle memory. Like home. Chelsea took a deep breath as she sipped on her glass of water and listened to the distant rumble of thunder.

Her phone buzzed in the pocket of her denim shorts, pulling her attention.

2 missed calls – Ryan.

1 new message – Chloe

1 voicemail

She quickly responded to her sister's message, which was letting her know that she had gone to work. But that she would be heading to Port Mac next week to catch up with her and the girls then. Chloe was a manager of a local clothing store, which, to her disgust, meant working some weekends. She mentioned something in her message about needing all the gossip from the party. Chelsea was kind of glad her sister wasn't here right now because she would be able to see straight through her.

She clicked on the voicemail from Ryan next before she could talk herself out of it.

"Hey, Chelsea. Just checking in. Let me know what time you're heading back tonight? I thought we could talk when you get back, and the girls are in bed. Really talk. Anyway, I will see you when you guys are back. Drive safe."

She deleted the message. Not out of anger, but more weariness. She knew something had changed with Ryan. Things had been slowly changing for some time now. But neither of them had voiced it, so it hadn't felt real. But that voice message and the realisations she had been having lately made it all feel very real.

Her mum quietly entered the kitchen behind her, wiping her hands on a tea towel.

"Everything alright?"

Chelsea turned, startled. "Yeah. Fine. Just...thinking."

Her mum tilted her head in that way only mothers could. "You didn't just have coffee with Emily."

"No," Chelsea admitted. "I saw him. Jake. At the beach."

Her mum didn't seem surprised. She just nodded, slowly. "And how did that feel?"

Chelsea leaned against the counter, the empty glass still in her hand. "Like the world folded in on itself. Like nothing had changed. And like everything had."

Her mum came to sit at the kitchen table. "You know," she said, "it's okay if you don't know what you want anymore. Life isn't a single decision. It's a thousand little choices every day. And it's okay if you change your mind."

Chelsea sank into the chair opposite her. "I think I've been living my life based on decisions I made when I was scared. Or sad. Or just trying to do the right thing."

"And now?"

"And now I'm starting to think I want something different. But I don't know what that is yet."

Her mum reached across the table and squeezed her hand. "Oh, darling. You'll figure it out. But don't forget you don't have to figure it out alone."

Chelsea blinked back a sudden sting in her eyes. "Thanks, Mum."

Chelsea had always had a close relationship with her parents. They had seen her when she was completely and utterly in love with the boy on the football team. They had then picked her up from the front porch that night after her entire world had crumbled around her. They gave her space to grieve her first love. They then supported her when she moved on far too quickly, even if they hadn't agreed with it. They had both always been her biggest supporters. Which was making this even harder. The last thing she wanted to do was disappoint them.

The girls appeared in the doorway a moment later, interrupting her thoughts, messy-haired and grinning.

"Mummy, Granddad said we can make pancakes for dinner!" Olivia squealed.

Chelsea smiled and stood. "You can. But we have to head home before it gets too late. So, you guys can do that while I get our things packed up."

A chorus of groans followed, but they didn't argue.

Chelsea gave them both a quick squeeze as they rushed past her to get started on the pancakes, their granddad following close behind them.

~

Later, after the bags were packed, the car was loaded, and the girls were full of pancakes, Chelsea hugged her parents goodbye. Her mum held her tightly; her lips close to Chelsea's ear.

"Be brave, my girl. Even if being brave just means being honest."

Chelsea nodded and squeezed her mum.

As she buckled the girls into their car seats and climbed into the front seat, her heart thudded hard in her chest. Not from fear. Not even from the anticipation of the conversation she needed to have with Ryan tonight.

But from the realisation that something had shifted. That she wasn't going home the same Chelsea that had left two days ago.

And whatever came next – it felt like it had already begun.

~

The drive home was quiet. The girls had fallen asleep ten minutes into the drive, slumped against their booster seats, mouths open. Lucy held onto her book, and Olivia clutched a random rock she had found in the driveway as they were getting into the car. Chelsea kept the radio low, fingers drumming against the steering wheel to her country music playlist, her mind caught somewhere between the hug on the beach and the house she was heading back to.

When she pulled into the driveway, the house looked exactly the same as when she had left.

But somehow it felt completely different. Like maybe this wasn't home anymore.

Ryan's car wasn't in the driveway, so she assumed that he wasn't home from work yet. Guilt took over her body as she felt briefly relieved that he wasn't home yet. Relieved that she had a little more time to prepare herself for seeing him.

She carried one daughter in each arm, the weight of them oddly comforting, out of the car and into the house. Inside, she tucked them into the couch with blankets and turned on the TV while they slowly woke up. Chelsea silently hoped to herself that the busy weekend they had would override that disaster nap when they went to bed for the night shortly.

Chelsea crouched down in front of them. "I'm just going to unpack the car and put away our things, okay?"

They both sleepily nodded. Olivia reached out and touched Chelsea's hair gently; her throat tightened. Her sweet little loving girl always knew what her heart needed or when she needed a little extra love.

In the girls' bedrooms, she unpacked slowly. Sorting out the clean clothes and throwing the dirty clothes into the washing baskets. The ordinary rhythm of it calmed her heartbeat. In that moment, she could almost pretend everything was normal. Like this was any other day, sorting through the washing.

Except…. it wasn't.

Nothing had felt normal for a while. And maybe now, she was finally ready to accept that. Finally ready to start accepting that what she was feeling about her marriage wasn't going to go away. And although being back home in Somerdale stirred up some confusing feelings and emotions, it couldn't be blamed for the breakdown in Chelsea and Ryan's marriage. That had been slowly simmering for a long time now. They both had just not wanted to give it a voice. That made it feel too real.

Back in the living room, the girls had perked up and were giggling at something Donkey had said in the movie Shrek. Chelsea slid down onto the couch between them, one child under each arm, and they both instinctively curled into her side.

They smelled like sleep and sweet pancakes. She kissed the top of each of their heads and wondered to herself why it was that babies and kids always smelled so delicious.

"Did you like seeing Grandma, Grandpa and Aunty Chlo?" She asked.

"Yup," Olivia mumbled, not wanting to take her attention away from the television.

"Can we go back next weekend, Mum? And maybe dad could come too." Lucy asked.

Chelsea smiled. "We'll see."

She didn't know what the following weekend would look like. She didn't even know what tomorrow looked like, really.

A sound at the front door pulled her attention, a key turning in the lock.

Ryan.

Chelsea sat up straighter, her stomach tightening slightly as the door opened and her husband walked in, dressed in his work scrubs and carrying a bag of groceries. He was wearing that same unreadable expression he'd started wearing more and more.

He looked up, and their eyes met across the room.

Something passed between them briefly.

Then his gaze dropped to the girls, and a smile slowly spread across his face.

"Hey," he said. "You're back."

"Yeah. We got in not long ago. The girls had a disaster nap in the car, so they are just watching a movie before they head to bed."

"Daddy!" The girls screamed in sync, bouncing off the couch to jump on him.

"Ahh, my girls. I missed you so much." Ryan said as he caught the two small humans diving at him.

"We missed you, Dad. Next time, you have to come." Lucy said as she squeezed her dad.

"Yes. Yes. Yes. Because Grandma and Grandpa let you have pancakes for dinner!" Olivia squealed.

Ryan laughed. "Pancakes for dinner? That's just crazy!"

Chelsea couldn't help but smile as she watched them. Even though things may be confusing and she doesn't know what will come next, she knows she could never regret marrying Ryan and choosing him to be her girl's dad. Although his work hours can be long, and some weeks it feels like they hardly see him, when he is home, he has always been present with the girls. Always given them all of his attention. And Chelsea couldn't fault him as a father.

Eventually, Ryan places the girls back down, and they run back to the couch to finish off their movie.

Ryan leaned over the back of the couch to kiss Chelsea's head. "We should talk later."

Chelsea nodded. "Yeah. Later."

And with that, he disappeared into the kitchen to unload the shopping bags. The quiet moment Chelsea had been having now felt almost fractured with what was coming. She felt the anxiety rise as she sat on the couch, trying to be present with the girls.

Chelsea stayed on the couch a little longer, letting the girls finish their movie while she tried to slow her thoughts and her heartbeat that was still thudding against her chest.

She listened as Ryan moved around the kitchen putting the shopping away without saying much. Just the sounds of the cupboard doors opening and shutting, and the occasional clink of glass.

As the credits of the movie began to roll, Chelsea stood up. "Alright, bath time for you little grots," she said, ruffling one head of curls and one straight head of hair. "Let's go."

The usual protest groans started, of course, but the routine kicked in like muscle memory. She filled the bath, got their pyjamas out, and listened to their stories from the weekend. Half of the bathroom got wet from splashing, and they fought over who would wash their hair first.

It was almost normal.

And yet, under every small moment, there was an ache.

An ache of not knowing how many more of these *normal* moments there would be.

Would they have to find a new normal?

Could they work through this?

Or was it already too far gone?

Chelsea shuddered at the thought of potentially not having Lucy and Olivia with her all of the time. She shook her head, trying to clear the thought. That was something she would deal with if the time came.

Later, after Ryan had tucked the girls into bed and said good-night, Chelsea went in and brushed Olivia's hair back from her warm forehead, kissed her and then did the same to Lucy before sitting at the edge of her bed. Lucy looked up at her sleepily.

"Are you happy, Mummy?"

Chelsea paused.

It was the kind of question only her sensitive and intuitive child could ask with such quiet, devastating honesty.

She almost answered as she usually would if anyone had asked that question, stating that, of course, she was. But in that moment with four sleepy but adoring eyes staring back at her, she couldn't say anything but the truth.

"I'm figuring that out, sweetie," she said softly.

Lucy nodded, already falling asleep. "Okay. You should be happy. Love you, mum."

Chelsea kissed them both goodnight again and waited until their breathing slowed and deepened. She walked to the door and stopped to glance back at the two unknowingly peaceful girls, softly snoring already. Her heart swelled as she clicked the door shut and made her way back to the kitchen.

She found Ryan sitting on the couch now, a half-poured glass of red wine in front of him, the bottle beside it, one of their favourite local wines. He held a second glass out to her as she walked in.

"Figured we could both use one," he said.

She took the glass without answering and sat down at the other end of the couch.

There was a silence between them as they sipped their wine, not angry, but heavy. Tired.

Ryan swirled his wine, then glanced at her. "So. Talk now?"

Chelsea nodded once, her fingers tightening around the stem of her glass.

"Yeah," she said. "Let's."

TWELVE
Chelsea

The wine bottle sat on the coffee table in front of them. Chelsea curled her legs up underneath herself on the couch, holding her glass of wine in both hands, more for comfort than for sipping. Ryan sat at the other end, his body turned slightly towards her, his arm draped across the back of the couch. He was wearing his grey track pants with a plain white tee. His blonde hair, which was usually neat and styled, now looked like he had run his hand through it countless times. The silence between them stretched, thick with years of things unsaid.

He spoke first, breaking the silence.

"You've been distant for a while now. I just thought… I don't know. That it was just life getting busy. The girls. My work."

Chelsea looked down at the rim of her glass. "It was. For a while."

"But not just that anymore?"

She shook her head.

Ryan leaned back with a sigh, scrubbing a hand over his face. "So, what is it then?"

She hesitated.

"I've spent years just…functioning. Surviving." She continued, "Raising the girls. Being your wife. Managing our home. And I love them. And I love you. And we have tried. But I think somewhere along the way, I lost track of myself."

She hesitated again.

It wasn't just about the beach. It wasn't about Jake, even if that moment had cracked open something inside of her. This conversation, this unravelling, had been coming long before that hug.

She continued, "I think we've been holding things together with duct tape and routines," she said quietly. "We're good parents, we get through the days, but we don't actually *see* each other anymore."

"That's not true," he said, almost too quickly. Then softer, "At least I didn't think it was true."

Chelsea turned her body towards his and met his eyes, "When's the last time we sat down and talked about anything real? About anything other than things to do with the girls or whose turn it was to hang the washing out?"

Ryan opened his mouth to respond, then closed it again. The silence between them answered for him.

There'd been a time, she thought, *when he would have followed her into the kitchen just to keep the conversation going, laughing, and joking like they couldn't get enough of each other. When they would never run out of things to say and could read each other better than they could read themselves.*

She stared into her wine. "It's like we're two people running side by side but on completely different tracks now."

He shifted, clearly fighting emotion. "I don't know when it got this bad. I guess I have just been so distracted at work that I didn't notice us slowly falling away from each other."

Chelsea nodded. "I know, and this next step in your career is important, so I don't want you to think this is all on you." She took a deep breath before continuing. "But I guess I didn't want to admit it to myself either, and it was easier for us just to continue the way we were, and hope things would change."

"But they haven't."

She paused, her voice catching, "But they haven't."

Ryan stopped and took a long, slow sip of his wine. Looking like he was lost in his own thoughts.

"I have to ask something, and I don't want you to get offended by this, okay?" He asked cautiously.

Chelsea gulped, suddenly nervous. "Of course."

Ryan nodded. "Did anything happen when you went back home this weekend?"

She paused before she lifted her eyes to meet his. "I saw Jake."

Ryan nodded. "I figured that was the case."

"At the engagement party," she added quickly. "I knew he would be there, but it was still weird. I hadn't seen him since we left high school."

Ryan leaned back slowly, processing. "And?"

Chelsea breathed in deeply. "To be honest, it shook me. Not because of *him* exactly.... but more so because of who I used to be when I was with him. Who I used to be before all of this."

Ryan's jaw tensed, but he didn't speak.

"Nothing else happened; we spoke a couple of times when we bumped into each other, and he did hug me, but nothing more than that happened." She took a breath before continuing, "I think just seeing him....it just made me *feel* something again. Something I didn't realise I'd stopped feeling."

The silence that followed was thick. Not explosive or negative. Just deep. Real. She honestly couldn't pinpoint a time when things had shifted between her and Ryan. She guessed it was just a gradual thing, but looking back now, she couldn't figure out when things started to change. It felt like one minute they were best friends who were married and wanted to be around each other every minute of every day, and then the next, they were roommates who lived their separate lives, only coming together to parent and sleep in the same bed at night.

Ryan finally let out a slow exhale and nodded. "So what? You saw your ex, and now we are falling apart?"

Chelsea shook her head. "No. It's not about him. This was already slowly falling apart. I think just being back home, seeing him…it just made it impossible for me to keep ignoring what was going on with us."

He looked at her, really looked, and for the first time in a long while, she saw hurt. Not anger. Not bitterness. Just hurt.

"I get it. It's just…. I didn't realise it was this bad," he said quietly. "You never said anything."

"You never asked," she said, gently.

A long silence settled between them, filled only by the hum of the fridge and a dog down the street barking. Crumpet, who was curled up on the carpet between them, lifted his head, contemplating whether to bark back at the dog, before he lay back down. Eventually, Ryan set his wine down.

"So, what do we do, Chels?"

"I don't know," she whispered. "But I think we need to stop pretending we're okay when we're not. I think I need to figure out who I am again."

Ryan nodded slowly, his jaw tensed. He looked down at his hands.

"I just wish you had told me sooner."

Chelsea put her glass on the coffee table and scooted over on the couch so that they were sitting with their knees touching. She grabbed Ryan's hands in hers. "I wasn't ready to see it until now. What we have…or what we had, was special. It gave us our beautiful daughters, and we truly did have a good relationship. But somewhere along the way, we lost ourselves. We got too comfortable… stopped putting in the effort that we needed to keep our relationship going."

Ryan squeezed her hands gently and nodded. "Yeah, you are right. I guess I have just taken for granted everything you have sacrificed for me and my job, whilst not giving you what you need from your husband."

Chelsea sat with that. Realising he was right, she hadn't been getting what she needed from her husband. She also knew she probably wasn't giving him what he needed from his wife. This wasn't something that was one-sided; they had both chosen to let the relationship slide for whatever reason.

"It's not all on you, Ry. I wasn't giving you what you needed either. I think we just fell into a roommate relationship and rather than work to fix it, we ignored it, hoping it would get better on its own."

"But instead, it feels like this is the end," Ryan said, his eyes glazed.

Chelsea felt her own eyes sting with tears. She moved even closer and tucked herself under his arm. A move that used to feel so natural when they would curl up on the couch to watch something together, but now she couldn't remember the last time they sat like this. She guessed that was part of the reason they were where they were.

Ryan moved his arm to hold her against him. They sat like that in silence. Listening to each other's heartbeats, wanting to hold onto this moment, as it felt so final.

"God, this sucks," Ryan said eventually as he let out a long breath.

Chelsea laughed, her voice cracking and a tear escaping her eye. "It really does."

"So, what do we do now?" Ryan asked with a slight sniffle.

Chelsea thought for a moment. "I guess we give each other some space to figure things out. Figure out what we want... or what we need."

Ryan nodded. "Whatever we do, we have to make sure the girls are okay. They are number one. I don't want them feeling like this was their fault."

Chelsea nodded against Ryan's side. "Agreed."

"And we have to have open communication with each other. I don't want to drag this out if we feel we are just delaying the inevitable. I'd rather you just tell me straight, as much as that might hurt me."

Chelsea nodded again.

"I'll take the couch tonight, and then we can figure out the rest tomorrow," Ryan said after a while, getting to his feet.

Chelsea looked up. "You don't have to."

He gave her a tired smile. "I think we both know I do."

And with that, he disappeared down the hall to their room, leaving Chelsea sitting alone in the glow of the living room lamp. She heard the shower start up down the hall as she picked up her wine glass and leaned back on the couch, wondering how something could hurt so much and still feel like relief all at once.

~

The house felt quieter than usual when Chelsea woke the next morning. Ryan was already gone – the blanket he used on the couch, neatly folded, his keys missing from the buffet. No note. No text. Just an empty space where he used to be.

They hadn't really spoken since Ryan had left the couch last night. Both processing the heaviness of their conversation. They had passed each other in the hallway, Chelsea on her way to bed and Ryan to the couch. They briefly paused before passing each other, where they would usually share a kiss or go to bed together; instead, they politely said goodnight before going their separate ways.

Now, she could hear the girls stirring. Chelsea heard the muffled footsteps and the creak of the bathroom door, followed by whispers and the faint hum of the morning cartoons. Chelsea sighed as she flicked on the coffee machine before she walked over to let Crumpet out into the backyard. Real life didn't pause for broken hearts.

She moved through the motions of their regular weekday mornings. Made breakfast. Braided hair. Packed lunchboxes. Smiled on autopilot.

"Mummy, you forgot my strawberries," Olivia said, poking at

her yoghurt.

"Oh – sorry, honey," Chelsea murmured, turning back towards the fridge. She was offbeat. There, but not fully there.

Later, once she had finished the school drop off, she got into the car and scrolled through her contacts on the screen in the car. She found Emily's name and hit call as she reversed out of the school car park, heading towards home.

Emily answered on the second ring. "Hey girl! How are ya?"

Chelsea exhaled. "Can you come over? I…I need to talk."

Emily didn't hesitate. "Be there in a bit."

Emily lived a couple of towns over from her, about a half an hour drive, so Chelsea assumed Emily must have been able to hear in her voice that she really needed her best friend right now.

Chelsea hung up the phone call and continued home, again feeling like she was on autopilot. Her sister had messaged her during the morning rush, checking in on her, but she hadn't replied yet. Still not able to come to terms with the fact that her marriage could be over. Saying it aloud or telling someone just made it feel all the more real. She wasn't ready to think about the fact that there was a very high possibility that she would soon be thirty years old and divorced. The thought made her shudder.

An hour later, Chelsea and Emily sat on the patio steps of Chelsea's house, just like they used to in high school, back at Chelsea's parents' house. Chelsea sipped her coffee while Emily twisted her engagement ring around her finger, sensing the weight of the conversation to come.

"So, I told Ryan," Chelsea said finally as she stroked Crumpet, who was flopped against her legs. "About everything. About how I've been feeling. About Jake.

Emily's eyes widened. "Oh hell, you told him."

"I had to," Chelsea said. "He deserved the truth. Even if the truth was messy, I couldn't walk around pretending everything was okay when it had been so far from okay."

Emily was quiet for a moment, then softly asked, "How did he take it?"

"Better than I expected, I guess. But it was hard. He looked so hurt and broken." Chelsea gave a small, sad smile.

Emily reached over and squeezed her hand. "I'm proud of you, Chels. That's a brave thing to do."

Chelsea blinked back the sting behind her eyes. "It doesn't feel brave. It just feels…sad."

"I know. And it probably will feel sad for a while. But one day it won't feel as sad anymore. And then eventually you will start to feel happy again."

Chelsea nodded while sniffling. "God, I hope you are right," she sniffed again before continuing. "I am just so worried about how the girls will cope."

Emily nodded, "I know it's hard. But they have the best parents, and as long as you guys keep that as a priority, they will be okay." She paused before continuing. "Don't you want to set an example for those girls? You wouldn't want them settling for something that doesn't make them genuinely happy. You would want them to find that love that sets them on fire. A love that doesn't fade into the routines of life."

Chelsea was beyond trying to hold back her tears; they were streaming down her face now. She leaned her head on her best friend's shoulder, nodding. "You are right…as always."

Emily laughed and leaned her head against hers. "Babe, when am I ever wrong?"

Chelsea managed a cracked laugh.

They sat like that for a minute before Emily broke the silence. "So now what?"

"Well, now he is at work, and then I don't know. We didn't really make a plan," she shrugged. "I guess I'll just see what happens when he gets home from work."

They sat like that, watching the clouds roll across the sky before Emily told her she had to go to work. She left, hugging her tightly, promising to check in with her later.

Chelsea lingered outside for a little longer. She pulled her phone out to text her sister back. She gave her a quick rundown of what was going on and that she would call her later.

She got a response almost immediately:

Oh Chels. Come home xx

Chelsea stared at the message for a while before putting her phone away.

Where was home now?

Everything in her life was shifting – and for the first time in a long time, she wasn't trying to hold it all still.

It was time to figure out where home was.

T he pub was busier than expected for a Monday arvo. The warm afternoon breeze was salty and fresh coming off the beach across the road. Jake leaned back in his chair, one hand wrapped around a half-drunk beer, the other lazily spinning a coaster between his fingers.

Across from him, Dean smirked. "You look like you slept all of three hours. That or you argued with your old man."

Dean was in town because he had a job for a local nearby. He worked as a carpenter, so whenever he was working in Somerdale, he and Jake always made sure to catch up for a beer before he headed home.

Jake chuckled. "Pretty accurate. We are driving each other nuts. He can't give up any control with the brewery, so he is hobbling around the place in pain by the end of the day because he isn't resting and taking it easy like his doc said." Jake took a swig of his beer. "Bloody annoying, I tell ya."

Dean laughed. "You need to get out of town more, mate," he said, raising his beer. "Being back here has made you all soft."

Jake rolled his eyes, "Says the man getting married."

Dean grinned. "Touché."

They sat in comfortable silence for a moment, the sound of other pub goers and the football game on the big screen in the beer garden filling the silence. The familiar smell of the beer and the salt from the ocean across the road, it all settled around them like old habits. This was one thing Jake did miss while he was galivanting around the world. Having a beer with his best mate on a random weekday afternoon. Even if said mate enjoyed digging into Jake's personal life, any chance he could get.

Jake tapped the edge of his glass. "So, how's Em? Still deep in the Pinterest wedding hole?"

Dean snorted. "Absolutely. She showed me seven different fonts for the welcome sign last night. I thought she was going to divorce me before we are even married because I picked the wrong one."

Jake laughed, leaning forward.

Dean took a swig of his beer before saying, "Also, I didn't want to make this a big soppy thing, but you know you are my best man for the wedding, right?"

Jake laughed again. "I hoped so, but it was fun watching you squirm, figuring out a way to tell me." He winked as he took a drink.

Dean scowled at him across the table. "Sometimes you are such a jerk. Emily wanted me to get these matching glasses engraved for you and my brothers to formally ask you, but I told her you all knew, so no need."

"To be fair, I would have liked a glass. I would have laughed at you, but I would have used it."

Dean shook his head, amused, but then his expression shifted – just slightly. He set his glass down and drummed his fingers against the edge of the table, contemplating.

"There's something else, actually. I didn't really want to ruin the moment right now, but I would rather you hear it from me."

Jake raised a brow. "What?"

Dean hesitated. "About Chelsea."

Jake's body stilled, his hand pausing mid-spin on the coaster.

"What about her?"

Dean leaned in a little, dropping his voice. "Em drove over to her place in Port Mac this morning. She told her that she and Ryan are separating. Or taking a break. I don't really know, but something happened."

Jake blinked. "What?"

Dean shrugged. "Yeah. They had a pretty serious chat when she got back. Chelsea was honest with him – told him seeing you again stirred some stuff up. Not just about you," he added quickly, "but about who she used to be. Who she *is*."

Jake leaned back in his seat, exhaling slowly. He stared past Dean for a moment, at nothing in particular. Just lost in his head. The coaster stopped spinning.

"She told him about me," Jake said quietly, almost a whisper.

Dean nodded slowly. "Not in a 'run back to Jake' way. More like...she saw something in herself again that she had lost... or forgotten."

Jake didn't say anything for a minute. The pub buzzed on around them, everyone completely unaware of how his heart had just dropped and surged all at the same time.

"She's not the kind of woman who does things halfway," Dean said. "If she's being honest and raw, it means something, Jake."

Jake gave a slight nod. "Yeah. I know."

Dean lifted his glass again. "Just thought you should hear it from me before you start hearing whispers around town."

Jake raised his own glass, clinking it gently against Dean's.

"Thanks," he said. "For not sugar-coating it."

Dean smirked. "Since when have I ever sugar-coated anything, best man?"

Jake smiled, but it didn't quite reach his eyes.

And in the quiet moments, or loud moments in the pub, between one sip of beer and the next, something inside him shifted.

This wasn't over.

Not by a long shot.

Until she told him that there was no chance of them ever being together in the future, Jake couldn't walk away. Not again. Not when, after all these years, he still felt as if he was the same eighteen-year-old boy madly in love with one of his best friends.

FOURTEEN
Chelsea

The front door opened softly just after four.

Chelsea looked up from the kitchen bench where she was slicing apples for the girls' after-school snack. Ryan stepped in, keys in one hand, his work uniform in the other, looking tired but still collected, as always.

"Hey," he said, setting his wallet and keys down on the kitchen table and hanging his uniform over the back of the chair.

Lucy and Olivia were in the living room, curled up on the couch in their school uniforms, absorbed in a cartoon they had seen a million times. Oblivious to the outside world.

She wiped her hands on a tea towel. "How was work?"

"I finished early," he said. "Took a few days off. I thought maybe I could spend some time with the girls. Give you some breathing room."

She blinked, surprised. "Oh. That's...thoughtful."

He offered a slight shrug. "Figured you might need it."

Chelsea nodded, her throat tight. "I was actually thinking

about going back to Mum and Dad's for a couple of nights. Just me. Reset a little. Give us both some space to figure things out."

Ryan didn't flinch. "Okay."

"I'm not running away," she added quickly.

"I know." His voice was gentle. "You're trying to figure things out. I get it. And honestly? I could really use some one-on-one time with the girls. Maybe let them skip school for a few days and head down the coast to see my family."

Chelsea gave him a grateful smile, her eyes slightly misty. "They would love that. Thank you."

They stood there for a moment, not reaching for each other, but also not stepping away. Each moment feeling so final, even without the weight of any words.

Then Olivia yelled from the lounge, "Mummy, don't forget I want the pink cup!"

Chelsea laughed as she exhaled, grabbing the requested cup and the plate of fruit. As she passed Ryan, he placed a hand lightly on her shoulder – just a touch. "We are doing the right thing, aren't we?"

Chelsea tilted her head and lifted her shoulder so that her chin was resting on his hand. "I think so."

He nodded before heading into the kitchen. Chelsea hesitated before continuing towards the girls. She hadn't been away from Lucy and Olivia for more than a night, their entire life. She placed the snack plate and water on the coffee table and settled on the couch between the girls, wanting to soak up as much of them as she could before she left later that night. Her heart ached from the heaviness of her marriage mixed with the guilt of leaving the girls. She knew they would be okay, and to be honest, uninterrupted time with Ryan would be good for them, but she couldn't help the guilt settling in the pit of her stomach. She supposed that was just a normal feeling that came with parenting, particularly in a tricky situation like this one.

~

She packed her overnight bag later that evening. Just a few things. Pyjamas. Her book that had been sitting on her bedside table, half-read for months. Her old hoodie from high school that she hadn't worn in years. She placed her bag in the hallway before heading into the lounge room to where the girls were sitting with Ryan.

When she kissed the girl's goodnight, Lucy clung to her for a moment longer than usual.

"Where are you going, Mummy?" She asked, worry lining her face.

She knelt so that she was at eye level with Lucy. "Just to Grandma and Grandad's for a bit. Daddy is going to be here with you and might even take you on a little trip."

Lucy frowned in confusion, "But why can't we all go?"

Chelsea opened her mouth to respond, but no words came out. She didn't know what she was feeling, let alone how to explain that to a nine-year-old. Thankfully, Ryan could see she didn't know how to respond and stepped in.

"Mummy just needs to take some time out for herself. You know how sometimes when you get home from school, you like to go to your room on your own to colour in or read?" Lucy nodded before Ryan continued. "Well, that's the same for adults. Mum just needs to go and have some time on her own, and then she will be back, feeling all recharged."

Chelsea smiled appreciatively at Ryan.

"Okay," Lucy whispered before turning back to Chelsea. "But come back soon, okay?"

Chelsea smiled, brushing her hair back from her daughter's face. "Always."

Lucy thought for a moment before she spoke again, "You should take Crumpet with you, Mum. So, you aren't alone."

Chelsea felt her heart swell at her daughter worrying about her being alone while the rest of them were together. "You know what? That's a great idea, Luce. Can you help me get his things?"

She said, standing back up.

She watched as both Olivia and Lucy ran off to gather all of their dogs' essentials. It wasn't long before they came charging back through the house holding a dog bed, lead, food bowl and numerous stuffed toys Chelsea knew would end up ripped apart. Ryan took Crumpet and his things out to the car while Chelsea said goodbye to the girls.

"Okay, be good for Dad," she said. "I'll FaceTime you in the morning."

Olivia hugged her legs, "Love you, Mumma." She said, and in the next breath, "Dad, can we have ice cream?" As she looked around, Chelsea at Ryan, who was now standing back in the doorway.

Chelsea laughed. Her youngest daughter never seemed to let things worry her. In her world, the most important things were ice cream and her favourite stuffed toy. "Love you guys, I'll see you soon." She gave them both another hug and kiss before making her way back to the hallway and to her packed bag. As she bent down to grab her bag, she felt Ryan behind her.

"I really hope you find what you are looking for, Chels." He said his words were genuine, but Chelsea could tell by his face that he was hurting.

She gave him a small smile, "You too, Ry."

As she got into the car and backed out of the driveway, she looked back up at the front window.

Ryan was standing there with one girl at each of his sides. The girls were enthusiastically waving at her. Ryan lifted his hand in an almost wave, but something was missing kind of way. Something she couldn't quite read, written on his face.

She waved back, then turned the corner. Fighting every urge not to turn around and go back. She knew she had to do this for herself and for her girls. She owed it to them and herself to truly find herself again.

She had given up everything to be the best mother and wife she could be for the past decade. But now she wasn't even sure if she was being the best she could be for them. Chelsea lost herself in her thoughts as Port Mac flashed past her windows, the sun setting and casting a golden glow over the sky.

Tomorrow, maybe, she would walk the beach again.

Maybe she'd read some of her book finally.

Maybe she would let herself wonder what comes next.

But for tonight, she would simply *breathe*.

And get a hug from her mum.

FIFTEEN
Chelsea

The kettle whistled softly through the empty kitchen, steam curling upward in the soft morning light that was filtering through the windows. Chelsea sat at the old wooden table, watching her mum move around the kitchen with quiet ease, her slippers shuffling like no time had passed since Chelsea used to sit in the same spot, telling her about school dramas or the boy she loved.

Her mum flicked on the coffee machine, holding up a mug to Chelsea in question.

Chelsea nodded, desperately needing a coffee more than a cup of tea to help wake her up. She had arrived at her parents' house quite late last night and caught them just before they went to bed. It wasn't long before Chelsea followed, heading to her childhood bedroom. She felt as if she fell asleep as soon as her head hit the pillow, but considering how exhausted she felt now, she guessed she didn't sleep as soundly as she had hoped.

"How'd the girls go last night with Ryan?" She asked gently while she made Chelsea a coffee.

"Good. He sent a photo of them all snuggled up together in our bed. I think he is going to take them down the coast to his parents' house for a few nights. Chelsea said with a soft smile. "It feels so strange. Being alone again."

Her mum put a steaming coffee in front of her, touching her shoulder gently before pulling out the chair opposite her. "You used to love your quiet mornings. Every morning, I would find you out on the back porch, coffee in one hand and a book in the other."

"Yeah. Back when quiet meant peace, not guilt."

They sat in silence for a few moments. Chelsea sat holding her coffee in both hands close to her face. The steam curled around her face, in an attempt to wash away the thoughts that were weighing heavily on her.

Her mum put her cup down on the old wooden kitchen table and leaned forward. "You don't have to tell me everything, love. But I can see the weight this has on you. You seem... lost."

Chelsea blinked hard, her hands wrapped around her mug. "It's just all a lot. Seeing Jake again...It cracked something open. Something I hadn't let myself think about in years. And not just about him. About *me*. About the version of myself I left behind all those years ago." She took a sip of her coffee before continuing, "And Ryan. I don't know where everything went wrong... when we stopped working."

Her mum nodded slowly, taking a sip of her tea. "You've carried a lot. Always did. You wanted so badly to build a life, you didn't stop to check if it fit. And I don't mean just in your relationship. Even university. You just did what you thought was the right thing to do. Or what you thought everyone expected from you."

Her mum's words hit harder than she expected. She swallowed, feeling the burn of tears.

"It wasn't that Ryan was a bad choice," Cheslea said. "It's just.... maybe I stopped choosing myself a long time ago." Chelsea hesitated before continuing, "Ryan is a good Dad. And he was a good husband. He hasn't done anything wrong...which just makes this even harder." Chelsea knew it was a toxic thought, but she couldn't help but think that if he had done something wrong by her, then it would make this situation a hell of a lot easier. She was also aware that this was probably entirely untrue.

Her mum reached across the table and squeezed her hand. "He is a good father. And a good husband. But it's also okay to admit that maybe you just aren't the right fit for each other anymore." She said, "And it's okay to start again. To start choosing yourself again."

Before she could say more, the back door creaked open, and a familiar voice filled the room, "Smells like I made it just in time for coffee."

Chelsea turned as her baby sister stepped into the kitchen, dressed in her running clothes, hair tied up in a messy bun. Chelsea laughed, genuinely this time, grateful for the lightness Chloe brought to the room. Her sister had chosen to travel after she finished school rather than go to university or start a career. Once she graduated, she set off travelling around the world, mostly on her own, but occasionally a friend would join her. She had always been social and found it easy to make friends wherever she went. Once Chelsea had Lucy, Chloe's trips became shorter as she didn't want to miss out on seeing her niece grow up. Chloe had been living at her parents' house because there was no point in paying rent or buying a place of her own when she was only there for a few weeks at a time. She had a few flings with guys over the years, but again, nothing ever stuck because she wasn't ever in a place long enough. But her trips seemed to have slowed down in the past year or so. Chelsea wondered if her baby sis was finally going to start thinking about settling down. The thought seemed wild to her.

Chloe flopped into the chair next to her. "I didn't think you would actually listen to my message and come home."

"Yeah, well, don't get used to it," Chelsea said with a wink.

Chloe rolled her eyes. "But seriously, you, okay?"

"Working on it."

Chloe studied her for a beat, trying to decide if she believed her, then nodded. "Good. You're allowed to."

Her mum stood, switching the coffee machine back on. The sound of coffee beans grinding filled the comfortable silence.

"Did mum tell you she saw Jake at the brewery yesterday?" Chloe asked, casually.

Chelsea's head snapped up. "Hmm, no, she didn't."

Her mum tensed briefly before snapping her head around to glare at Chloe. She turned back around to continue brewing more coffee. "I was getting there, Chloe. But yes, I did see him. Your dad and I popped in for some lunch, and he was there. He has been helping his dad out since he had surgery, he said. He looked good. Taller, maybe?"

Chloe smirked. "You mean hotter, Mum."

"Oh, stop it," her mum said, but didn't deny it.

Chelsea shook her head, chuckling, trying to act like her heart wasn't thudding all over again. She knew logically they would bump into each other somewhere around town, but she hadn't expected the ghost of him to return when she hadn't even been here 12 hours yet. She guessed this was the reality of a small country town.

"So, what are we going to do today then?" Chloe asked as her mum placed a cup of coffee in front of her and returned to the kitchen.

Chelsea shrugged, "I was thinking I would head to the beach and read for a bit."

Chloe scrunched her nose up, "Boring," she said as she took a sip of her coffee. "Okay, I have some work to do, so while you go do your wholesome healing, I'll do that, and then we are having drinks tonight in town."

"Chloe... I don't know if I want – "

"Girl, you do. Plus, I have already spoken to Emily, and she is coming up this afternoon and thinks drinks are a great idea." Chloe said with a smirk.

Chelsea rolled her eyes, sipping from her cup. "Fine. I'll go, but only if we go to The Sandbar."

"Now you are talkin' my language, sister," Chloe said as she got up, walked past her sister and headed down the hallway.

Chelsea smiled to herself while she finished off her coffee. She couldn't remember the last time she went out for drinks with her sister or friends. She wasn't sure if this was a good idea, and usually, she would feel guilty about going out.

But for the first time in forever, she felt free. Free to make her own choices and not feel guilty. Okay, so she might still feel guilty, but she was working on that.

SIXTEEN
Chelsea

The mid-morning sun kissed the shoreline, soft and golden, as Chelsea dug her toes into the cool sand and flipped the page of her book while Crumpet splashed in the shallow water. The rhythmic hush of the waves was the only sound, except for the occasional bird cry overhead and panting from Crumpet as he ran past her. She hadn't read uninterrupted like this in years. Every time she would try to pull her book out these days, someone would need something from her – the girls wanting a snack or an argument broken up, or Ryan asking her where something was. Sitting here in silence with no one needing her felt liberating.

The breeze gently brushed against her face, playing with strands of hair that had fallen loose from her braid. She tucked her hair behind her ear without looking up from the page. She wasn't even sure what the book was about anymore; she'd read the same paragraph three times now. Her mind just kept wandering. To Jake. To Ryan. To how her life had somehow become something she wasn't sure she wanted anymore.

She stared out at the sparkling water for a long moment, closing the book gently on her lap. Crumpet was now lying beside her on the cool sand, snoring away after spending the past hour chasing birds and flies.

This beach had always been the place she came when she needed to think. And now, after all these years, it still felt like the only place quiet enough for her thoughts to land.

She had given up everything the moment she found out she was pregnant with Lucy. Her relationship with Ryan was still fresh, and they were still very much in the honeymoon phase, but they both were excited. There was never a question of whether they would go through with the pregnancy despite how new their relationship was. They immediately moved towns together for Ryan's job because he would be the one supporting them financially while she took the time to stay home with the baby. This was what she had wanted at the time. But now she was realising she didn't know what she wanted. She had given up her dreams. Her career. Everything. To be the best mum she could be. But now she was beginning to think she needed to figure out what her new dreams were so that she could continue to be the mum she wanted to be. The Chelsea she wanted to be again. She needed something for herself. A purpose other than being a mother.

She sat there zoned out in her thoughts for some time, just watching the water edge in closer to her feet. Eventually, the sun crept higher, and her phone buzzing in her tote bag dragged her from her thoughts. A message from Emily:

"Hey, babes. Are you home? I have something I want to give you before tonight xx."

Chelsea smiled faintly. She sent off a reply letting her know she would be home shortly and then packed up her things. She could already guess what was coming. Emily couldn't keep a secret to save her life. She was surprised she had lasted this long.

~

Back at the house, Chloe was napping on the couch, a half-eaten bowl of cereal on the coffee table and a rerun of Grey's Anatomy playing on the television. Chelsea tiptoed past with a grin and headed for the kitchen, wondering how much *work* Chloe had done this morning. Chelsea smiled at Crumpet as she entered the kitchen, where he was already passed out again on the cool floors. She knew he probably wouldn't move for the rest of the day after using up all his energy at the beach. Chelsea had just poured herself a glass of water as the doorbell rang.

When she answered it, Emily stood there in a denim skirt and a cute top, grinning like a kid with a secret who was about to explode.

"Oh God," Chelsea laughed, taking in the sight of her best friend squirming, "You're about to cry, aren't you?"

Emily held up a small pink envelope and a bottle of champagne. "Open it before I burst."

Chelsea raised an eyebrow but took the envelope from her. Inside was a little handmade card covered in glitter and gold ink. The words were scrawled in Emily's neatest handwriting:

"I am sure you were expecting this, but let's make it official. Will you be my Maid of Honour?"

Chelsea looked up at her best friend, already teary. "You're seriously asking?"

Emily nodded, looking like she was truly about to burst. "We both knew you always would be, but I wanted to make it special."

Chelsea pulled her into a hug, pretty much jumping on her. "YES. YES. YES. Of course I will be. I bloody love you!"

Emily laughed, tears dropping from her eyes. "I love you too." She pulled her back, eyes bright. "And now that we have cried a little, we are celebrating tonight. Me, You, and Chloe." She said, waving the bottle of champagne.

Chelsea laughed. "Chloe's idea of fun is tequila and flirting with the DJ."

"Exactly," Emily said with a grin. "You need a night of that." Emily stepped into the house, putting her arm around Chelsea's shoulders and guiding her down the hallway. "Now, go wash off that sunscreen and sand, and I'll go get us some glasses so we can have some champagne while we get ready. Like the good old days." She basically pushed Chelsea towards her room, with a smack on the ass.

Chloe was sitting up on the couch now, probably woken by the squealing and crying that had just happened, or she could smell the champagne through the bottle. She got up and followed Emily into the kitchen while Chelsea headed to the shower.

In this moment, her mind was clear. She was feeling overjoyed for her best friend and just full of so much love and gratitude that she would get to stand by her side for one of the best days of her life.

Maybe Chloe and Emily were right.

This night out could be exactly what she needed.

~

The Sandbar was exactly how Chelsea remembered it. Fairy lights tangled around the timber rafters, the scent of salty air and citrus cocktails floating through the space, and the familiar thud of the music playing on an overworked speaker system. She didn't think the place had changed at all since she was last here ten years ago.

Chelsea stepped in between Emily and Chloe, immediately hit with the buzz of laughter and clinking glasses. Her boots tapped against the worn timber floor as she took in the space around her. Everything exactly the same.

She was feeling good, relaxed. That could have something to do with the bottle of champagne they had polished off while they were getting ready, but she really was feeling confident. She had decided to wear her blue denim mini skirt, paired with a black halter top that always made her feel confident. She chose her black knee-high boots, which may have been slightly overdressed for this place, but she didn't care. It had been a long time since she had felt the confidence to dress this way. Her usual uniform had been bike shorts and an oversized tee for far too long.

Chloe made a beeline for the bar. "I'm getting the first round.

No arguments."

Emily slid into a high-top table near the window; Chelsea slid into the chair next to her.

"Oh god, I probably should have eased up on the wine. Not sure I have even recovered from your party yet."

Emily laughed. "Me either, to be honest. But you look hot tonight, girl. Glowing might I say." She said, nudging her shoulder with hers.

They both giggled, and Chelsea realised how long it had been since she'd laughed like this. How long had it been since she truly felt this relaxed?

Chloe returned quickly with three drinks: a mojito for herself, a gin and tonic for Emily, and a spicy margarita for Chelsea.

"Oh, you remembered!" Chelsea said, going straight for her drink.

Chloe shrugged, "Hard to forget when you told the bartender, who mind you still works here," she said, pointing towards the bar, "that you were going to marry him based on how good he could mix tequila and lime."

The three of them looked back at the bartender, who was, sure enough, the same one who had worked there when the girls had first turned eighteen. They all cracked up laughing.

Chelsea scrunched her nose up, "I remember him a lot younger. And a lot hotter."

"Well, yeah, it was ten years ago, babe." Emily winked at her.

They all laughed again before Chloe stood from her chair, raising her glass. "Okay, we need a toast. To Emily, somehow tying Hotshots down," she raised her glass to Emily. "And to my big sister, finally putting herself first and looking hot while doing it." She raised her glass to Chelsea.

Both girls jumped up to clink their glasses with Chloe, a choir of "cheers" following. They all fell silent as they took a drink before sitting back down.

As the evening wore on, the bar filled up, locals mingling with tourists. Some familiar faces gave them polite smiles, a few second glances. She saw at least three former classmates, all a little older, but still recognisable. One thing about this town was that everyone was very social. It was hard to believe it was a Tuesday night. Back home, or back in Port Mac, the town would be quiet and empty at this time of the night. But here, everyone loved a drink and made the most of the warm summer nights.

Conversations moved between light-hearted gossip, Chloe's love life, and wedding talk. At one point, they were all up and dancing to a 2000s throwback hit. When the song finished, Chelsea and Emily left Chloe on the dance floor with some random surfy-looking guy to go to the bar for another round of drinks. Emily ordered the round and then put her arm around Chelsea's shoulder while they waited for their drinks. "I missed this," she said. "You. Us."

Chelsea leaned into her best friend. "Me too. I didn't realise how much."

"You seem more…. *you*, tonight."

Chelsea gave a faint smile. "Maybe I'm remembering who that is."

"Good," Emily said. "Because I bloody love her. Well, I love every version of you, but I miss seeing you this happy."

Chelsea squeezed Emily's hand as the bartender arrived with their drinks at the same time that Chloe joined them.

"That guy said he will take me out to teach me how to surf tomorrow," Chloe said, grinning as she grabbed her drink from the bar.

Emily and Chelsea laughed, picking up their drinks before turning back to look at the dance floor that was starting to fill up. "But you already know how to surf? Dad taught us both before we could walk." Chelsea said as she sipped her drink.

"Yeah, but he doesn't know that," Chloe responded with a wink.

Chelsea shook her head at her sister as she looked over the dance floor.

Someone familiar caught Chelsea's eye from across the room.

She tensed. But as they turned around, she realised it wasn't Jake.

Just someone who looked like him enough to jolt her chest for a second. Chelsea laughed to herself. She must be drunker than she thought. Looking now at the guy across the bar, she realised he looked nothing like Jake. She wondered if it was just her brain, hoping she would see him tonight.

Emily grabbed her hand and pulled her back through the crowd to the dance floor. The three of them danced to throwback tunes, sang badly, and took a blurry selfie that Chloe put up on her Instagram story. Chelsea was sure she would look at that in the morning with a bittersweet smile, laughing at their drunk eyes; they didn't realise they had.

Despite the heaviness of her life at the moment, Chelsea felt carefree and light, dancing with her best friend and sister.

She was sure it could be a different story in the morning once the tequila was out of her system, but tonight she felt like no matter how things worked out, she would be okay.

SEVENTEEN
Chelsea

The balmy night air hit Chelsea like a soft slap as the girls spilt out of The Sandbar, laughter and the hum of the music trailing behind them. The sound of waves crashing across the road was magnetic, drawing them in.

Chloe flung her arms around both Emily and Chelsea. "Beach walk. It's tradition."

"What! No, it's not." Chelsea laughed. But neither of them protested when Chloe started dragging them in that direction.

"It is now," Chloe said with a shrug as they made their way towards the sound of the salty water crashing against the sand. It somehow always sounded louder at night.

Chelsea thought that a beach walk might help sober her up. Now that she was out of the bar, she knew if she went home, she would find the room spinning as she climbed into bed. Some fresh air would do her some good. Besides, she wasn't quite ready for the night to be over.

They all took off their shoes as they stepped onto the sand, letting their bare feet sink into the cool grains. Chelsea felt loose, warm from the drinks, dizzy in the way that was half alcohol and half happiness. There was a buzz in her chest she hadn't felt in years – light, free, and kind of reckless.

The girls laughed and sang as they walked along the beach. It was mostly empty since it was quite late now, just the occasional couple or group gathered around phone flashlights or half-dug out firepits. As they neared the path that cut back towards the street, they heard a low murmur of voices and a sudden burst of laughter.

Emily squinted ahead. "That sounds like – "

Chelsea froze.

As if she could feel him before she could see him.

Jake.

Dean. And a few other guys from their high school group.

They were walking towards the same path, beer bottles in hand, casual and unaware. Chelsea felt her stomach turn. Not sure if it was the margaritas or the uncertainty of seeing Jake again so soon.

Before she could turn around and run the other way, Jake looked up, noticing them first. She watched his expression shift in real time – from relaxed to surprise to…unreadable as his eyes drank her in.

God, she felt sick now.

Dean let out a low whistle. "Well, well, well. Fancy seeing you three here."

Chloe laughed, completely unfazed. "What can we say? The beach calls."

Emily stepped forward, always the peacekeeper. "Hi, babe. We were just heading this way." She said, giving him a pointed look.

Dean wrapped an arm around her waist without hesitation, his eyes softening. "You look incredible, by the way." He said, softly nibbling at her ear.

Emily giggled as she wrapped her arms around his neck, "And you are drunk."

Jake had stayed a step behind, but now his eyes were locked on Chelsea. She hadn't seen him since the beach. Since the hug. Since that heartbeat of a moment when he hadn't let her go.

"Hey," he said softly to her now that the group had broken away.

"Hey, yourself." She said, trying to ground herself in the sand so she didn't fall over and make a fool of herself.

The others talked around them, Emily teasing Dean, Chloe flirting with one of the other guys, but the noise seemed to fade away. Nothing else mattering.

Chelsea tucked her hair behind her ear. "Didn't expect to see you out tonight."

Jake smirked. "Didn't expect to hear *Spice Girls* being sung down the beach, but here we are."

Her cheeks flushed. "Oh no, you heard that?"

He nodded. "Could've sworn I was seventeen again for a second."

Chelsea laughed, soft and a little breathless. "Yeah…something about tonight feels a lot like that."

Jake took a small step closer, "Are you…okay?"

The question was simple. But it landed heavily.

And Chelsea was too drunk to answer it how he probably expected her to.

Chelsea looked at him, into those familiar eyes, and for a second, she truly did feel like she was seventeen again.

"Well, I could go for another margarita. And maybe a swim." She said, trying to lighten the vibe after such a heavy question.

Jake looked at her, his eyes shining, raking over her face. Before a massive grin spread across his face. "Chelsea Quinn. Are you drunk?"

Chelsea hesitated. His smile literally took her breath away for a second, and she couldn't make any words. Before she cracked up laughing, with a slight hiccup. "I guess I am."

Dean called back to Jake, motioning toward a shortcut. "We're heading down to the firepit for one last drink."

Jake looked at Chelsea. "You coming, drunko?" He said playfully.

Chelsea hesitated. Emily looked at her. Chloe raised an eyebrow with a smirk, waiting for her to decide.

Chelsea turned back to Jake. "Lead the way." She said as she took a step towards him, stumbling slightly.

He grabbed her instinctively, "Oh Jesus, you are drunk." He said with a laugh. "Here, give me those." He said, pointing to her boots that were tucked under her arm.

Chelsea laughed as she handed her shoes to him without a thought. He tucked her boots under one arm and wrapped the other around her shoulder to steady her. She let herself lean into him slightly. Mainly because she didn't trust herself to walk on the soft sand in her state. They followed the others up the shortcut towards the same fire pit where they used to hang out when they were in high school.

The firepit wasn't much, just a circle of mismatched stones and driftwood logs, the flames licking at the night air with a quiet crackle. Chelsea wasn't sure if this was where the guys had been hanging out before bumping into the girls, or if they had just hijacked someone else's fire pit, but no one else seemed to care. Someone had brought a portable speaker and was playing old acoustic covers at a volume low enough to talk over. As they approached the firepit, Chelsea felt a rush of nostalgia at being back here. The same place, mostly the same people. It felt like she had been pulled straight back into her high school days.

Chelsea dropped down onto a log with a soft oof, hugging her knees as the breeze swept through her hair. She was tipsy, no doubt about it. Her skin warm, her head light, her heart entirely unsure. But for once, she didn't care.

Jake sat beside her, just close enough that their shoulders were pressed lightly together. Chelsea felt the ping of electricity where his shoulder rested against hers, but neither of them made a move to pull away.

"Didn't peg you for a firepit kind of guy still," Chelsea teased, glancing at him sideways.

Jake smiled, holding a beer loosely in one hand. "Didn't peg you for a girl who still sings the second verse of 'Wannabe' with full confidence."

Chelsea gasped. "It's a classic. Don't insult my craft." She said as she took his beer from his hand and drank.

"Wouldn't dream of it," he said, eyes glinting as they briefly dropped to her lips as she drank.

Chelsea passed his beer back to him, biting her bottom lip to hold back her smile.

They sat and watched the flames for a moment, the world around them quiet except for the low murmur of the music and the others chatting around the fire.

Jake leaned forward slightly, elbows on his knees. "You seem different from when I saw you last weekend," he said, voice soft.

Chelsea blinked at the flames. "Different how?"

He glanced at her. "Lighter. A little wild again, like the old Chels who used to sneak out to watch the stars with me."

Chelsea huffed a laugh. "You mean the version of me that got grounded after falling asleep in the back of your Ute?"

Jake chuckled. "Best nap of my life."

They both grinned, and for a second, it was so easy. So, them. Like no time at all had passed. One of Chelsea's favourite parts of their relationship, and arguably the hardest part to get over, was that they were best friends first. Their relationship came so naturally because they were already so comfortable around each other. Although losing her first love was heartbreaking, losing her best friend had been devastating.

Chelsea picked up a twig and threw it onto the fire. "I forgot what this felt like," she admitted. "Not just...being here. But being me."

Jake didn't say anything right away. Then he said, "I never forgot."

She turned to him, surprised.

Jake shrugged, eyes fixed on the fire now. "Even when I tried. I'd hear a song. Drive past the old bakery we always went to. See someone laugh the way you used to. It all brought you back. No matter where in the world I was, or how hard I was trying to forget. I never could."

Chelsea's heart twisted in a painfully beautiful way. "Jake..."

He looked over at her, eyes searching her face. "I know it's messy. I'm not trying to make it harder."

"You're not," she said quickly, too quickly. She lowered her voice. "I just... I'm still figuring things out."

Jake gave a slow nod. "I get it."

A breeze swept her hair into her face, and she laughed, brushing it away. Jake reached out instinctively and tucked a piece behind her ear.

His fingers lingered for a second longer than necessary. Chelsea didn't pull away. She leaned into his hand ever so slightly. She hardly even realised she had done it.

"I missed you, Chels," he said, just loud enough for her to hear.

Chelsea swallowed. Her whole body felt electric. She knew in this moment she could very easily tell him she had missed him and fall into whatever it was with him again. But she knew she owed it to herself to take the time to figure this out properly. Figure out what she wanted. Who she really was now. So instead of answering, she reached out and plucked his hat off his head with a grin.

"You still wear this thing?"

Jake laughed, catching her wrist gently. "Only when I want to impress beautiful women on the beach."

Chelsea slipped it onto her own head with her other hand. "Well. It's working." She said with a wink.

They sat there, grinning like idiots, surrounded by the flames and salt air and ghosts of who they used to be. They chatted lightly, their friends joining them. Everyone feeling light, slightly tipsy, and just enjoying each other's company.

Chelsea didn't know what would happen next. Didn't know how much of this was real, safe, or smart. Or how much she would even remember the next morning.

But in that moment, warm, spinning slightly, toes in the sand and heart cracked wide open, she didn't care.

She was just *there* with him.

EIGHTEEN
Jake

J ake knew this feeling well. It was familiar.

The buzz in his chest that wasn't from the beers. The weightless, untethered way Chelsea's laugh made him feel like he was back in his body for the first time in years.

He felt drunk. Not on the beers. He had only had a couple of drinks throughout the night. No, he felt drunk on the feeling of having Chelsea next to him again. The smell of her shampoo hit him in waves as the breeze brushed through her hair. The feel of her shoulder pressed against his. The sight of her wearing his cap. It was like they were right back in high school. Like no time at all had passed.

Her cheeks were flushed from the alcohol, curled in on herself beside the fire, wearing a small smile, like this is exactly where she belonged.

Like nothing had changed.

Like everything had changed.

He watched her as she gazed at the fire, swaying a little to the music. The group had thinned out now; Dean was whispering something into Emily's ear that made her giggle. Chloe had drifted towards Billy Elliot, who looked entirely too pleased with himself.

Chelsea let out a dramatic yawn and stretch. Her eyes suddenly looked very tired and heavy.

Jake leaned in. "Come on, let's get you home."

Chelsea looked up at him, blinking like she hadn't realised the night was ending. An expression on her face that he couldn't quite read. Like she was in a battle with herself.

She eventually nodded and sighed. "Yeah. I should probably go before I start singing again. Or I fall asleep out here."

He smiled. "Pity. I was holding out for your rendition of 'No Scrubs'."

She stood, wobbling slightly on her feet. Jake instinctively reached out, steadying her with one hand on her waist.

Chelsea looked up at him, hair slightly tousled around his hat, mouth parted slightly. Too close. Too easy to forget himself.

"Careful," he murmured.

"I'm okay," she said, smiling. "Just...think those margaritas have hit me."

Jake chuckled. "You were always a sucker for some tequila. Come on. I'll take you home."

Chelsea looked up at him with a scowl from beneath the brim of his hat. "Haven't you been drinking?"

Jake shook his head, still very aware that his hand hadn't dropped from her waist. "Nah. I only had a couple, so I'm all good."

Chelsea thought for a moment before letting out a groan that did something to Jake's body. "Great. So, I am the only one who is going to have a hangover tomorrow."

Jake laughed, "Something like that." He had to hold back from adding that he was sure he would feel hungover tomorrow. But it wouldn't be from the alcohol.

They said their goodbyes, Emily already tucked under Dean's

arm, eyes sleepy but content. "Text me when you get back," she whispered to Chelsea, then turned to Jake, wearing a scowl that Jake assumed was supposed to be intimidating. "Drive safe."

Chloe was still laughing and getting awfully close to Billy near the street. She threw Chelsea a wink and a thumbs-up that made Jake raise an eyebrow.

Chelsea rolled her eyes. "She'll regret that in the morning."

"Probably. But I don't think he will. Swear he has been waiting for this day since we graduated." Jake said with a laugh.

They walked closely back to his car, making small conversation. Not awkward, but both slightly holding back. Jake found himself walking close to her, convincing himself it was for Chelsea's benefit, ready to steady her if she stumbled again. But really, he was just selfishly making the most of being this close to her. To be honest, the few times he had seen her, it was clear she had some big walls built up around herself. He could tell she had been holding back, trying to keep her distance. So, it was nice to see her with her guard down. Even if it was only for a couple of hours, or the margaritas were entirely to blame.

The car ride was quiet. Not tense, just comfortable. Chelsea rested her head back on the seat, gazing out the window. Jake stole glances at her every few seconds, drinking her in like he hadn't already spent the entire night doing it. He hoped she was drunk enough not to realise just how much he had been looking at her. But at the same time, he didn't really care anymore. Watching her sitting in the front seat of his car felt way too normal. And there was a time when this was normal. Once Jake got his licence in high school, Chelsea became a permanent fixture in his car. Always going for drives, belting out songs together with her hair flowing in the breeze.

He pulled up outside her parents' house and left the engine running for a moment before switching it off. The porch light cast a warm glow across the driveway.

Chelsea unbuckled her seatbelt but didn't move to get out.

"I had fun tonight," she said finally.

"Me too."

She looked at him. Really looked. "I don't know what any of this means, Jake." She paused before continuing, "I don't know what I want. I don't know what you want. What if we are just getting caught up in reliving our high school days? We don't even really know each other anymore."

"I know." His voice was steady. "I'm not expecting anything. I just...wanted to see you. Be around you. That's enough for me right now." He paused. "And for what it's worth, I think we will always know each other. Yes, we may have lived different lives and changed in some ways, but being around you tonight definitely didn't feel like I was hanging out with a stranger." He said with a smile.

Chelsea nodded, searching his face with her eyes. "No. No, it didn't."

Jake reached into the console and pulled out the pebble he'd kept from the beach.

She smiled softly, recognising it immediately. "You kept that?"

He shrugged. "Some things are hard to let go of."

There was a pause. Chelsea reached out her hand to cup his face, staring deep into his eyes. He leaned into her hand slightly, heart thumping away in his chest.

After what felt like a lifetime, Chelsea finally pulled her hand away. "I guess I should go inside."

Jake nodded. Instantly feeling cold where her hand was just a moment ago.

She opened her door and stumbled as she tried to get out. Jake unbuckled his seat belt, got out of the car, and rushed around to the side of the car at lightning speed.

"God, you really have done a number on yourself tonight. Impressive." He said playfully as he reached her and helped her out of the car.

She shook her head. "Oh boy, I am going to have some regrets in the morning."

Jake helped her up to the front door of her parents' house. They stood and faced each other, standing awfully close, almost out of habit.

Chelsea looked up at him. "Thank you," she whispered. "For being you."

"Always." He said softly.

Then she rose on her toes and leaned forward. Jake's heart felt like it was going to beat out of his chest. He thought for sure she was going to kiss him. And as much as he wanted it, he didn't want her to regret it in the morning. He also wanted her to remember it when they did finally kiss again.

As if she could read his mind, she paused, her face inches away from his. Instead, she rested her forehead against his, closed her eyes and sighed.

They stood like that for a moment, held there by the weight of the moment and how close they had come to falling back into being Jake and Chels.

Chelsea lowered herself and wrapped her arms around Jake's waist, resting her head on his chest. "Goodnight, Jakey."

His heart swelled. She was the only one who ever called him that. He wrapped his arms around her shoulders and kissed the top of her head. "Goodnight, Chels."

He closed his eyes as she pulled away and opened the front door.

He walked back to his car slowly. The imprint of her still burning against him.

And as he got back into the car and made his way home, he felt the weight of the whole night catching up to him, bringing back memories and emotions he had tried to ignore over the years.

He knew one thing with certainty:

He was in trouble.

Big, beautiful, impossible trouble.

NINETEEN
High School: Second Year
Jake

*T*he bonfire crackled against the sound of the waves, mixed with the music travelling through the warm, salty air from one of their friends' portable speakers. Their friends were scattered along the sand, some dancing to the music, others passing around marsh-mallows to toast or a beer to share, everyone laughing.

Jake had been sitting with a few of the guys around the fire for a while now, his gaze constantly seeking Chelsea, who was standing near the speaker with Emily. Her eyes would flick towards Jake's now and then, but it almost seemed like she was trying to go out of her way not to look at him or to avoid him.

Jake was vaguely aware that some extras had joined them here to-night, some girls from another school. People he didn't know. People he didn't really care to know. Not when his person was standing only a few metres away from him, pouting.

He stood up from the log he was sitting on, dusting off the sand from the back of his jeans. The brunette girl sitting next to him grabbed his hand as he stood, asking him where he was going. He didn't even respond; he just shook his hand free as he made his way over to his girl.

He wandered over to Chelsea, his hands shoved in his pockets, a grin taking over his face as he looked at his girl. Emily noticed and slyly backed away, giving them space.

"What's with the pouting, babe?" He asked, nudging her shoulder with his.

She glared at him.

Oh shit, he thought, *what have I done?*

"You looked like you were having a great time over there, with your new friend."

Jake blinked, caught off guard. Trying to retrace his steps. He looked back over to the fire pit, where the brunette who had grabbed his hand earlier had her gaze locked on Jake. "You mean her? The brunette? I have no idea who she is. I didn't even – "

"Don't," Chelsea snapped, her cheeks reddening. "I'm not stupid, Jake. I saw the way she grabbed your hand."

He ran a hand through his hair, frustrated. "Then you would have seen me pull away. Seriously? You think I care about her?"

"I don't know what to think!" Chelsea's voice cracked, causing Jake to flinch. A couple of their friends turned their heads towards them. Chelsea spun away, storming through the sand toward the water.

Jake jogged after her, not caring if they had an audience. He caught her wrist just before she reached the water. "Chelsea, stop."

She shook her head, blinking fast. "Maybe this was a mistake. Maybe we should have just stayed friends. Maybe you'll realise you want someone else, and I'll just be left – "

"Hey." His voice cut her off, sharp and desperate. He stepped in front of her, forcing her to look at him. He felt his heart thumping in his chest. "Don't you get it? I don't care about her. Or anyone else, for that matter. I only want you."

Chelsea blinked up at him; her chest was heaving. Jake didn't know how to get her to understand what she meant to him. That he hadn't so much as looked at a girl since that night they kissed for the first *time. Hell, probably since well before then. He had eyes only for her, for as long as he could remember.*

"Then why didn't you – "

"Because I'm an idiot," Jake cut in, almost breathless. He raked his hand through his hair before stepping forward and cupping her face with his hands. He felt her melt slightly into his touch as she usually did. Her body not listening to her mind, or her face that still had a slight frown to it. Jake couldn't stop the words from tumbling out now. "Because sometimes I don't always say the right things. Or know how to talk about my feelings as well as you do. But don't you get it? You are it for me, Chelsea."

Jake exhaled deeply before continuing, "I don't give a crap about any other girl. I don't care who looks at me or who tries to grab my hand. You are the only person I am looking at. The only girl I want to hold my hand. I hardly even noticed that girl sitting beside me because all I was doing was looking at you. Waiting for the moment I could be back with you."

He closed his eyes, drawing in another deep breath. He knew what he wanted to say next. He had wanted to say it for weeks, but he had never said it to anyone besides his family, so the thought kind of freaked him out. He never expected to feel this way about someone so young. He opened his eyes to find Chelsea's big blue eyes searching his face. She locked her gaze onto his, giving him the confidence to continue.

"I don't know what I am doing, and sometimes I mess things up, but I love you, Chelsea. Okay? I love you."

The world seemed to still. He could still hear the waves crashing behind him and the fire popping in the distance, but all he could focus on was Chelsea and watching her absorb his words. It felt like time stretched forever before she finally reacted. The anger on her face melted as she launched forward. Her fists bunched his shirt as she crashed her lips to his. Jake wrapped his arms tightly around her as their kiss deepened. As if their whole future rode on this one moment. Chelsea pulled back slightly, their lips only inches apart as she whispered the words Jake had dreamt he would hear.

"I love you."

He hardly let her finish before he brought his lips to hers again, causing her to laugh against his mouth.

He realised they were young and that life would likely be against them, but at that moment, Jake felt he was on cloud nine. He knew this was the girl he wanted to grow up with, to experience going into adulthood with. He didn't know where they would end up once they had finished school, but in this moment, he wanted to believe so badly that they would be able to handle whatever life threw at them.

TWENTY
Chelsea

T he next morning, Chelsea was woken by the morning sun stretching across the room through her open curtains. She cursed herself for forgetting to shut the curtains before she drunkenly fell into bed the night before.

Now that she was slowly waking up, her pounding head and dry mouth were increasingly obvious. She felt around her bedside table without opening her eyes for her water bottle. She grabbed it and took a huge swig, silently thanking drunk Chelsea for at least remembering that. She could feel a heavy lump on her feet, which she guessed, by the snoring filling the room, was Crumpet, who had decided he didn't want to sleep on his bed anymore. When they first got him as a puppy, she and Ryan made a pact to train him to stay off the furniture. That lasted about five minutes, and now Chelsea was sure he had slept on theirs or the girls' beds more than his own.

Once the water had soothed her throat, she risked slowly opening her eyes.

Not too bad, she thought. She could hear her phone vibrating on the bedside table, so she felt around and picked it up.

8:17 am.

She noticed her notifications.

1 message from Ryan: *Hey Chels, hope you are relaxing. Just letting you know the girls and I have made it to Mum and Dad's last night. We are going to stay here for a couple of nights. Girls want to FaceTime you, so let us know when you are up x*

1 message from Emily: *Coffee is on its way xx*

1 notification from Instagram: *ChloeQuinnxx tagged you in a story.*

Chelsea groaned. She wasn't sure if she was ready to see what her sister had posted on her Instagram story. She love heart reacted to Emily's message. Then tapped on the Instagram notification. A picture filled her screen. Her, Emily & Chloe. Looking so carefree and happy. Chelsea couldn't draw her eyes away from her own face. She found herself smiling back at herself. She couldn't believe how happy and genuine her smile looked. Despite the extremely obvious drunk eyes.

The following story loaded, showing a selfie of Chloe in bed with Billy. Chelsea laughed to herself. She had forgotten Chloe hadn't come home with her.

Home.

Oh god.

Chelsea had flashbacks of the car ride home.

Jake.

The long goodbye they had.

The kiss they almost had.

Chelsea groaned and pulled the covers over her face.

In that same moment, her bedroom door sprang open. She pulled the covers off her face and saw Emily standing in the doorway with three takeaway coffee cups and Chloe beside her. They bounded into her room and sat on her bed. Emily passed Chelsea and Chloe their coffees.

"God, how are you both so lively this morning?" Chelsea said, sitting up to take her coffee from Emily. "Thanks, Em, I bloody need this."

Emily laughed, "Thought you would."

Chelsea turned to Chloe, "I'm surprised to see you back already. How was the rest of your night?" She asked with a wink.

Chloe took a long sip of her coffee. "Well, to be honest, I am mad at you guys for not introducing me sooner." She paused, glaring at them both, then continued. "That man is seriously hot, and boy does he know what he is doing." She said with a grin.

Emily almost choked on her coffee as she laughed, "Oh god, that's like my brother you are talking about."

Chelsea shook her head and chuckled.

"What about you, Chels. How was the rest of your night?" Chloe asked, sipping her coffee.

Chelsea leaned her head back against the bedhead. "Ugh. It was good. Confusing. Weird. I don't know." She looked up at the ceiling. "I almost kissed him. I think I was drunker than I thought."

She expected them to be shocked when she looked back at them, but they both just looked at her, smirking.

She scowled at them, "Why are you both looking at me like that?"

Emily huffed out a laugh. "Mate, no one who saw you two together would be surprised."

Chloe nodded. "She is right. I had forgotten what it was like to be in the same space as you two. It's like…. magnetic. Like the rest of us aren't there at all."

Chelsea threw a pillow at her sister. "It is not." But she secretly agreed that's exactly what it felt like. "Anyway, we didn't. He just dropped me off at home, and we said goodnight."

"Mmhm. I am sure that's all that happened." Emily said, raising her eyebrow.

Chelsea rolled her eyes and sipped her coffee.

"Anyway, enough about you two. I have news. We discussed it last night before bed, and we have decided we are going to get married in a month!" Emily said excitedly.

Chelsea almost choked on her coffee. "One month!?" She asked, in shock. "Are you okay? Are you still drunk?"

"Yep, one month. And no, I'm not drunk. So, maid of honour, we have to get to work." She said, looking at Chelsea expectantly.

Chloe got up off the bed, "and that's my cue to leave. Good luck with that. I am going to go shower and get ready for work."

Chelsea watched her leave. Before she looked back at Emily, who was still looking at her, waiting for her to say something.

Chelsea sighed. "Ok, where do we start?"

Emily squealed. "Well, we are having it at Jake's dad's brewery. So, their wedding planner is taking over most of that; we just have the finer details to work out, and we obviously need to find some hot dresses for us."

"Em, I think we just need to focus on you looking hot. It is your day."

Emily shrugged, "Yes, but I can't have my maid of honour not looking hot next to me. Besides, you might want to have slutty wedding sex with the best man." She said as she wiggled her eyebrows.

"Oh my god!" Chelsea said as she threw a pillow from beside her at her best friend. They both cracked up laughing, careful not to spill their coffees.

Chelsea couldn't help but smile at her best friend's happiness. This wedding planning could be the perfect distraction.

~

Once Emily had finally left her bed, after showing her hundreds of Pinterest wedding pages, Chelsea facetimed the girls to catch up on what they had been up to. The conversation made Chelsea feel motion sick because Olivia was running around the house with the phone, showing her things she had seen a million times before. After a while, once she had been given a minute-by-minute rundown of the past couple of days, she told the girls she loved them and would see them in a couple of days before asking them to put their dad on.

As much as she needed this time on her own, a call back home was a sure way to make her miss the girls, but she felt lighter seeing how happy they both seemed. Even Lucy seemed happy and less worried. Before she hung up, Ryan told her that they would be home in two days, which Chelsea agreed so would she. They had quickly confirmed they would need to then make a plan on how to move forward. Which honestly scared her. She wasn't sure how she was going to cope with being away from the girls on a more regular basis. She briefly lay there after the phone screen went black, looking up at the ceiling.

How was this going to work? she thought to herself.

She couldn't be away from the girls this much. But was her home really Port Mac? Or was it here?

Was it just because she was here right now that it felt like home, or was there something much deeper keeping her here? She covered her face with her hands as she groaned. Her hangover was kicking in, and it was not making it easy to make these huge life decisions.

She had a feeling the only way she was going to figure it out was to go back to Port Mac and face Ryan and their life.

TWENTY ONE

High School: Third Year
Jake

It had been one week since Jake's mum, Susan, had passed away. Jake was overcome with grief. He had never really lost anyone close to him, so this was his first significant loss and potentially the biggest he would ever endure. But one week on, and he wasn't sure there was any way he could survive this. He couldn't understand how, at sixteen, he had just lost his mother. It was a quick battle with breast cancer, which had unfortunately been found too late. His mum had been too busy, she said. She kept putting off getting checked out because why would someone in their thirty's have breast cancer? But of course, when she finally did go to the doctor, expecting them to just tell her that she needed to slow down, she was told it had progressed too far. Jake didn't understand a lot of it, and he expected that his parents had purposely done that to protect him. He and his dad had sat by her side throughout it all, but last week she went to sleep one night and never woke up. He had never believed in much after life, but he felt that his mum chose to pass away peacefully like that, so she didn't suffer through relentless treatment that wouldn't work, and so that he and his dad didn't have to suffer slowly watching her disappear.

They had spent the night as a family, watching a movie and reminiscing on past family holidays. Chelsea had been there for the movie, but once it started getting late, she went home. As much as Jake had wanted her to stay, she had told him to enjoy the night with his mum. So, he did. And then he went to bed. Not knowing that would be the last time he would see his mum.

The past week had been a blur. They had the funeral and an endless line of support from their community, but Jake felt numb. He didn't know how to act. He didn't want to be around anyone but Chelsea. He felt guilty for relying on her so heavily to survive right now, but Chelsea, being Chelsea, had taken it in her stride. She automatically stepped up for Jake and his dad, doing all the cooking and cleaning at their house. He wasn't sure what her parents thought of the fact that Chelsea had basically moved into his home, but he couldn't think about it right now. He needed her with him; otherwise, he was worried he would drown in his grief.

Right on cue, as if she could sense he needed her desperately, Jake heard Chelsea approach him. He was sitting on the wet sand by the beach. He had his hoodie pulled over his head, shoulders hunched over. The bottoms of his jeans were getting wet now since the tide had crept in, but he didn't have the energy to move.

Chelsea sat down beside him without a word, their knees touching. For a long time, Jake didn't look at her; he just stared out at the water, his jaw tight and eyes red and swollen from days without sleep. When he finally spoke, his voice was raw.

"I keep thinking she's going to walk in the door. Like... none of this is real. Like I'll wake up, and she'll be right there making a cup of tea and telling me to clean my room." His voice cracked on the last word.

Chelsea reached out to thread her fingers through his. "It's real, Jake. And it sucks. It's not fair at all. But you aren't alone. I'm here."

He shook his head, trying to shake the new tears that were threatening to fall. He had cried so much the past week that he didn't know how he still had tears to shed. "What if I forget her? Her voice, her laugh. What if she just...disappears?"

"You won't," she whispered, squeezing his hand hard. "Because I'll remember her too. Every story you tell me, every time you smile her

smile, I'll keep it with me. For you."

The dam he was trying to hold back completely broke then. Jake pulled her against him, clutching her like she was the only thing keeping him afloat. He felt his chest heaving against her, silent sobs shuddering through him. She held on tight to him, letting his tears soak her shirt, rubbing slow circles against his back.

After a while, the tide had crept higher and the sun lower. Jake sat up and pulled Chelsea towards him, kissing her hard. It wasn't a wild, breathless kind of kiss they usually had; it was a soft, desperate kiss.

When they pulled apart, Jake rested his forehead against hers. "I don't know how to do this, Chels."

Chelsea pressed her lips to his jaw, "You don't have to know, baby. We'll figure this out together." She stood slowly, dusting the sand from the backs of her legs before reaching her hand out to him. "Come on. Let's go check on your dad, and I'll cook you some dinner."

Jake reached up to grab her hand, feeling an enormous rush of gratitude for this girl as they walked hand in hand down the beach.

~

When they entered the back door of his house, the first thing Jake noticed was how quiet it was. It wasn't that his mum was loud, but since she had been gone, the house had a completely different presence to it. An empty feeling.

Jake hadn't let go of Chelsea's hand the whole way home. He was worried that if he let go, she would disappear. As they walked through the house to the kitchen, they noticed Jake's dad sitting at the kitchen table, hunched over a beer bottle. His eyes lifted when they came in, tired and red-rimmed.

"Hey, Dad."

"Hey. Hey, Chels."

Chelsea made a beeline for his dad, dropping Jake's hand. She wrapped her arm around his shoulder, giving him a squeeze.

"Hey, Barry." Jake's heart melted slightly, taking in his girl hugging his dad. Here she was not only taking care of him, but also his dad.

"*Alright, boys, what do we feel like for dinner? Spaghetti?*" *She asked lightly.*

"*Darl, you don't need to cook for us. Thank you, but you have done enough.*" *His dad said sadly.*

"*Nonsense,*" *Chelsea waved her hand in his direction.* "*Spaghetti it is.*" *She said as she made her way to the kitchen and started organising her ingredients.*

Jake's dad brought his beer to his lips to drain the last of the liquid before he stood from his chair.

"*I'm going to go take a shower.*" *He said as he put his bottle in the recycling bin, he paused beside Chelsea.* "*Sue loved you, Chels. She loved how happy you made our boy. And she would love that you are here looking after both of us for her.*"

Jake's throat tightened as he watched his dad's eyes glaze over with tears.

"*I loved her. And I love both her boys.*"

Jake's dad nodded as he walked away down the hallway towards the bathroom.

Jake walked over to Chelsea, who was standing at the stove. He slipped his arms around her waist, hugging her tight. "*Thank you.*"

She didn't say anything, just squeezed his arm with her free hand while she continued cooking for them.

Jake already knew he loved her before this, but having her here with him through the most immense grief he had ever gone through changed things. This didn't just feel like a first love anymore. No, this ran a hell of a lot deeper now.

TWENTY TWO

Chelsea

The rest of the previous day had involved Chelsea sitting out on the back patio, reading her book and napping off her hangover. Her phone had been blowing up from Emily, sending her wedding inspo pictures and lists of things they had to do. Her best friend was a type A bride, so really, she had most of it under control. She had already decided on the style of her dress and would be going to try it on next week. Emily had her two sisters as her other bridesmaids, so they had set up a group chat with the four of them. They had sent through countless options of bridesmaids' dresses and had already managed to narrow the list down to a few to decide between.

Today, they were meeting at the brewery to finalise the wedding plans with the venue staff before Chelsea had to go home the next morning. Emily's sisters were working, so it was just Chelsea and Emily who were meeting Dean and Jake at the venue.

The day was warm, the air feeling moist with the rain forecasted to hit later that afternoon. Chelsea stood outside the repurposed brewery, arms crossed, heart thudding away in her chest. She could hear the faint music inside and the low hum of conversation. The wide wooden doors were open, revealing warm timber floors, strings of lights hanging above repurposed timber tables set for lunch, and an open bar tucked beneath the lofted ceiling beams. Outside, the decking opened up onto lush green grass, with an arbour set up down by the pond for another wedding.

It really was beautiful. Different from how she remembered it as a teenager sneaking in through the back doors. But Jake's dad had always had a vision, and apparently, so did Dean and Emily.

"Ready?" Emily asked beside her, oblivious to the churning in Chelsea's stomach. She was practically glowing. Her happiness and excitement radiated off her.

Chelsea smiled, "As I'll ever be."

They stepped inside, and Chelsea let the familiar scent of the oak and alcohol settle around her. It was nostalgic in the most disorientating way. Like walking into a dream she'd had a hundred times, only everything was slightly different.

Dean waved to them from the back near the bar. And beside him, laughing at something one of the bar staff said, stood Jake.

He looked relaxed. Chelsea let herself soak him in for a moment. He wore a fitted white t-shirt, jeans, and had a rag tucked into his back pocket, clearly mid-shift, or mid-fix, or just mid-life, because he looked settled in a way she didn't feel at all. She had to admit, he looked good. Very good.

His gaze shifted and found hers like it always did.

And there it was again.

The pause. The undercurrent. The thing neither of them could name, but both could feel whenever they were around each other.

As he stepped forward, Chelsea heard a familiar voice come from somewhere behind her.

"Are my eyes deceiving me, or is Chelsea Quinn standing in my brewery?"

Chelsea turned. A huge grin already plastered on her face.

Jake's dad stood there, beaming back at her.

"Barry!" Chelsea said as she almost threw herself at him.

He caught her and squeezed her back. Before stepping back and holding her at arm's length. "Bloody hell, girlie, let me get a look at you."

Chelsea blushed. Smiling like an idiot. She had spent so much time at their house when she and Jake were growing up. Even before they began dating, they were good friends and had spent a lot of time as a large group or on their own at each other's houses. Jake's parents had always been like her second family. When they were sixteen, Jake's mum had passed away after a short battle with breast cancer. It was unexpected and fast, and she had felt almost as though she had lost her second mum; it was the most grief she had ever felt, still to this day. They had grown close, and Chelsea, being the protector she was, took it upon herself to help Jake and his dad through their grief by making sure they had cooked meals and a clean house. Seeing him now brought back a flood of emotions. She felt happy and warm seeing Barry again, sure, but she was also smacked with the feelings of homesickness and guilt. Guilt, she had left this place and not looked back. When she lost Jake, she also thought that meant she would lose her second family. Now standing here, she felt overwhelmed with guilt that she didn't so much as call Barry.

Barry smiled at Chelsea. "You still look like our little Chelsea. A ray of sunshine. God, how long has it been?"

Chelsea gave him a soft smile. "Too long."

"Right there you are. Come on, let's get you a drink," he said, leading her towards the bar. "Maybe now that boy of mine can stop moping around the joint and biting people's heads off."

Chelsea laughed and looked up towards the bar where her gaze crashed into Jake's. He was watching them with a look that she couldn't entirely read.

"Come on, Jake, don't just stare at her, get the girl a drink." His dad said playfully as they approached the bar where Emily and Dean were now sitting.

"Yeah, Jake, get the girl a drink, would ya?" Chelsea said with a wink as she sat down on the barstool next to Emily.

Chelsea spent the next little while catching up with Barry while Jake floated behind the bar, half serving other customers, half eavesdropping on their conversation. Every time Chelsea looked up, she found Jake's eyes already on her.

He wasn't even trying to hide it. And he looked.... happy. Content maybe. Like this was the most normal thing in the world.

Eventually, Emily whisked her away to run her through how everything would be set up on the day. They talked fairy lights, drinks, and music for the next hour. Chelsea tried to focus on her best friend's excited voice, but every so often, she would feel her gaze be dragged across the room. Across the room to where two dark green eyes were already locked on her.

She didn't get to speak to him for the rest of the day as his shift picked up, apart from when they all said their goodbyes. She left the brewery feeling slightly disappointed that they didn't get to talk much, considering what had almost happened the other night. However, as she got in the car ready to head back to her parents' house, she couldn't shake the feeling of being happy and light.

~

Later that afternoon, back at her parents' house, Chelsea stood in the kitchen, hands wrapped around a mug of tea. Her mum was slicing vegetables for dinner, the knife rhythmically tapping the cutting board.

"I can hear your brain thinking from here," her mum said without looking up. "Do you want to talk about it?

Chelsea sighed. "I went to the brewery."

Her mum raised an eyebrow as she looked up briefly, "How did that feel?"

Chelsea gave a tight smile. "Like walking back through my memories. I saw Barry, which was great. I had really missed him."

Her mum nodded, wiping her hands on a tea towel. "I bet. He was like another father figure to you. I know he missed you."

"How?" Chelsea asked, slightly tilting her head.

Her mum huffed a laugh. "Just because you two broke up, didn't mean we had to stop being friends with Barry."

Chelsea looked at her mum, stunned. "I just assumed you didn't see him much anymore. You never mentioned it."

"No, we didn't. We didn't want to make it more difficult for you," she said as she leaned against the counter. "But we did. We still do. And he would often ask about you, reminiscing on how much of a godsend you were for him and Jake and their grief when Susan passed away."

Chelsea looked up at the ceiling, tears stinging her eyes. She was starting to think she really did run away from her life when she met Ryan. She had convinced herself that leaving it all behind and not looking back was the best way to move on. But after seeing Barry today and listening to her Mum now, she realised that she had really missed out on so much and even worse, left behind the people she loved.

"It's okay, darling," her mum said, reaching across the counter to grab her hand. "We all understand why you left. You were doing what was best for you and your family at the time. We have our beautiful granddaughters because of that, so we can't be mad at you for doing it."

Chelsea nodded and let out a sigh. "Gosh, I don't know what to do, Mum."

Her mum looked at her with that motherly look. The one where it seems like they already know what you are going to do, before you do. "You don't have to decide anything today. Or tomorrow. But don't talk yourself out of what you want just because it scares you."

Chelsea blinked back tears that were back again. "What if I don't even know what that is?"

Her mum shrugged, "Then give yourself time to figure it out."

~

The next morning, Chelsea enjoyed breakfast with her sister and parents before packing up her things. Her dad loaded her bags and Crumpet into her car while she hugged her mum goodbye. She pulled away and held Chelsea at arm's length. "Take your time and figure things out. But it's time to put your happiness further up the list."

Her dad appeared next to her, pulling her in for a hug. "Your mum's right, as always," he laughed. "Everything will work out. And you know you and the girls have rooms here if you are ready to come back home."

"Thanks, Dad. I have a feeling I will be back soon." She said as she squeezed him back, something telling her to hold on for a little longer. She had missed so much time with her parents over the years; one thing she knew for sure was that she didn't want to miss anymore.

Eventually, she stepped away and waved to her parents as she got into her car, Crumpet panting in her ear from the backseat. Chelsea felt a strange knot of dread and calm settle into her chest as she pulled out of the driveway and started her drive back to Port Mac.

She was going back home.

Back to her girls.

Back to Ryan.

Back to some hard conversations.

But part of her, the part that had been awakened on the beach, the part that stood silent in the brewery, wasn't quite ready to leave this town behind again.

TWENTY THREE
Chelsea

Chelsea pulled into the driveway of her house just after eleven a.m., the hot sun already beaming down across the front lawn. Neither Chelsea nor Ryan were gardening people, so when they purchased this house, the first thing they did was transform the garden into a low-maintenance yard. This meant lots of grass and a few trees for shade. The tropical weather meant everything stayed nice and green despite the heat, so thanks to a few recent heavy rainfalls, the lawn was looking particularly lush against the white picket fence surrounding the yard.

Ryan's car was already in the driveway, which meant he and the girls must have also not long returned home. She looked up at the house and spotted Olivia and Lucy waiting in the front window, waving at her and bouncing up and down. Chelsea's heart tugged as she stepped out of the car, Crumpet rushing out behind her.

They burst out the front door before she had even reached the porch steps.

"Mummy!"

Chelsea dropped to her knees as their arms wrapped around her, their voices overlapping in a rush of stories, giggles, and something about pancakes for breakfast. She held both girls tight in her arms, not realising how much she had missed the chaos that came with the two young girls.

Ryan stepped out a beat later, mug of coffee in hand. He looked tired but gathered. Familiar. He smiled down at the sight of the girls wrapped in Chelsea's arms on the ground.

"Hey," he said. "They have been sitting by the window since we got home an hour ago. Counting down the minutes."

Chelsea stood smiling. "I can tell."

"Come on, girls, let's let mum get inside."

They moved inside with ease, the morning routine quickly slipping back over her like an old jacket. But something felt different now – quieter, more conscious.

Later, once Chelsea had unpacked her bags and the girls were fed and distracted, playing out on the trampoline, Chelsea and Ryan sat on the back step, side by side, two steaming cups of coffee between them, looking out over the backyard.

Ryan was the one who spoke first.

"So, how were your couple of days back home?"

"It was good. Good to reset. Emily and Dean have decided to get married in a month," Chelsea shook her head as she let out a quiet laugh. "Typical Emily. So, I ended up spending a bit of time helping her with that. It was a good distraction."

Ryan nodded as he took a sip of his coffee.

"How was your time with your parents?"

"Oh, you know, good for the girls to spend some time with them, but I quickly remembered why I moved away. Feel like I am a little boy again as soon as I enter that house."

Chelsea huffed a laugh.

Ryan looked out at the yard vaguely in the direction of the girls playing, but she could tell he was miles away in his mind.

After a minute, he turned slightly towards her. "So, what now,

Chels?"

Chelsea sighed, rubbing a thumb along the rim of her cup. "I don't know exactly. But I know we can't keep doing this limbo thing."

He nodded. "Agreed." He continued, "I got a call from one of the guys I went through medical school with yesterday. He said their hospital in Watervale has an opening for a surgical rotation position. He encouraged me to apply and said he would put in a good word."

Chelsea's head turned. "Seriously?"

Ryan gave a small smile. "It's not a guarantee, but it sounded promising. The boss said he had heard my name and was keen to meet with me," he shrugged. "It would mean I would be closer to Somerdale. Not all the way – but close enough to co-parent properly. And give the girls a sense of consistency since I am guessing you will want to move back home."

Chelsea nodded; the word co-parent had shocked her. It sounded final. She thought for a moment. "I was thinking... maybe I'll stay at Mum and Dad's for a little while. Not forever. Just a few weeks. Give us both some time to breathe."

Ryan watched the girls playing for a long moment before he said, "It means we will have to move the girls' school. And I will have to find somewhere to stay. Sell this house, I guess."

Chelsea nodded, hardly believing everything was moving this fast. She stared at Ryan for a moment. "You would really do that? Move from this town? From this house?"

"I'm not moving for *us*," he said honestly. "I am doing it for them. But... I also want to see you happy again. And you're not happy here, Chels. You haven't been for a long time." He took a sip of his coffee before continuing, "You left behind your home. You gave up working so that you could be there for the girls while I pursued my career. You have given me everything." He paused. "Now it's your turn."

His words were harsh but true. They didn't hurt. They felt honest. Gentle. Kind.

"Thank you," she said quietly. "How do you feel?" Chelsea asked cautiously.

Ryan shrugged, "I don't really know yet. But…" he turned to look at her, "don't take this the wrong way, but when I was at mum and dad's, I felt… relieved. I think being here, in this house, with the way we are, I felt like I was always holding my breath. Like I could feel this coming, but I didn't know how to fix it."

Chelsea nodded, "I know what you mean. Do you think we should talk to the girls?"

"I think we owe it to them. They are smart, they can tell things are changing."

Chelsea nodded, agreeing that they needed to be open and honest with the girls. The last thing she wanted was for them to grow and resent them for shutting them out. It may be Chelsea and Ryan's relationship that is changing, but their lives would be changing as well.

"You should take Crumpet with you," Ryan said as he sipped his coffee.

Chelsea looked at him, shocked. She hadn't really considered what they would do about him, but she had spent most days at home with him, and when the girls were asleep or at school, Crumpet kept her company. So having to leave him would have added a whole new level of heartbreak.

"Are you sure?"

Ryan shrugged. "We both know he is more your dog than he is mine. I'll miss him, of course. But it wouldn't be fair to him to be with me when I work so much. He would be alone too much. But I'll still get to see him, yeah?"

Chelsea smiled, "Yeah, of course. He is part of the family."

They sat in silence, sipping their coffee and watching their girls play. The warm breeze rustling through the trees.

Chelsea broke it this time. "We'll figure it out, right?"

Ryan nodded. "One step at a time."

Over at the trampoline, Olivia was now underneath the trampoline, giving herself a mud facial thanks to the rain they had had overnight.

Chelsea laughed under her breath. "First step might be getting them inside without a mud fight breaking out."

Ryan grinned. "I'll start prepping the emergency bath."

They stood, moving in harmony. Partners in the way they'd always been best: as parents.

And even though things still felt uncertain and slightly scary, Chelsea felt a weight lift off her shoulders.

Leaving space.

Space for something new to begin.

Space for the new Chelsea to grow.

~

The afternoon sun cast long shadows across the living room as Chelsea folded a blanket across the back of the couch. The girls were curled up on the rug, surrounded by building blocks and half-dressed Barbies. Mid-drama, in a world of their own, oblivious to the impending changes coming to shake up their worlds.

Ryan walked in from the kitchen with two small glasses of apple juice, setting them on the coffee table.

"Girls," Chelsea said gently, brushing a crumb from Lucy's cheek. "Can we talk to you for a minute?"

Lucy glanced up first, suspicious. "Are we in trouble?"

"No, baby," Chelsea said with a smile. "It's just something important."

Ryan sat down on the couch, and Chelsea knelt beside him. She reached out and tucked a strand of hair behind Olivia's ear.

"So… you know how mummy went to visit Grandma and Grandad for a few days?"

Both girls nodded.

"Well," Chelsea continued, "while I was there, I had a lot of thinking time. And daddy and I have been talking as well. We have been thinking about what's best for *all* of us."

Lucy, who had started braiding a doll's hair, looked up slowly. "What do you mean?"

Ryan jumped in, calm and gentle. "We've been thinking about moving. Not too far. But closer to where Grandma and Grandad live. Mummy and daddy are going to live in different houses for now. And this will be easier for us all to see each other. Easier for *you two* to have both of us close by."

Chelsea held her breath waiting for the outburst of emotion at the thought of us living in separate houses.

Lucy frowned. "But what about our school?"

Chelsea took a deep breath. "That's part of it. If we move, we'd probably start at a new school. A smaller one. I saw it the other day. It had a huge playground and chickens."

Olivia's eyes widened. "Real chickens?"

Chelsea smiled. "Real life chickens."

Lucy's voice was smaller. "But my best friend is here."

Chelsea's heart tugged. "I know, sweetie. And we'd never do anything without talking to you about it. This isn't happening right this second. It's just something we're thinking about."

Ryan added, "We'd still visit here. And your friends could visit too. It doesn't mean goodbye forever. Just a new chapter."

Lucy looked at Olivia, then back to Chelsea. "We will still live close to each other?"

Chelsea glanced at Ryan.

He nodded. "Yep, that's the plan. Super close. Just in different houses. You'll still have your own rooms at both houses. And you can see us whenever you want. Nothing else will change; you will just have two houses instead of one."

Olivia wriggled closer to lay her head in Chelsea's lap. "Can we still have pancakes at both houses?"

Chelsea laughed softly. "Always."

Lucy was quiet for a long moment. She had always been a deep thinker, so Chelsea knew her daughter was processing everything. She would probably be the one to take the changes the hardest. Then she said, "I think I'd miss Ms Porter most. But... I would like a school with chickens."

Ryan reached out and stroked his daughter's hair. "That's okay. Missing people is part of life," his gaze briefly flicking to Chelsea before back to Lucy, "but we'll always make sure you feel safe, wherever we are."

They sat like that for a while – the late sunlight washing through the windows. The girls returned to their imaginative world. Although the girls seemed to take the news pretty well, Chelsea knew it was just words to them at the moment. The real test would be when they began making the changes. She knew that was when the big emotions would come out.

Chelsea glanced at Ryan and gave him a small smile.

One step at a time.

TWENTY FOUR
Chelsea

The days passed by in a blur of quiet logistics. Chelsea barely had any time to think. The girls returned to school, happy to go back and show their friends pictures of their trip down the coast. They all fell back into their routine while gradually making changes to move forward.

Ryan applied for the position that his old colleague had mentioned the day after they discussed the move to the girls. She heard him on the phone in the next room; his voice was low but steady. Chelsea didn't ask for details; she didn't want to hope too quickly or get involved in something that was no longer hers to manage. But when he stepped out afterwards and gave her a slight nod, she returned it with something close to appreciation. Ryan was doing the things he said he would, but Chelsea couldn't help but feel some guilt that he was doing this for her benefit when they were no longer... well, she wasn't really sure what they were or weren't right now. She tried to shake off the feeling and remind herself that she had done this for him throughout their entire marriage.

They took the girls for a tour of the new school that Thursday

– a small, welcoming country school with bright classrooms and warm teachers. Lucy had clung to Chelsea's hand at first, more apprehensive than her sister, who had asked the principal 'Where were the chickens?' as soon as they had met her. But by the time they had left, Lucy was much more relaxed and asked if they had noticed how big the library was.

The girls didn't completely understand the weight of the transition yet. But they were adapting. Kids always did. More resilient than adults gave them credit for. She was sure there would be challenging moments filled with emotions to come, and they would deal with them together. However, as they left the school, Chelsea felt like things were slowly falling into place.

Ryan spoke to a real estate agent that afternoon after they arrived home from visiting the school. Chelsea overheard him muttering about the market value and the timing. Once he was off the phone, he let her know that the agent had mentioned it was a good time to sell because the market was picking up in this area. She nodded, not asking for any more details. Ryan had always been the one to handle this type of thing, and to be honest, she only knew the basics about real estate. Another thing she guessed she was going to have to take control of in her own life now. She mentally added that to her never-ending list of things she needed to start figuring out.

She and Ryan were both staying in the house, Ryan sleeping between the couch and Olivia's bed, and Chelsea staying in their master bedroom, often joined by a tiny human or two. They spoke to each other when they needed to, but things felt uncertain. They were coexisting, orbiting the same house, but no longer colliding. Dinner times were managed in turns. School lunches were prepared in silence. Evenings passed with the sounds of splashing in the bath and laughter from their daughters.

Chelsea tried to keep herself busy, trying to ignore the unease she felt with her life being so up in the air. She had briefly called her mum after Ryan spoke to the real estate agent to explain what was happening. She told her she didn't know what was next, but that she would keep her updated, mentioning that she and the girls would probably need a place to stay while they figured out the house here. Her sister and Emily checked in on her via text message every couple of hours, like they were just waiting for Chelsea to fall apart. Between wedding planning, Chloe's dating updates, and the daily mum duties, she didn't really have the time to feel lonely.

~

On Friday afternoon, Chelsea was busy folding the laundry in the living room while the girls were out in the backyard playing. The television buzzed softly in the background, a trashy reality show she was hardly watching on the screen just to fill the silence.

She heard her phone buzzing on the kitchen bench.

As she walked over and picked it up, she saw it was Chloe. She answered as she wandered back into the living room towards the never-ending pile of washing.

"Hey, sister, what's up?"

"Chels."

Chloe's tone made her stand up straighter; she felt the hairs on the back of her neck stand up instantly.

"What's wrong?"

There was a pause.

Then, "It's Dad."

The way Chloe's voice broke on those two words told her everything.

Chelsea's knees gave slightly. "What happened?"

"He collapsed at the supermarket this morning. An ambulance took him straight in. Mum is at the hospital, and I am heading in now. They... they said it's not looking good. They think he had a brain aneurysm. He is in surgery."

Chelsea pressed a hand to her forehead, trying to slow her breathing. "No. No, no, he was fine a couple of days – "

"I know. Chelsea… It's bad. It's really bad. They're saying… You should come now. Tonight."

Chelsea's world blurred. She could still hear the girls laughing and playing out in the backyard. The pile of clean clothes waiting to be folded, sitting at her feet.

"I'm coming," she said. "I'll leave now."

"Okay," Chloe whispered. "Just drive safe, yeah?"

"I will."

They hung up.

Chelsea stood in the middle of the living room, unmoving for a moment. She held her phone to her chest, using all of her control not to fall apart right there on the living room floor. Then she called out to Ryan, her voice sharp, uneven, as she made her way to her bedroom and began frantically gathering the pieces of her world into a bag she hadn't planned to pack.

Ryan appeared in the hallway, looking confused until his expression changed to concern when he saw Chelsea packing a bag.

"What's going on?"

Chelsea stopped and looked at him. The pause allowed reality to catch her, and suddenly she felt like she couldn't breathe. She fell onto the bed and dropped her head into her hands.

"It's Dad…he is in surgery. A brain aneurysm, they think." She felt the bed dip beside her.

"Oh shit." He put his arm around her shoulders as she began to shake.

"I don't know… I…this has to be a mistake." Chelsea felt like she couldn't catch her breath. She felt like she was on the verge of a panic attack. She closed her eyes, focusing on her breathing.

This had to be a mistake. Her dad was the glue of the family. Always cracking dad jokes at inappropriate times. He made their home a safe place. No, this had to be a mistake. There was no way this could be happening.

"I have to go. Can you – "

"Don't worry, I've got everything here. Just go."

Chelsea leaned into him for a moment before she got back up to finish packing her bag. She needed to leave now.

Everything else suddenly seemed unimportant.

Everything else could wait.

TWENTY FIVE
Chelsea

The hospital lights were bright and white, giving Chelsea an instant headache as she stood in the corridor outside the ICU wing of the Somerdale hospital. It was hard to tell in here whether it was night or day. Chelsea was wearing her old blue hoodie. The one she used to always wear when she was younger. It was the first thing she grabbed when she rushed out the door with a half-packed bag. Chelsea stood there in an almost state of shock, her arms wrapped tightly around her body, trying to prepare herself for what would be waiting for her inside the hospital room.

She and Ryan, well, mostly Ryan, because she was silent and in shock when he came running to her, calling his name, had decided she would drive here now while he stayed with the girls and packed them a bag. Then, once she had arrived at the hospital and assessed the situation, they would decide if he should bring the girls.

She'd driven straight to the hospital without thinking, without blinking. The moment she'd pulled into the parking lot, her chest started to ache. Now, she pushed through the ICU doors, searching the room numbers for the one that matched the text Chloe had sent her while she was driving.

Her mum looked up at her as she entered the hospital room. The room was pretty bare, except for some machines, a few plastic chairs, and the bed where her dad lay, with her mum beside him. Her eyes were red and puffy, her hands clenched around a takeaway coffee cup like it was the only thing holding her together.

"He just got out of surgery... they aren't sure..." she sniffed. "They aren't sure if he will wake up."

Chelsea blinked, her eyes felt raw even though she hadn't let herself cry yet. "But – he was fine. A couple of days ago. He was whistling in the garden. Telling me some of his terrible dad jokes."

"I know," her mum whispered. "It was fast. He just... dropped. In the middle of the supermarket." She sniffled as she wiped her eyes with her sleeve. "I was off getting bread while he was browsing for a snack. Sam, the cashier, called the ambulance."

Chloe was sitting beside their mum, cheeks damp and silent. She looked up and gave Chelsea a shaky, wordless shake of her head as tears dripped down her cheeks.

Chelsea stood there for a moment, still, trying to process the scene in front of her. Hoping that maybe if she stood still for long enough, the grief wouldn't notice her.

But it noticed her.

It slowly wrapped its fingers around her ribs and started to squeeze. She felt like she couldn't breathe. She was no stranger to panic attacks. She had experienced plenty of them when she was younger, but she hadn't had one in a while. But now she could feel it grabbing hold of her again.

She couldn't be here.

Not yet.

"I just – I need a minute," she said, turning around and running out of the room.

She heard her mum call out her name, but she didn't stop. She didn't stop until she got into her car and started driving. She looked straight ahead in silence, hardly blinking. Just working hard to catch her breath.

She didn't know where she was going.

Until she did.

~

The gravel crunched beneath her tyres as she pulled up in front of Jake's dad's old weatherboard house. It looked like nothing had really been changed in the past decade. The gardens were well-maintained still, but the house itself could do with a coat of paint. It almost looked exactly the same as the first night she came to Jake's house with all of their friends after a football match. It still had the old wooden porch swing on the front porch. She had always loved that swing.

Chelsea got out of her car, completely on autopilot, hardly even registering where she was or how she had gotten there. She didn't bother closing the car door behind her; she just started to make her way towards the house when she stopped abruptly. Like she suddenly realised where she was.

At that exact moment, she heard the front door of the house creak open. She looked up to see Jake basically running down the front porch steps towards her.

"It's... It's my dad." She tried to say more, but no sound came out. Her breath hitched, her mouth opened, and then... she broke.

Tears came flooding out in a rush, like someone had torn a dam open. Her hands trembled as she covered her face, her knees giving way.

Jake caught her instantly. No hesitation. Just there to catch her as she completely fell apart in the middle of his front yard.

He pulled her to his chest, holding up her weight, and she clung to him like she was drowning, sobs wracking her body as the weight of everything collapsed on top of her. Her father, her girls, Ryan, the entire impossible world.

Jake just held her. One hand tangled in her hair, the other firmly around her back, holding her up. His breath was steady and slow against her ear. She held onto his shirt with her fists, her face pressed against his chest. Her tears were soaking his shirt, but he didn't let her go. He just held her tightly as she let everything she had been holding in, out.

After a long while of standing in Jake's front garden, her breathing had slowed, and the tears had dulled into silent shudders. Jake slowly turned and walked them towards the porch swing. Still holding up the majority of her weight.

He lowered her gently onto the old swing and sat beside her, his hand automatically grabbed hers as they sat down, lacing their fingers together.

After a moment of silence, Chelsea spoke, her voice hoarse. "I didn't know where else to go."

Jake squeezed her hand in response.

"He's dying," she whispered.

Jake didn't flinch. "I know." He said as he stroked his thumb over her hand.

Chelsea didn't know how he knew, but she didn't have the energy to care right now.

He didn't say it would be okay. He didn't try to fix it.

He just sat with her and let her feel what she needed to feel.

J ake had just walked through the front door after finishing
the lunchshift at the brewery when his phone buzzed with a
call from Dean. He told him that Emily had just received a message from Ryan, telling her that Chelsea's dad was in the hospital
and that Chelsea was on her way to Somerdale. He said it wasn't
good and wanted to make sure Chelsea had someone there with
her. Emily told Ryan that she and Dean would head to Somerdale
to meet Chelsea at the hospital. On the phone, Dean had told Jake
that he wanted to tell him since Jake had been close with Chelsea's dad when he and Chelsea had been together, and that he
would update him once they arrived at the hospital.

Once Jake had hung up the phone, he stood in the kitchen in
disbelief for a long while. He was just about to grab his car keys
when he heard the familiar crunch of gravel in the driveway. He
wasn't expecting anyone, and his dad wouldn't be home from the
brewery until after dinnertime, but something pulled him to go
out the front.

He bolted out the front door just in time to see Chelsea standing
beside her car in his dad's front yard, staring at the house.

Her hair was tangled from the wind, her eyes red and wide, her whole body shaking, wearing his old blue hoodie she had claimed as her own when they were teenagers. Something inside of him cracked open at the sight of her standing there, broken. Or breaking.

He didn't need to say anything. She didn't need to say anything. He could feel her emotions rolling off her in waves.

She didn't even have time to open her mouth before he was moving again and jogging down the porch steps towards her.

"It's... It's my dad." Her voice broke as tears fell from her eyes.

And then she was falling at the same time as her tears. Both physically and emotionally, completing collapsing into his arms.

Jake caught her like muscle memory. He held her like he had done a hundred times before. She was sobbing now, huge heart-breaking sobs wracking her body, hands fisted into his shirt, her breath broken and fast.

He didn't speak. He knew better than anyone that there was nothing he could say to make this better.

He just held her tighter, one hand against her head, the other wrapped around her body, holding her up. His shirt was damp from her tears, his own heartbeat hammering against his chest.

None of it mattered.

Only she did.

He felt his heart break.

For her.

For her family.

For himself.

His eyes were wet, and he could feel the tears dripping down his cheeks, but he couldn't bring himself to let go of Chelsea to wipe his eyes. So, he let the tears fall silently onto her golden hair.

They stood like that for a while in the middle of his front yard until her sobs began to slow down. He was sure that if he were to look around, he would find a few nosy neighbours watching them, but he didn't care enough to check. Once they had reduced to the occasional sharp breath, he led her back up towards the house. To the porch swing. The old wooden swing where they used to sit together for hours watching the stars, talking about everything and anything.

Jake sat down beside her on the swing, instantly reaching for her hand. They laced their fingers together, and Chelsea held on tight.

"I didn't know where else to go," she whispered finally.

Jake squeezed her hand in response.

She looked up at him, eyes raw. "He's dying."

"I know," he said quietly. "I'm so sorry, Chels."

She squeezed her eyes shut, like even hearing it out loud was too much.

His heart cracked open.

Jake squeezed her hand again, firm but gently. "Do you want to go back? To the hospital?"

She hesitated. Her lips parted, but no words came. She looked exhausted, shattered, like the grief had completely ripped through her, leaving her hollow.

"You don't have to go alone, I'll drive you. Stay with you. Sit in the waiting room. Whatever you need me to do."

Her fingers tightened around his.

And he saw it in her face, that deep, hidden part of her that had always needed to be strong for everyone else, finally giving in. His eyes searched her face, trying to figure out how he could take this pain away. But there was nothing he could do. Nothing could fix this. But he knew she needed to be back at the hospital. He knew her well enough to know that she would regret not being there with her family.

"Okay," she whispered.

He stood, squeezing her hand, "Wait here, okay?"

She gave a very small, hardly there nod. Jake bolted inside the house to grab his phone and keys. He almost tripped over on his way back to the front door, moving too fast for his own feet, worried that Chelsea would disappear if he took too long.

Once he made it back to the front door, he silently let out the breath he was holding when he saw Chelsea sitting in the same position as when he left. He flicked the lock on the front door and pulled it shut behind him before moving to stand in front of Chelsea.

"Let's go." He said, reaching for her hand again.

She let him lead her back towards her car, without protest. Just like old times, when she didn't need to speak for him to understand exactly what she needed.

He walked her back towards her SUV, this time helping her into the passenger seat before he closed the door and made his way around to the driver's side, where the door was still wide open. He took a moment before he got into the car. He scrubbed his hands over his face, wiping away the latest tears that were escaping his eyes as he tried to control his own grief.

As they drove through the darkening, quiet streets back to the hospital, Jake didn't say much. Chelsea didn't either. She just stared out the window, silent tears falling down her face.

Jake kept his hand resting gently over hers on the centre console, trying his best to anchor her as her world crumbled around her, just like she had for him.

~

The hospital looked different at night, with the building lit up against the dark sky. It had an eerie feeling to it.

Jake parked right outside the emergency entrance before jogging around to the passenger side to help Chelsea out. She hadn't said much during the drive, just stared out the window, the only sign of movement was her chest heaving heavily and the tears falling from her eyes.

His heart hadn't stopped aching since the moment he saw her in the front yard. And he was sure it wouldn't stop aching anytime soon.

They walked inside side by side, footsteps soft but echoing in the empty hallways.

"I'll stay in the waiting room," Jake said quietly as they approached the ICU. "I don't want to crowd – "

But Chelsea didn't even stop walking. She didn't turn, didn't hesitate, didn't respond. She just reached back and grabbed his hand, lacing their fingers together, and kept going.

He followed without hesitation.

Chloe looked up first when they turned the corner. Her red, glassy eyes went wide with surprise at the sight of him, but she didn't question it. She just nodded, like, of course *he* was there.

Chelsea's mum stood, face drawn and pale, clutching a tissue in one hand.

Jake offered her the softest nod. "Maggie… I'm so sorry."

For a fleeting moment, Jake felt like he shouldn't be there. Like, why wouldn't Chelsea's mum throw him out of this hospital room? He wasn't Chelsea's husband. He wasn't… well, anything to them anymore.

But the thought left almost as fast as it came when Maggie gave him a tired smile and pulled him in for a hug. "Jake." Her voice cracked. "Thank you for being here. For bringing her back."

Jake nodded as he hugged her back with one arm, while his other hand tightly held onto Chelsea. He swallowed hard.

Chelsea dropped Jake's hand only long enough to fold herself into her mother's arms. Jake stood just behind, giving them space but ready to catch her again if she fell.

A nurse came into the room then, eyes kind. "Mrs Quinn?"

Jake saw Chelsea's mum straighten. "Yes?"

"The doctor will be in shortly with an update. You're welcome to wait here or step into the family room just across the hall."

They chose to stay in the room, not wanting to lose any time they could be in their dad's and husband's presence.

Jake stayed quiet. He stood tucked behind Chelsea, not touching her, but close enough to let her feel his presence. To be honest, he felt helpless. He didn't know what else he could do.

Moments later, the doctor entered the room, nodding to them out of respect.

He was tall with dark hair that looked like he had run his hand through it multiple times on his way to the room. His voice was calm and practised as he spoke.

"Mr Quinn's condition is very serious," he began gently. "We were able to stabilise him temporarily, but the damage to his brain is extensive. At this stage, it is unlikely that he will wake up. And if he does, it is unclear what damage the bleeding has done to his brain."

Chelsea inhaled sharply, her shoulders tightening in front of him. Jake instinctively placed his hand on her shoulder, squeezing gently.

The doctor continued, "We have some more tests we will run on his brain over the next couple of hours. We'll keep him comfortable. You're welcome to sit with him tonight." he paused before continuing, "If there are family members who would like to see him, I recommend they come soon."

The silence was deafening.

Chelsea nodded, her shoulders trembling. "Thank you," she whispered.

The doctor gave her a soft look before glancing at her sister and then her mum. "I am very sorry." He said, before quietly stepping out of the room.

Jake didn't move. He just waited, hand still gently resting on Chelsea's shoulder. Waiting for her to fall apart again, or take control, or bolt. He didn't know which version would show up this time.

Chelsea stood slowly. Then she turned to look at him. Her usual piercing blue eyes were watery and red now. His heart cracked a little bit more, seeing the pain etched on her face.

"You don't have to stay," she said, voice hoarse.

"I know," he replied. "But I'm not going anywhere. Not until you tell me to."

And just like before, she didn't argue.

She nodded once before turning back to her dad. She pulled her chair closer and leaned on his bed, holding his hand in both of hers.

Jake stood right behind her. He was heartbroken more than he thought was possible. He couldn't leave her. Because even in grief, even in this impossibly heavy moment, she still chose him. And after all she did for him and his dad when his mum died, Jake felt like he owed it to Chelsea to be here for her.

And even if, after this, she said she never wanted to see him again, he would always show up.

TWENTY SEVEN
Chelsea

The beeping of the machines in her dad's room was constant and steady. The only noise filling the quiet room.

Chelsea sat in a hard plastic chair beside her father's hospital bed; her fingers laced through his motionless hand. He looked smaller somehow – not physically, but in his presence. He seemed... vulnerable. His chest rose and fell with the rhythm of the ventilator while the machines clicked softly around them. The hum of the machines had a cruel kind of calm to it.

Chloe was curled up in a chair on the other side of the hospital bed, legs tucked underneath her, eyes closed but not sleeping. Their mum hadn't sat once since the doctor had left the room. She stood in the corner, arms crossed, eyes fixed on the small window, even though there was nothing to see but darkness.

Jake had stayed in the room for a while after the doctor had left, silently standing behind Chelsea. He didn't touch her apart from a squeeze on the shoulder now and then. But he didn't need to. She knew he was there, grounding her with his presence. He left the room a little while ago under the premise of getting coffee, but she knew him. He was giving her the space to grieve with her family. She had no concept of time, but she assumed they had been here for hours. She vaguely registered that he was sitting right outside the doors to the ICU room, only moving when a doctor or nurse entered or exited her dad's room.

A doctor had come in not long ago to run some more tests. Chelsea had been zoning out the whole time, so she hadn't understood exactly what they were doing, but she did hear the words 'reflexes' and 'brain activity' being thrown around.

Now they were waiting on the results. Waiting for words that no one wanted to hear but needed to. Hanging onto a sliver of hope that this was all just a big misunderstanding and her dad would wake up and ask what all the fuss was about.

Chelsea reached up and brushed a stray piece of hair from her father's forehead. "It's okay," she whispered. "If you are tired, you can go. You don't have to hold on for us." Her tears fell down her cheeks as she spoke. She swallowed hard. "I promise we'll be okay. I'll take care of Mum. And the girls. You don't have to stay for us."

But even as she said the words, her grip tightened on his hand. Tears silently falling onto the hospital bed.

The door opened, and the neurologist stepped in. Jake followed closely behind, his glassy eyes matching hers. Sensing this was something he needed to be here for.

Chelsea found his hand with hers as soon as he stood next to her. His thumb instantly stroked her skin.

The whole room tensed, everyone bracing themselves to hear what they already knew.

"I'm sorry," he said gently. "We've completed all the tests, and unfortunately, there aren't any signs of brain activity. At this stage, we have to declare that he is no longer neurologically responsive. I am very sorry for your loss."

Chelsea's breath caught in her throat.

Her mother turned, slowly, her hands pressed over her mouth. "No," she whispered.

Chloe covered her face and let out a broken sob on the other side of the hospital bed.

Chelsea closed her eyes for a long moment. She gripped Jake's hand tightly, trying to hold on for dear life while the doctors' words echoed around her the room.

No brain activity.

No coming back.

Loss.

She stood up; her throat felt thick. "I need to call Ryan," she murmured, letting go of Jake's hand and stepping out into the hallway. She pulled her phone out of the pocket of her shorts. She glanced at the screen, ignoring all of the unread messages and notifications.

1:21 am.

This felt like the longest night in history. Chelsea opened up her contacts and clicked on Ryan's name. The call barely rang twice before Ryan picked up, despite it being the middle of the night.

"Chels?"

Her voice cracked immediately. "Can you bring the girls to Somerdale?"

There was a pause on the other end. "Oh god."

Chelsea nodded, though he couldn't see it. "It's bad. They… they need to come and say goodbye."

Ryan's voice was soft. "We'll leave now."

"Thank you."

She hung up before she could cry again. She turned around to go back into the room when she collided with a hard, warm chest. Arms wrapped around her instantly. She buried her face into Jake's chest, allowing herself a minute to fall apart again before going back into the room. His hand stroked her hair, the other holding her strong.

Here he was again.

Knowing she needed a moment to breathe, to feel what she needed to feel before going back into the hospital room and holding herself together for her family. Giving her a safe space to do it, without saying a word.

They stood like that for a moment before Chelsea let go and stepped back, looking up at him. His face mirrored something similar to what she imagined hers did. He had clearly been crying, his eyes red and slightly wet. She reached up to cup his cheek with her hand. Although her whole world was crumbling, she still wanted to take his pain away. He turned his face slightly to kiss the palm of her hand lightly. She lingered there in the hall, holding his face for a moment before she dropped her hand and stepped around him.

Back inside her father's room, her mum had sat down in the chair Chelsea had just left. Her head bent, cradling his hand in hers.

"I can't do it," she whispered. "He's still breathing."

Chelsea crouched beside her. "I know, Mum. But it's the machines now. It's not… he isn't here anymore."

Her mum turned, face streaked with silent tears. "How do I say goodbye?"

Chelsea's own heart split. "We'll do it together."

~

The next couple of hours passed in pieces. Quiet words, shaking hands, the soft sound of the ventilator filling the space like a ticking clock. Jake had waited outside the room again, letting them have the moment, but Chelsea felt him nearby. Somehow, it was enough to help hold her together. It was like a comforting soft pull giving her the strength she needed to keep going.

She didn't know how she would cope when she needed to tell the girls when they arrived. How she would hold it together for them. Their grandad was one of their favourite people in the whole world. God, he was one of Chelsea's favourite people. She had been going through the motions of the night, but she hadn't really let herself think further ahead. She had no idea how she was going to survive this. How was she going to not only continue to parent but also support her daughters through their grief when she herself would be grieving an unimaginable loss?

She wasn't afraid to show emotion in front of her children; she had never hidden from them. But she knew their little worlds were about to crumble. They were both so little still. Too little to have to grieve and watch their mum grieve.

So, she had to hold herself together for them. Or at least try to.

TWENTY EIGHT
Jake

Jake sat on the uncomfortable chairs just outside Chelsea's dad's ICU room, elbows resting on his knees. The ICU rooms were all surrounded by glass, he assumed, so the staff could easily keep an eye on all the patients and their machines. Unfortunately, this meant there was hardly any privacy for a grieving family. He felt oddly protective of the grieving Quinn family in the room, where everyone could see. So, he stayed sitting right where he was.

Jake had no idea how much time had actually passed since Chelsea turned up at his dad's house, but it felt like a lifetime. But somehow at the same time, not long enough.

The halls were quieter at this time of night. There were a few nurses who floated through the ICU floor, checking on patients and doing their paperwork. A couple of doctors had gone in and out of Chelsea's dad's room throughout the night, but that had slowed down now. The coffee in Jake's takeaway cup had turned stone cold, but he was hardly drinking it anyway. He just needed something in his hands to stop him from barging into the hospital room behind him.

He wanted to be in there holding Chelsea through the worst moment of her life, like she had done for him all those years ago when his mother had passed away when he was a teenager. But he knew she needed to be in there with her family to say goodbye. He didn't know exactly what was going on behind the closed door, but he could feel it. The finality of the moment.

Chelsea hadn't come out in a while. Not since he had followed her out of the room and watched as she called Ryan. Not since she turned around and collided with him. Not since he wrapped his arms around her and held her tightly for a minute. Giving her the space to fall apart again before re-entering the room.

She hadn't asked him to stay.

But she hadn't asked him to leave, either.

So, he stayed.

A soft voice pulled him from his thoughts.

"Jake?"

He looked up.

Emily stood in front of him, flanked by Dean. Her eyes were red but warm, her hand linked tightly with her fiancé's. She sat beside Jake without hesitation. Dean on his other side.

"We couldn't sleep at home knowing what was going on here," Emily said quietly. "We figured we would come and wait here."

Jake nodded, running a hand over his face. "She's sitting with her dad. Guys, it's... not good. The doctors said there is no brain activity."

Emily gripped Jake's hand, her eyes holding back tears that threatened to fall. "We'll wait here. Wait until she needs us."

Dean gave Jake a light clap on the shoulder. "Do you need anything?"

Jake shook his head softly but didn't respond. He just stared straight ahead at the sterile white wall in front of them.

He didn't need anything they could give him.

But he needed everything.

He needed her to be okay.

He needed him to be okay.

He needed this to be some sick nightmare.

But he knew none of that was going to happen.

She was in there, saying goodbye to the man who'd once taught her to surf, who'd come to every one of his footy games and shouted from the sidelines, and still called him "Jakey-boy" years after high school had ended.

He wasn't sure if he had the right to grieve for that man, but the ache in his chest told him otherwise.

The elevator chimed softly down the hall, cutting through his thoughts. Jake lifted his gaze to the elevator as the doors opened.

Chelsea's husband, Ryan, stepped out, one small child on his hip, still half asleep, and another beside him gripping his hand tightly. They looked tired, blinking in the bright, sterile hallway light.

Jake stood instinctively.

He hadn't met Ryan, not properly. But he knew this was him. And the girls with him were Chelsea's whole heart, beating outside of her chest.

Ryan met his eyes across the hall. Something filtered across his face. Something like recognition.

Jake gave a slight nod before sitting back down.

Ryan returned the nod, moving forward towards the ICU room beside Jake.

Emily stood to hug Ryan and the girls before guiding them towards the room.

Jake watched as they made their way to the room. It was quiet, but there was a heaviness in the air that he was sure even children could feel. His heart broke all over again seeing Lucy and Olivia. Knowing they had no idea the pain they were going to face. Knowing how much pain Chelsea would be in seeing her daughters go through their first heartbreak, whilst she is grieving her first love, her dad.

Jake dropped his head into his hands.

The protective streak running through him wanted to be right there with her, protecting her from this pain.

But he couldn't.

It killed him that he was out in the hall, rather than in there with her. But it wasn't his place. He couldn't stomach the fact that, really, he wasn't anything to her anymore. He wasn't sure if that was true, but what was true was that Ryan and those girls were her family, and they needed to be in there with her.

So, he would give her the space and wait out in the hall.

He just hoped that was enough.

TWENTY NINE
Chelsea

Chelsea was pulled from her thoughts when she heard a small tap on the glass doors to her father's ICU room. She looked up to see Ryan standing there holding Olivia on his hip, his other hand holding onto Lucy's shoulder, quietly reassuring them. Her heart felt a tiny bit lighter seeing the girls. Although their faces were etched with worry, Chelsea just needed to hold them.

She got up from the plastic hospital chair as they entered the room, bracing herself.

"Mummy!" Olivia ran straight into her arms, clutching her old bunny in one hand.

Chelsea dropped to her knees and wrapped her up, Lucy close behind, her little face serious, assessing the room. Ryan stood a few steps back, giving them some space.

Chelsea kissed their heads, one after the other, not wanting to let them go. "Hey, my girls."

"We got to drive here in the middle of the night!" Olivia said with excitement. "It was kind of...spooky." She said, obviously too young to understand the heaviness of the moment.

Chelsea let out a small laugh, the air feeling lighter with Olivia's bright energy filling the room.

"Is Grandad ok?" Lucy asked, looking behind her mum to the hospital bed. Lucy was very intuitive. She always felt other people's emotions almost as intensely as they did. She was the one Chelsea was worried would take this the hardest. Her eyes pricked with tears, not wanting to lie to her daughter but not quite ready to break their hearts. "He is sleeping at the moment, baby. But you can talk to him if you want. I think he can hear us."

They shuffled closer to the hospital bed, Chelsea holding both girls' hands, Ryan closely behind them.

Her father's breathing was mechanical, slow, and steady, the sound filling the otherwise quiet room. Her mum and sister were cuddled up together on the other side of the hospital bed, watching as Lucy and Olivia approached.

The girls didn't speak at first. They both stood near the bed, looking up at their grandad, as if trying to figure out what they were seeing. Tightly gripping Chelsea's hands.

Chelsea knelt beside them. "You can talk to him if you want," she whispered. "I have. We all have been."

Olivia stepped forward first, her voice small. "Hi Grandad. I bought Mr Bunny. He says hi, too." She set the toy gently near his arm "You can cuddle him. He always makes me feel better, so he can fix you, too."

Lucy reached out and touched her grandad's hand, then leaned close. "I'm going to be brave," she whispered. "Like you always said. I'll look after Mum and Olivia. And Grandma. And Aunty Chloe."

Chelsea felt tears sliding down her cheeks, silent and unstoppable. She didn't need to tell her daughter the seriousness of this situation. Lucy had always been so emotionally mature for her age. Always able to read the emotions in a room. She knew he wasn't going to get better.

Ryan knelt beside her then, placing a steady hand on her back.

"They're okay," he murmured. "They needed this. So did you. I prepared them before we got here, so they had an idea of what they were walking into. They are okay."

She nodded, unable to speak. Grateful for him being able to hold space for the girls. For her as well.

After about an hour of the girls taking it in turns talking to their grandad, the energy had somehow turned lighter as they spoke about their favourite memories with their grandad. Chelsea sat beside them, laughing at their stories and admiring how brave they were, while Ryan stood behind them. But eventually, the girls began to tire, both yawning and their eyes growing heavy.

Chelsea stood and brushed their hair back.

"Daddy's going to take you back to Grandma and Grandad's house now, okay? Get some sleep. I'll be back in a couple of hours."

Lucy looked like she wanted to argue, but she eventually nodded.

"I love you, Grandad," Lucy said, squeezing his hand before walking over to Ryan and grabbing his hand, burying her face in his side.

Olivia climbed up onto the bed to kiss her grandad's cheek. "I hope you feel better soon." She then climbed down and hugged her mum tightly. "Don't be sad, Mummy."

Chelsea smiled through her tears. "I'll try, baby."

Ryan gave her a soft look as he took the girls' hands. "I've got them, Chels. Take all the time you need."

Chelsea's mum and sister gave the girls and Ryan a quick hug before they left the room. She watched them walk out of the room and down the hall, noticing her best friend, Dean and Jake, still sitting outside of the room. Dean had his head leaned back against the wall, Emily on his side, head on his shoulder, eyes closed. And Jake. Jake had his gaze locked on her. Searching her face with his eyes. Worry etched all across his face.

Her people. Waiting for her. Not expecting anything. Just waiting for the moment she needed them.

She gave Jake a small, sad smile as she turned back to her father.

Her mother was holding her husband's hand; her lips pressed to his knuckles. Chloe sat at the foot of the bed now, tears silently slipping down her face.

Chelsea sat back into the crappy hospital chair beside the bed.

The heaviness of the moment was suddenly weighing her down now that the girls had left. She had been holding back, focusing on them arriving rather than what would come once they left.

But this was it.

She could feel it.

No more doctors.

No more decisions.

Just time.

Just goodbye.

~

After the girls and Ryan had left. The room had shifted again. It had lightened slightly while the girls were there, but now the heaviness had retaken charge.

It was still and warm, dim except for the low light above the bed. The hum of the machines was steady but somehow felt softer now. Almost background noise against the rhythm of three women sitting beside the man they loved most.

Chelsea sat on one side of her father, one hand on his arm. His skin was warm but slack. She tried not to focus on the way his chest moved mechanically up and down. It wasn't natural anymore. She could feel him slipping away.

Now and then, Chloe would mention something she remembered from their childhood, and they would all laugh at the memories together.

"Remember when we used to go to the beach, and he would carry one of us on his shoulders and the other on his back, all the way back to the car if we refused to wear shoes," Chloe murmured, a faint smile pulling at her lips.

"He said shoes were a 'government scam'," Chelsea added with a soft laugh.

Their mother shook her head fondly. "He was always saying the most ridiculous things to make you two laugh."

Silence followed, but it was warm, wrapped in memories of the life they had lived with him. It wasn't nearly enough, though.

Chelsea leaned forward and took his hand in hers again. "Dad…" she began. "You were the best. Pure sunshine. The clown of the family. Our safe space. Our best friend."

Her throat tightened as she blinked back tears. "I don't know how to do this without you."

"You don't need to know right now," her mother said from across the bed. "You just have to love him."

And so, they did.

They sat with him, the minutes blurring together. Telling stories and memories, whispering the things they were thankful for and the things they would miss about him most.

And then the doctor came in, followed closely by a nurse. They slowly nodded when he asked if they were ready. Tears silently slipped down Chelsea's cheeks. Her mother kissed him once more. Chloe held his hand to her lips.

Chelsea moved and leaned in to kiss her dad's forehead, wanting to feel his warmth one last time. "I love you, Dad," she whispered. "So much."

The nurse quietly floated around the room. Silencing the machines one by one.

The room fell into a heavy silence.

No sound apart from her father's final breath and the silent tears falling from all three women beside him.

THIRTY

Chelsea

T he sun was shining as Chelsea's car pulled into the driveway of the Quinn family home a few hours later. Jake had driven them home since all three women were struggling to remember how to breathe, let alone drive a car. Chelsea vaguely noticed Dean's car parked across the road; she assumed he was there to take Jake home. But she didn't have the energy to think about the logistics of it all.

Everything looked the same. The white picket fence around the front yard, the garden beds her parents were always pottering in, the neighbours out watering their lawns before the hot summer day set in.

But Chelsea felt entirely different.

No one had spoken the whole car ride. Chloe and their mum were sitting in the back seat, both staring out the back windows, their hands entwined across the seat. Chelsea sat in the front seat next to Jake, staring straight ahead. They didn't speak, but she could feel Jake's gaze flicking to her the whole car ride, the worry radiating off of him.

Jake put the car in park and glanced at her, reaching for her hand gently.

Chelsea turned to him, eyes swollen but soft. "Thank you. For everything."

He nodded, giving her hand a quick squeeze. "Of course."

Chelsea hesitated, just for a second, wanting to give him more but having nothing left to give in this moment. She eventually opened the car door and stepped out, her body aching, heart heavy. Her mum and Chloe followed slowly, moving like shadows behind her. Jake met her at the front of the car, placing her car keys into her hand. He gently squeezed her hand before she walked around him to her sister and mum. She turned to look back at Jake as she walked towards the house, Jake already watching her. She knew him well enough to know he was fighting an internal battle with himself to walk away from her and go to Dean's car. He had always been the one who wanted to take away her pain or fix her problems, so she knew that it would be eating him alive that there was nothing he could do right now apart from letting her walk away.

She turned back towards the house with her mum and sister as they walked up the front steps. The front door creaked open before they could open it. Lucy and Olivia stood there, looking like they had just woken up. Hair wild and still in their pyjamas. Chelsea still had no idea what the time was or when the girls would have gotten to bed, but their tired little eyes told her that they hadn't gotten nearly enough sleep.

"Mummy," Olivia said softly.

Both girls threw themselves at Chelsea. She wrapped her arms around the girls when she felt her mum and sister join. They stood there for a few moments. All five girls holding and grounding each other in the midst of their grief.

Ryan appeared at the door quietly, giving them space.

Lucy pulled back and looked behind Chelsea before looking back at her, "Mummy," she whispered. "Did Grandad wake up?"

Chelsea swallowed hard. Her eyes instantly glazed. She had thought for sure she would have run out of tears by now.

Chloe knelt to look at her niece. "No, babe. He didn't." She said as she held her little hands in hers.

Both girls' eyes went wide.

"But… that means…" Lucy's voice trailed off.

Chelsea nodded. "He passed away a couple of hours ago, sweetheart. Very peacefully. With all of us holding his hands."

Olivia, who was now holding her grandma's hand, with watery eyes, thought for a moment before she said, "Can we still talk about him?"

"Always," Chelsea whispered. "We will always talk about him. Or to him. I think he will still be able to hear us wherever we are."

They shuffled their way inside the house. Chelsea's mum murmured that she was going to take a shower and lie down. Chloe saying something to the same effect.

Chelsea followed her daughters into the lounge room, feeling like a zombie. Torn between her grief and the guilt of not having the energy to give the girls what they need through their own grief.

Ryan stepped towards her, gently pulling her to him. "I'm so sorry, Chels."

Chelsea nodded, her head against his chest. Tears threatening to fall again. She wrapped her arms around him, and they stood together for a moment. Chelsea's mind was racing with thoughts of how she was going to possibly get through this grief. How was her mum ever going to recover from the biggest heartbreak of her life? She turned her face into Ryan's chest as the tears she tried to stop fell over her eyes. Ryan rubbed his hands up and down her back as she quietly sobbed into his chest.

Ryan eventually stepped back to look at her. "You go and rest. I've got the girls."

She looked at him, gratitude rushing over her. "Thank you."

She kissed the girls once more, telling them she was going to lie down, but if they needed her, they could come and join her in the bedroom. Then she turned and headed down the hall to her bedroom with slow, dragging steps.

Chelsea sat on the edge of her bed and let out a long breath. Letting the emotions of the past twenty-four hours wash over her. She didn't know how long she sat there on the edge of the bed staring out the window, but eventually she lay down, fully clothed, curled up on top of the quilt.

She finally let the exhaustion take her completely.

T he local football club had been packed full of people for the celebration of James Quinn's life.

Even through the fog of the past few days, with the endless stream of condolences, flowers filling their home, and home-made meals in the fridge, Chelsea was still overwhelmed by the number of people who came to celebrate her dad.

Old friends. Neighbours. Former footy teammates. People who had worked with her dad over the years. All of them with plenty of stories to tell.

The service was exactly what her dad would have wanted. Fond memories shared, with a few dad jokes thrown in. He was never serious, and he would have been mortified if they had a service in a church with poems and readings.

Chloe and Chelsea stood together, re-telling funny stories from their childhood, voices trembling but proud. Their mum had spoken, barely, before breaking down. Her parents had been high school sweethearts, each other's only love. Her mum had lost not only her love but also her best friend, and her grief was deep. So,

Chelsea stepped in when she was unable to continue, holding her mum and finishing the words. She didn't remember everything she had said; it had all gone by in a blur. The same as every day since he had left them.

After the funeral, they all headed back to the family house to continue the celebration of her dad's life. The house filled up quickly, people in every room, laughter mixing with grief in the strange, bittersweet way it does. Her mum was pottering around in the kitchen as usual, Chelsea assumed, trying to keep busy. But also, probably to avoid the continuous flow of people wanting to give her their condolences. Chelsea had seen her sister floating around, but she noticed she kept disappearing. She wasn't all that surprised, though. Chloe had never been the best at communicating her emotions and tended to keep to herself when going through something. Chelsea made a note to check in on her later.

Chelsea had hugged so many people she lost count. Smiled when she really didn't feel like smiling. Thanked them for their kindness, listened to stories and the same sentence over and over again *"He was a good man."*

They weren't wrong. He was a good man.

And now he was gone.

She couldn't wrap her head around how someone who had such a positive impact on so many people could just be gone. He was a constant fixture in her life, and she knew it wasn't realistic, but she had never thought she would have to live without him. Lucy and Olivia had spent the day following their parents or grandmother around, still partly their energetic, happy selves, but also dulled by their own grief and the grief of those around them.

Late in the afternoon, as the house began to slowly empty except for their close family and friends, Chelsea stepped outside onto the back porch to get some fresh air and have a moment to breathe. The light was golden, and the air was slowly cooling down after another warm tropical day.

Ryan had taken Lucy and Olivia to the second lounge room to watch a movie and to have a break from the sadness filling the house. They were overwhelmed with everything catching up to them from the past couple of days. So much grief for two little girls. Chelsea was grateful she had Ryan there to hold them up for her as she was struggling to hold herself in her own grief.

She stood on the back porch quietly, arms crossed over her black dress, watching the way the breeze moved through the trees. Watching the sun begin to drop towards the horizon. Her dad had always made a point to watch the sunset when he could. So, watching the sun dip now made her feel close to him again. Something she guessed she would be reaching for often in the days, months, and years to come.

"Hey."

She startled at a voice coming from behind her. A voice she would recognise anywhere. She turned.

Jake was standing at the back door behind her. He walked over to join her, hands buried in his pockets. He was dressed simply but neatly in black pants, a white shirt, and no tie. His eyes were soft, tired, and worried.

"Hey," she said, giving him a tired smile.

He walked over and stood beside her. Close, but not quite touching. They both turned to look out over the garden.

Chelsea exhaled slowly. "Thank you for being there today. Dad really loved you. Especially calling you Jakey-Boy in front of your footy team." She huffed a small laugh.

Jake looked at her, something tender in his expression. "I wouldn't have been anywhere else." Then he smiled, "And there is no one else I would have let call me that. The boys always gave me so much shit for that nickname."

Chelsea smiled at that. There was a silence for a moment. Not awkward – just thick with everything they wanted to say but didn't know how to. "I wanted to say thank you," she said. "For that night. For being there when I didn't even know what I needed."

He gave a slight nod. "You don't have to thank me for that, Chels."

"I do." She turned toward him, really looking. "Because I didn't know who else to run to. I didn't even know where I was going until I pulled up at your dad's house. That means something."

Jake's jaw tightened slightly. "It does mean something."

Chelsea had thought about that night countless times over the past few days. Obviously, her father passing away in front of her was something she would never forget. But Jake being there, supporting her, not questioning her when she turned up at his place, was something she wasn't sure she could ever forget, either. She still didn't completely understand why she chose to go there, and to be honest, she hadn't had the emotional capacity or energy to work it out yet.

She looked down at her hands and sighed. "I feel like I've aged ten years this week."

"You've been so strong. For everyone."

Chelsea let out a breath. "I don't feel strong at all."

Jake tilted his head. "You showed your girls how to say goodbye, helped your mum through the hardest moment of her life. You held your whole family together when you were crumbling. That's not weakness." Jake sighed, running his hand through his hair. "God Chels, I'm so sorry. Sitting in the hospital, I wanted nothing more than to take away your pain. Do what you did for me all those years ago."

Her eyes filled again, but this time the tears didn't fall. "I'm so tired, Jake."

"I know," he said quietly. "You don't have to carry it alone. I'm here."

She nodded and looked into his eyes, eyes searching each other, before stepping forward and resting her head gently against his chest. She felt him place his hand on her back, silently showing her that he really was there.

Chelsea closed her eyes as they stood like that for a moment until her eyes started to feel heavy. The weight of the week catching up to her. She had to force herself to step away before she fell asleep standing up outside. As she stepped back, she looked up at Jake and reached up to cup his cheek with her hand. Jake's eyes softened as he slightly leaned into her hand. Neither of them said anything, their eyes just searching each other's. Something had definitely shifted between them in the past week. Chelsea couldn't quite put her finger on what had changed, and as much as she wanted to stay out on the deck with him to figure it out, she felt like a walking zombie.

She gave him a soft smile before dropping her hand and walking back towards the house. What she needed right now was to go and cuddle up with her two little girls and hopefully fall asleep.

She needed to be with them and to start rebuilding their lives and piecing back together their broken hearts.

THIRTY TWO
Chelsea

The morning after the funeral was grey and still. Like the world around them was also grieving the loss of a significant presence. The kind of day where even the birds seemed to be quieter than usual.

Chelsea stood in the hallway of her childhood home, one hand resting on the doorframe of her father's study. It hadn't changed much since she was a teenager. It still had the same wooden desk, the same framed footy jerseys and team photos, the books lining the shelves.

She stood there quietly inhaling the smell of the old books and the lingering scent of his aftershave.

It was strange how someone could be gone, yet their presence lingered in the corners of the spaces they once occupied. Logically, she knew he was no longer here, but in certain places, she would get an overwhelming feeling of him being nearby. His office seemed to be one of those places.

Behind her, the rest of the house was quiet, except for her mother talking softly to Chloe in the kitchen. Chelsea felt a pang of guilt when her thoughts drifted to Lucy and Olivia. They had been shut in the house, hardly leaving, surrounded by so much grief. But Chelsea didn't have it in her to put on a happy face and pretend she was okay. Everything was weighing on her, and when she stopped to think about it, she felt as if she couldn't breathe. She felt mentally and physically drained, with not much else left to give. She felt guilty for the girls. And evidently so did Ryan. So, he had taken them out to the park and to get ice cream this morning. Chelsea also suspected he did it to give her some time. He was giving her a lot of that lately – space.

She wasn't sure what had shifted, or if it was the grief making things unclear, but things had felt different with Ryan. Like he was holding back or hiding something from her. She wasn't exactly sure where their relationship stood or if she had the right to know what was bothering him. She guessed there were things she was holding back as well. She also understood that staying in her childhood home after only ever being here a handful of times would be weird for him, especially when it was filled with so much grief. She guessed that taking the girls out for the morning would also be an excuse for him to get himself out of the house. To have some breathing space.

Chelsea was pulled from her thoughts as the front door opened and Emily's voice floated down the hall. "Chels? You home?"

"In here," Chelsea called back.

Emily appeared next to her, holding a coffee tray that held four coffees and a paper bag.

"Emergency pastry and coffee drop for you ladies." She said with a small smile.

"Just what we need," Chelsea said gratefully, putting her arm around her best friend and leading her to the kitchen, where her mum and sister were.

"Did I hear coffee and pastries?" Chloe said, looking up as they entered the kitchen.

"Sure did, thought you all might need it," Emily said, walking in and placing the coffees and paper bag on the kitchen counter.

"You weren't wrong there. Thank you, Sweetheart." Her mum

said with a soft smile, reaching for a coffee.

They stood in silence for a few sips. Everyone lost in their own thoughts.

Emily sat down at the kitchen table. "Dean and I were talking last night. About whether we should postpone the wedding."

Chelsea looked at her, surprised, and dropped into the chair opposite her. "What? No. Em, absolutely not."

Emily hesitated, looking to Chelsea's mum briefly. "It just feels… weird. With everything going on."

Chelsea shook her head firmly. "Don't. You deserve your moment. You deserve the joy. And honestly? We could all use something to look forward to."

Chelsea's mum spoke up then, "She's right, Emily. If you waited for the perfect time when nothing was going on, you would never get married."

Emily let out a small laugh. "You're sure?"

"I want to be your maid of honour," Chelsea said, softer now. "Plus, we have already got our dresses, so that would be a huge waste." She said playfully.

Emilly nodded, a smile on her face. "That's true," she paused briefly. "You'll tell me though if things get too much, right?"

Chelsea smiled. "Of course. But it's not too much. I am excited."

They sat at the kitchen table, the four of them, sipping their coffees, eating pastries, and chatting about all things wedding. It was the first time in days that Chelsea had managed to think about things other than her grief for longer than a couple of minutes. She even managed to smile and have a few laughs. It was a good distraction and probably exactly what they all needed, without realising.

After Emily got up and gave each of them a quick hug goodbye before leaving, Chelsea stayed sitting at the table for a while longer, thinking.

So much was changing.

The funeral had nudged everything slightly forward. Ryan had started packing boxes at their house between being in Somerdale. The school transfer forms were nearly done. The real estate agent was scheduled to come on Monday to list their house for sale. Ryan had an interview scheduled for the surgical position at another hospital.

They were really doing it.

They were really moving.

Chelsea wasn't exactly sure what came next for her personally. She didn't know if she'd stay in Somerdale forever, or just long enough to breathe. Long enough to figure out her next step.

But for the first time in weeks, she didn't feel overwhelmed by the unknown.

She was… ready.

Or getting there at least.

One foot in front of the other.

THIRTY THREE
Jake

Jake had been keeping himself busy over the past week. Doing everything he could to keep himself from driving over to Chelsea's parents' house and ambushing them, just so that he could lay his eyes on Chelsea. Just to see that she was okay.

It was taking all of his willpower to give her space to grieve and be with her family. He didn't understand how a decade could pass, and he still felt just as protective and territorial of her as he did when she was actually his. He thought that travelling the world, filling the voids in his life with different countries, experiences, and even different girls, would help him get over her.

He was wrong.

So very wrong.

It was like no time had passed at all. He was still as hooked on her as he had been all those years ago when he walked away from her on the front porch of her house. He was just waiting for the moment she realised she was too.

Jake shook his head, trying to clear his head. His dad had run out of coffee beans at the brewery, so Jake offered to run into town to get them. More so as an excuse to get out of the office. He was going crazy, and he wasn't sure if it had to do with working in close proximity to his dad for so long or that he couldn't concentrate on anything other than Chelsea.

He needed to work out a plan. Figure out his life and what he was going to do next. Figure out where he wanted to be. But something inside of him kept stopping him from moving forward. Like he couldn't move forward until he knew where he stood with Chelsea. Or maybe he just didn't want to.

He shook his head, trying to clear his mind again, as he pushed the door to the café open, the bell overhead chiming softly.

Jake looked up and stopped mid-step.

His heart suddenly slammed against his chest.

Cheslea stood by the counter where the takeaway orders were collected.

Her hair was tied back in a low ponytail, and she wore an oversized t-shirt half-tucked into her denim shorts, with her long golden legs on display. Effortlessly beautiful.

God, she looks good, Jake thought to himself.

She was holding her phone in one hand, talking to her eldest daughter as the little one spun slowly in circles behind her, singing softly to herself.

Jake's chest pulled at the sight.

Something about seeing her there, her kids, her coffee order, the way she just looked like she belonged, felt permanent. Like this was their everyday routine.

She turned slightly as he stepped in, and the door shut behind him.

Their eyes met.

For a second, everything around them stilled.

Then she smiled, soft and familiar. "Hey."

He stepped toward her slowly. "Hey. Didn't expect to see you here."

She nodded. "We came into town to grab some lunch and boxes. We're heading back to Port Mac this afternoon to pack up our house."

He blinked, his stomach dropping. "Wait – pack up?"

She glanced down briefly, then back at him. "We're moving. Here. For good. Well... for now."

He didn't speak for a moment, letting it settle in.

Chelsea Quinn was coming home.

He tried his best to hold back the huge schoolboy grin that was threatening to spread across his face at that news. "Since when?"

"A few weeks. But after Dad... things just felt clear. We had been making plans before, but that just accelerated the whole thing." She shrugged. "I want to be here for Mum. Ryan has an interview at a hospital nearby. It made sense. For the girls. For all of us."

Jake nodded slowly. "Wow... that's big."

"It is."

"You okay?"

She looked at him. Jake's eyes searched her face, holding himself back from closing the space between them when her gaze stayed on his for a beat longer than necessary. He was trying to play it cool, but he really just needed to know that she was okay.

"Not really. Not yet. But I will be." She said, finally.

He smiled gently. "You always were, Chels."

Interrupting them briefly, the barista called her name, and she stepped forward to collect the tray of drinks, a coffee and what looked like two small hot chocolates topped with marshmallows.

Lucy stood up straighter beside her mum and looked up at Jake curiously.

Chelsea turned toward the girls. "Oh, girls, this is Jake," she said casually. "He's an old friend of mine. We went to school together."

Jake tried to ignore the disappointment he felt at the term 'friend' being thrown around. Instead, he bent down so that he was at their level and offered a friendly smile. "Hey there. You must be Lucy and Olivia."

Lucy gave him a cautious once-over, but her voice was clear. "Mum talks about you."

Chelsea blinked, her cheeks slightly turning a shade of pink. "I do?"

"You said your friend Jake taught you how to kick the footy. But the ball hit you in the nose, and you cried, and then he cried because you got blood on his new shirt."

Jake laughed, rubbing the back of his neck. "I forgot about that."

Jake smirked, looking up at Chelsea, whose gaze was already locked on him. She squinted her eyes slightly. "I was sure you did that on purpose." She laughed.

Olivia stepped forward confidently. "You better not have hurt my mum."

Chelsea laughed, "Olivia!"

Jake's face reddened, flustered that he was getting the third degree from a 6-year-old for something that happened over a decade ago. "I promise you, it was an accident." He laughed nervously.

Olivia nodded, accepting. "Good."

Chelsea laughed again, shaking her head.

Jake stood, his eyes locking onto Chelsea's. "Well, I don't know how to feel about getting in trouble with your daughter, but she definitely takes after her mum."

Chelsea grinned at him, "God help me then."

They stood there for a moment, Jake not wanting her to leave but knowing he had to get back to the brewery for the lunchtime rush.

Chelsea cleared her throat, "We should get going," she said. "Long afternoon ahead for us."

Jake nodded, straightening. "Well... good luck with the packing. Let me know if you need any help at your parents' place."

Chelsea nodded as she passed him, the girls rushing ahead to the door. "Thanks, Jake."

She paused as she got to the door and turned back to Jake. "I'll see you soon, yeah?"

Jake's stomach filled with something. Something close to nerves. Or excitement. Or hope. He wasn't sure anymore.

He met her eyes. "Of course. I'm not going anywhere."

She gave him a look, quiet and knowing, then turned and followed the girls out of the door and into the sunshine.

Jake just stood there watching them disappear. Feet grounded to the spot. Forgetting why he was even there for a minute.

"We're moving here."

Those words echoed around his body.

And now he'd met her daughters.

This wasn't just nostalgia anymore.

This was real.

Jake felt a rush of emotions.

He had told her he wasn't going anywhere.

And it was true.

He had left her here once before, and there was no way he was making that mistake again.

He was so screwed.

THIRTY FOUR

High School: Last Year
Jake

*C*helsea was lying in the tray of Jake's old Ute. This was one of their favourite things to do after a game. The back of the Ute was filled with pillows and blankets where they would lie together, watch the stars and talk for hours. Jake smiled as he looked up at Chelsea, lying on her back, staring at the sky. He loved the way she looked when it was just them.

Jake climbed up beside her; his hair still damp from the post-game shower. He lowered himself down next to her, but instead of looking at the sky, he propped himself up on his side, elbow pressing into the pillows, and watched her. The field lights had gone out now, leaving the glow from the full moon in the dark sky.

"You're quiet," he said finally, reaching out to tuck a strand of hair behind her ear.

Chelsea smiled and turned her head toward him. "I'm just thinking."

"Care to elaborate?" Jake said, raising an eyebrow.

"Just about how weird it is that this is almost over. School. Every-

thing."

Jake leaned closer to her, laying his head down so they were face to face. "Hey. We've got time. Don't go getting all deep on me just yet, Quinn." He said, trying to lighten the mood, even though his leaving had been all he could think about lately. Trying to figure out if he was making the biggest mistake of his life, leaving this behind to go and travel the world. Or if it is exactly what he needs to do to figure out who he is or who he wants to be.

Chelsea let out a small laugh before turning away from him to look back at the stars. "You're the one who's leaving. Travelling. Working away. All of that."

"And you're staying," he said simply, still trying to convince himself that they were doing the right thing. "You'll go to university. Write that book you're always talking about. Or open your little bookstore and café that you've always dreamt of. You'll be amazing."

She nodded slowly. Jake noticed her chest rising faster than before. "You really think so? You really think this is the right thing to do?"

Jake propped himself back onto his elbow, reaching across to tilt her head back towards his so that she was looking at him. "Do I know this is the right thing to do? No. I don't know for sure. I think it is, but I won't know until I do it. But do I think you'll be amazing? Babe, I know you will be."

Jake heard Chelsea's breath catch, her eyes going glossy. Before she had a chance to respond, Jake leaned in and pressed his mouth to hers. Soft at first, testing, then as soon as she kissed him back, the kiss deepened. Her lips were warm and soft, with the faint taste of vanilla from her lip balm. Jake cupped her jaw with his hand, tilting her head slightly to deepen the kiss again.

After a moment, he pulled back, resting his forehead against hers, their chests heaving. She flashed him one of her smiles that always undid him.

"See? I don't know where we will end up for sure, Chels, but I don't think what we have will ever go away. We will probably end up coming straight back together." He rested back down beside her, sliding his arm underneath her shoulders and pulling her to his chest. "I bet we will end up back here, married with a heap of kids." He kissed the top

of her head as she chuckled against his chest.

He didn't know if it was fair to say those things to her when things felt so uncertain. But in this moment, he needed it as much as her. He needed to hold on to the hope that his leaving and her staying wasn't going to be the end of them forever.

God, he really hoped this wasn't it.

THIRTY FIVE
Chelsea

The house was quieter than usual. It felt bigger somehow... empty.

The girls were already in bed, with their mattresses on the floor of one of their bedrooms. They had gone to bed easily as they treated it like a slumber party, camping out on the floor. They had spent the past couple of days packing up the house. Mostly everything had been packed into boxes, ready to move over the weekend. Boxes lined the hallway. The walls were bare. Even the kitchen, once cluttered with drawings, reminders, and kids' birthday invitations on the fridge, now looked stripped bare of personality.

Chelsea stood at the kitchen counter, wiping the bench for the hundredth time this evening, for no other reason than it gave her something to do with her hands.

Ryan stepped into the kitchen. He didn't say anything at first. Just leaned against the counter, watching her. She turned to face him, raising an eyebrow at him.

"What's up?"

"I just got a call from the head of surgery at Watervale," he paused. "I got the job."

Chelsea looked up at Ryan, then threw the dishcloth into the sink and walked to stand across from him. "That's amazing, Ry! I knew you would get it."

Ryan nodded, giving her a small smile. "Yeah, they said they finished up the interviews today, but I had some good references from my bosses here, so it was a no-brainer."

"That's so good. When do you start?"

He shrugged, "They said they will email me the contract over the weekend, and then I will call into the hospital next week to go over the paperwork, and I guess I will find out then."

Chelsea nodded, a grin on her face. She was genuinely happy for him. That his hard work and long hours had paid off.

Ryan let out a sigh before saying, "Liv said they met Jake the other day."

Chelsea felt her stomach drop. She hadn't done anything wrong; she had just bumped into him on her way out of town, so why did she still feel so guilty?

"We bumped into him at the coffee shop before we made the drive here."

He nodded again, running his hand through his hair.

Chelsea watched him in silence. Her heart tugged at the sight of the man she married. The man she once loved… Still loved. Just not in the same way she once did. She hadn't noticed lately with everything going on, but he looked tired. Tired and broken.

Ryan pushed off the counter and moved closer to her slowly.

"You're really going to stay in Somerdale."

It wasn't a question. More of a realisation.

Chelsea's eyes locked onto his as he stopped in front of her. "Yeah…I think I am."

He nodded slowly, his eyes darting around the room before landing on her again, like he was trying to memorise it all. "You know, I thought packing this house would be the hardest part."

Chelsea waited, her heart thumping in her chest at the anticipation of what he was going to say next.

"It's not," he said. "It's standing here with you. Knowing once you leave, it's not just a move. It's the end of us. For real."

She blinked, throat thick. "Ryan… "

He held up a hand, not to stop her, but to steady himself. "I need to say this, Chels. Please."

She nodded.

"I've loved you. I… still do. But I have loved you from the moment we met. I loved you when we found out we were expecting Lucy and decided to make it work. I've loved you every day since then." He sighed.

Her heart twisted as she watched him run his hand through his hair again.

"But somewhere along the way," he continued, voice breaking, "you stopped being mine. And I kept hoping it was just a phase, or stress, or time. I was always working, and I am sorry for that. For not giving you what you needed. But now I see that maybe you weren't ever completely mine. I don't know if it's him… maybe it's just you remembering who you used to be before you were thrown into motherhood so young."

She was crying now, not even sure when it started, but the tears were silently rolling down her cheeks.

"God, I don't know," he took a shaky breath. "I don't hate him. I don't even hate that it's him." Ryan said. "Because when I saw you at your dad's funeral, with him, I saw you soften in a way I haven't seen in years. I can't be mad at you because I think deep down, I always knew that he was more to you than just your high school boyfriend. It was like I could feel that you weren't ever completely mine. Like, there was a small piece of your heart that you could never give me because you didn't even have it anymore. And I just pushed that feeling down. Hoping I was wrong."

Chelsea stepped forward, tears falling freely now. She hadn't realised that he had seen her with Jake at the funeral. Jake had kept his distance until that moment they shared on the back deck of her parents' house. Her heart broke that Ryan had seen her and that, despite him hurting, he still hadn't said anything to her.

"I'm sorry. I didn't plan this, Ryan. I didn't even realise I felt like this." She swiped at her tears before continuing, "I never wanted to hurt you. I just… I don't know how to explain it. It's like I've been holding my breath for years, and suddenly I can breathe again."

He looked at her, eyes glistening. Broken and calm all at once.

"I think you were trying to be everything for everyone. And in doing that, you forgot who you were. And I could tell. I knew you were missing something. But I selfishly wanted you to be mine, so I ignored it. I hoped that if I just kept going, I could give you everything you needed. But I think I am starting to realise that what you were missing is something I can't give you."

She nodded, unable to speak. The realisation that this was it. They had been in limbo for some time now, not really knowing where they stood with each other. Or where they would end up. But it was clear now. This was final. They were really separating.

"I don't want to fight," he said softly, taking a small step towards her. "I want us to raise our girls well. I want us to be the kind of divorced parents that they don't have to recover from."

A sad laugh escaped her. "You're still a better man than I deserve."

Ryan smiled faintly. "Don't say that. You deserve everything good, Chels. You deserve a love that fills you. And if it's not me… I am just grateful I got to be yours for as long as I did."

They stood quietly for a moment, the weight of the goodbye resting gently between them.

Then he stepped forward and wrapped his arms around her.

And she let him. She wrapped her arms around his waist, resting her head against his chest.

"I'll always love you, Chels. But it's time for us to step away and let ourselves find ourselves again."

She sniffled against his chest, "I love you too, Ry."

They held each other in the middle of the empty kitchen, surrounded by cardboard boxes and ten years of memories.

And then, after a few moments, they let go.

Not of the love. Or even the past.

But of each other.

Chelsea felt emotionally drained, but it was as if a weight had been lifted off her shoulders.

THIRTY SIX
Chelsea

T he past two weeks had been a whirlwind.

Boxes had been unpacked, school uniforms ordered, and new routines established. Chelsea, the girls and Crumpet were officially settled in at her parents' house. Somehow, it was both a strange and comforting feeling to be back in her childhood bedroom. It felt the same, but also so different.

The house had an underlying emptiness feel to it without her father whistling around the place. Chelsea had spent most of her time with her mum and sister, holding each other up through their grief. Having Lucy and Olivia in the house had brought some joy back to her mum's life and provided a good distraction.

Ryan had managed to secure a rental a few suburbs over. Not far from them, but far enough to both have their own space. The place was a cosy unit along the beach with a garden for Crumpet when he visited and a second bedroom for the girls. Their house back in Port Mac had gone under contract surprisingly quickly, and they were now waiting for the settlement to be finalised. Because they had purchased the house for a reasonable price early in their relationship and had then spent the years slowly chipping away at the renovations, the offer that had been put on the house was significant and would mean that after paying off the leftover mortgage, they would still have plenty left over to split and put towards new house deposits.

Everything felt like it was moving at double speed. It only felt like yesterday that Chelsea was packing the car to come to Somerdale to spend the weekend with her family for Emily's engagement party. And now here she was, living back in the town she thought she never would again after experiencing some of the most significant losses in her life.

Chelsea had started thinking about what she wanted to do next once the dust had settled. Where she wanted her life to go. She had spent her whole twenties being a stay-at-home mum. She had applied for university straight after school to become a teacher, but that got put on hold when she found out she was pregnant. With Ryan's job being shift work, it made sense for her to be the stay-at-home parent. She was grateful for the years she got to spend with the girls at home without the responsibility of a career, but she was ready now.

Could she go back to university and get her teaching degree?

Could she open her dream bookstore? Or do something completely different.

She didn't know. But it was exciting to think about.

The thought would have to wait for now, though, because it was wedding week.

Emily had turned into a surprisingly chill bride, considering she was a type A kind of girl. She had her two sisters as her other bridesmaids, so between them all, the flower trials, playlist negotiations, and the last-minute dress fittings, everything fell into place quickly.

Tonight, though, it was the hen's night. A celebration with just the girls. Cocktails, dancing and maybe a little chaos since Chloe would be there and chaos seemed to follow her. The only condition Emily had was that it had to be a country and western theme, so everyone had to dress in their best cowgirl outfit. This meant their group was full of glittery cowboy hats and a variety of different coloured western boots.

The plan had been simple: start with dinner and cocktails at the local Italian place, then head to The Sandbar for more drinks and dancing.

What no one had planned on was Dean's bucks' night ending at the same bar. Chelsea only noticed when she spotted a familiar figure at the bar.

Her heart did a completely unnecessary flip.

Jake.

He was laughing, a beer in one hand, looking unfairly good in a black tee and jeans. Hair slightly tousled. Jawline sharp. She hadn't seen him since that morning at the café, since she'd told him they were moving.

Her mouth went dry just looking at him.

"Uh-oh," Emily murmured beside her. "Don't look now... or actually do. The boys are here."

Chelsea rolled her eyes. "Really? This town has three bars, and they pick this one?"

Emily shrugged. "It's fate. Or a sign. Or terrible communication."

Chelsea laughed, and then Jake's head turned sharply, scanning the room before locking his eyes on hers.

Everything else disappeared around her.

Chelsea watched as a smile crept across Jake's face, eyes briefly dropping to scan her body before meeting hers again.

She quickly did a mental check of her outfit, feeling the weight of his gaze on her body. She was wearing a denim skirt that was probably too short, a tight black tank top, finished off with a pink glittery cowboy hat and brown cowboy boots. She had to admit that when she did a final check in the mirror before they left, she looked hot. She thanked herself silently for deciding on this outfit.

She smiled back at Jake; her face flushed slightly as his eyes blazed on her. Before she turned back to the girls and her drink, trying to play it cool and ignore the heat that was rapidly crawling up her body from his gaze.

Later, after too many tequila shots and a dance floor detour with her sister, when the girls had scattered in various directions, Chelsea found herself at the bar ordering another drink. She was flushed, glowing, and slightly tipsy. Okay, she was more than tipsy.

Suddenly, she felt warmth next to her. She didn't have to turn to know Jake was next to her.

"Fancy seeing you here," Jake said, voice teasing.

Chelsea grinned, turning to him. "You stalking me now?"

He tilted his head. "I think I was here first. So, I guess technically you are the stalker." He winked at her and brought his beer to his mouth, a smile hiding behind the bottle.

She raised an eyebrow. "Sure, whatever you say, mate." She said with a smirk.

His smile widened behind his beer.

The bartender put Chelsea's margarita between them, holding out the card machine for payment.

Jake scanned his card before Chelsea could even blink.

"You didn't need to buy me a drink," she said, looking at him, narrowing her eyes.

He gave her a soft smile. "I think I owe you a drink or two, cowgirl." He said, gently tapping her hat with his beer.

She smiled before raising her drink to clink with his.

They both took a slow drink, turning around to observe the growing dance floor. The hens and bucks party had meshed together, a dance circle starting to form.

Jake nudged Chelsea's shoulder with his. "You look happy."

She shrugged. "I'm trying."

"Well, trying looks good on you. Very good." He said as his eyes raked down her body again.

She laughed softly, tucking her hair behind her ear. "God, someone is flirty tonight."

He flashed her a smile. "I've only had a few beers tonight, and then one of Em's friends tried to arm wrestle me. So, I am feeling confident."

She laughed, nudging him playfully. "Dean keeping it together?"

"Barely. He cried during his own speech to the guys earlier."

"Classic."

They both laughed. Then something in the air softened.

Jake turned to face her, his arm resting on the bar, crowding her with his body, more serious now. "You really moved back."

"I really did."

"How's it feel?"

"Strange," she admitted. "Good. Like… beginning again. But with all the same people watching. Like I can breathe again."

Jake nodded slowly. He reached out to touch her hand. Not quite holding it, but enough for the fingers to instinctively hook together before letting go. "Well, I'm one of those people. Watching. Just so you know."

Her breath caught.

"I mean it," he said gently. "No pressure. No expectations. But I'm here."

She felt those words smack into her.

I'm here.

She didn't know what to say back to them, but she could hear them echoing around her body,

"I'm glad." She finally said, leaning over to squeeze his arm briefly.

Jake grinned at her before asking, "How's your mum?"

Chelsea swallowed hard, "She is…okay. As good as she can be, I guess. I think it's been a blessing that we moved back when we did. Healing for us all to grieve together, you know?"

Jake nodded, "Yeah, I bet. And you? You're looking after your-self?"

Chelsea smiled, "Course."

Jake gave her a pointed look. He opened his mouth to say some-thing more when Dean appeared in front of them, slightly red-faced, claiming they needed him for a dance challenge.

Jake looked at Chelsea, as if asking for permission. Or perhaps a cry for help.

Chelsea laughed, waving him off. "Go get 'em, tiger," she said with a wink.

She watched Dean drag Jake away from her. Almost thankful for the interruption so that she didn't burst into tears talking about her dad in the middle of the bar. She watched as they made it to their group of friends, Jake still casting glances back at her. Something in his eyes blazing.

Chelsea took a deep breath, pushing away the thoughts of her grief as she made her way across the dance floor back to her friends, heart buzzing.

She danced the night away, celebrating her best friend and throwing glances at Jake across the dance floor, feeling free.

Suddenly, this weekend felt like more than just a wedding.

It felt like a possibility and a new beginning.

Or that could just be the tequila talking.

THIRTY SEVEN
High School: Final Year
Chelsea

*T*he crowd around them roared as the final siren sounded, signalling the end of the football grand final. Chelsea, who had been sitting on the hill cheering the boys on, jumped up with her friends, screaming and clapping along with the rest of the crowd. Jake and the team had won the first grand final for Somerdale in over ten years. Chelsea spotted Jake somewhere in the centre of the field under a sea of football guernseys, his teammates clapping him on the back and throwing their arms around him.

"Your boyfriend totally just won them the game, Chels," Emily teased, putting her arm around her shoulder. "He's going to be unbearable tonight."

Chelsea grinned, eyes locked on number 23, who had his arms around his best mate, Dean. "He already is."

Chelsea, along with her best friends Emily, Brooke and Mel, made their way down to the football field. The air was thick with post-game energy, and everyone was ecstatic with the win. As the girls made their way onto the field, a few of the boys from their group spotted them and hugged the girls. Chelsea stood waiting, shifting from foot to foot as she watched Jake's dad throw his arms around Jake before Chelsea's dad stepped forward to do the same. Both of them had not missed one game all season; they were Jake's biggest fans, right behind Chelsea.

Jake spotted Chelsea watching him over her dad's shoulder. He pulled away, squeezing her dad's shoulder before he jogged over to her. His hair was messy and sticking to his forehead from the sweat. His face was flushed, eyes gleaming as he made his way over to Chelsea, wrapping his arms around her waist and lifting her off the ground. He spun her around once, laughing breathlessly as Chelsea wrapped her arms around his neck. The adrenaline was pulsing off of him, and she had to admit it was pretty intoxicating seeing him like this.

"Jake!" she squealed, clinging to his shoulders as he placed her back on the ground. "You're gross. So sweaty." She grinned.

He smirked, his hands resting on her waist. "Yeah, but you love it."

She rolled her eyes. "Good game, baby."

He leaned in to rest his forehead against hers, his grin softening into something smaller, something softer. "Only because my lucky charm was watching."

Chelsea lifted onto her toes and pressed her lips to his, tasting the sweetness and saltiness of his sweat. Behind them, Chelsea heard Dean call out something teasing them about "getting a room." Jake pulled back slightly to flip him off before pressing another quick, lingering kiss to Chelsea's lips.

"Wait for me?" He asked as he started backing away, flashing her his boyish grin that always seemed to melt her.

"Always." She said as she watched him walk away, not turning around until he was at the entrance to the change rooms. Chelsea didn't understand how, even after they had been together for years now, he still made her feel like a giddy little girl whenever she was around him.

~

It had been almost an hour since Jake had gone into the change rooms with his team. The girls had all wandered back over to the hill *to pack up their picnic rug and bags. They had heard the cheers and singing coming from the change rooms as the boys celebrated their win. It had settled down now, though, so Chelsea assumed they were all having showers and getting changed, ready to continue the celebrations over at the club rooms with their friends and family. Once they had packed up and some of the team had started trickling out, the rest of the girls headed into the club rooms while Chelsea made her way over to the half wall that was located by the change rooms. It had become their little ritual after any home game. Chelsea would wait for Jake to come out, sitting on the wall, her legs dangling over. She didn't know why it started, but she did it one game after he had taken a nasty knock, and then it just never stopped. It was just another one of those small, quiet moments that they had kept for themselves.*

The night was quiet now, just the sound of crickets and the distant laughter from their friends in the club rooms. The oval lights buzzed low against the night sky now that the sun had set. Chelsea looked out at the field where Jake had just played one of the best games of his season. Finally achieving his goal of winning a grand final with his best friends by his side. Chelsea felt an overwhelming mix of pride, love and fear as Jake finally emerged from the change rooms. She jumped down from the wall to meet him as he held his hand out to her.

"Ready?" He asked, lacing their fingers together.

She nodded as they walked together towards the clubrooms and their friends. She wasn't ready, really. She knew what was coming in the next few months. She knew that school was going to end, and things were going to change.

She knew she would remember this night for years to come, feeling overwhelmingly proud and full of love, yet at the same time, terrified of what was to come. Afraid of losing him. Of losing their relationship.

Because even though she was still in the moment right now, it was already beginning to feel like a distant memory.

THIRTY EIGHT
Chelsea

The morning sun filtered softly through the kitchen, warming the house the following morning. A warm golden glow cast over the old, worn wooden table.

It was wedding day.

They had danced and laughed until midnight before Emily gathered them all up to head home to get their beauty sleep before the big day, including the boys. The boys had gone back to Dean's parents' house to stay and were getting up this morning to go and finish setting up at the brewery before getting ready for the wedding. Emily's sisters had gone back to their own houses to sleep and were planning to meet them at their parents' house this morning so that they could all get ready together. That left Chelsea, Emily and Chloe, who decided to stay at Chelsea and Chloe's parents' house. Emily had said it was so that Chelsea could see Olivia and Lucy in the morning, but Chelsea suspected it was to give herself a break from being at her parents' house. Emily had a pretty good relationship with her parents when they weren't living together. But when they were together in the same house for longer than a couple of days, things could be…tense.

Now Chelsea sat barefoot in her pyjamas, her hands gripping a hot cup of coffee. Her hair was still tangled from the night before, her voice still scratchy from too much laughing and singing. It had been a good night. A night with no worries, just setting the mood for the rest of the weekend, she hoped.

Chelsea watched her mum at the stove, flipping pancakes, while Chloe sat in the lounge room with her coffee, watching whatever cartoon the girls had on the television. Emily sat across from Chelsea, chin resting on her hand, eyes still lined with leftover mascara.

"You're not hungover," Emily said, mildly impressed. "How?"

"I think adrenaline is keeping me upright," Chelsea murmured. "Ask me again in an hour. But I am glad you dragged us out of there when you did. Imagine if we had stayed."

"We probably wouldn't have made the wedding if we stayed on that dance floor any longer." Emily laughed.

Chloe walked into the kitchen and sat down next to Chelsea at the table. "Jake looked hot last night, Chels."

Chelsea almost spat out her coffee in response to her sister's non-existent filter.

Chloe shrugged. "What? He did."

"She's right, he did," Emily added, taking a sip of her coffee.

Chelsea's mum walked over and placed a plate of pancakes on the table. "I can imagine. He has always been easy on the eye, that boy."

"Oh my god, guys. Stop."

"Oh, relax, it's ok to admit he is hot. Plus, you looked good too, Chels. Happy." Chloe said as she picked at a fluffy pancake.

Chelsea didn't respond straight away. She watched her coffee for a moment.

"I think I've spent the last ten years doing everything I was 'supposed' to do," she said finally. "Be a wife. Be a mum. Be the constant. And I don't regret any of it. But somewhere along the way I just... stopped checking in with myself."

"Preach it, sister," Chloe said in agreement.

Emily reached for her hand. "You don't have to explain anything to us. It was just nice seeing you enjoy yourself with no expectations or responsibilities."

"I know," Chelsea said. "But I think I need to explain it for myself. Or at least say it out loud to make it real. I don't know what comes next, but I want it to be mine. Mine by choice, not because it's the right thing to do."

Her mum leaned back against the kitchen counter, smiling softly. "That's the strongest thing I've ever heard you say."

Chelsea blinked, caught off guard. "Really?"

Her mum nodded. "You always think strength has to be loud," she said gently. "But sometimes, it's just being honest."

A lump formed in Chelsea's throat.

"Wow, this has gotten deep for Emily's wedding morning," Chloe said in amusement.

The buzz of Emily's phone on the table interrupted the conversation.

Emily's eyes widened as she glanced at the screen. "Oh shit!"

"What?" Chelsea said, her heart rate spiking as she watched her best friend's face drop.

"The florist's car has broken down, so she can't drop off the flowers at the brewery."

Chelsea stood. "I'll go get the flowers."

"I was going to send my sister, Bec, but…" Emily smirked, looking up from her phone. "Jake already offered to drive into town to grab something else for the setup. So, I told him you'd go with him."

Chelsea froze. "You what?"

Chloe laughed, looking far too entertained. "This is better than coffee."

"Well, I don't trust him to take care of the flowers like you would," Emily said innocently, sipping her coffee. "But he has the

Ute to fit them in."

Chelsea sighed and rolled her eyes at Emily. "You're really pulling the maid of honour card early."

Emily winked. "I'm a bride. It's in my job description, babe."

"Don't worry, Chels. I have an ice cream date with the girls this morning before the wedding, so take your time." Her mum said, cleaning up the empty coffee mugs.

"Just get Jake to drop you off at my mum and dad's, and I'll meet you there to start getting ready," Emily said as she picked at the pancake on the plate in front of her.

Chelsea let out a small laugh before heading past the girls, giving them a quick kiss on the heads before heading to the bathroom to jump in the shower and get dressed, heart already thudding.

~

Jake was already waiting when Chelsea stepped out of the house half an hour later, arms crossed casually over the roof of his Ute, sunglasses on, the hint of a smile curling up one side of his mouth. Looking unfairly good, compared to Chelsea, whose hair was still wet from the shower, fresh-faced and dressed in an oversized tee and activewear shorts.

"On time," he said, smirking. "Maybe some things really do change."

Chelsea raised an eyebrow. "Are you implying I was flaky?"

"I'm implying you used to make us late for everything in high school. Especially school or the movies."

She smirked. "Well, I guess I did change then."

Jake walked around the car to open the passenger door for her. "Let's find out, shall we?"

"You'd better bring my girl back on time, Jake. We have hair and makeup to deal with," Emily called out to them from the porch.

"Yeah, yeah, we'll see," Jake called back with a wink as he shut the door behind Chelsea.

They drove in easy silence at first, the windows down, the early sun pouring over the green hills and palm trees as Somerdale blurred past them. Chelsea glanced over at Jake as he adjusted the radio, the scent of pine and coffee drifting across from his side. He seemed annoyingly relaxed and not at all hungover. Like this was a totally normal thing they did on a Saturday morning. Perhaps in another lifetime, it would have been.

Jake made another quick stop on their way to the florist. Apparently, Dean had sent him on a secret mission to pick up some cigars for him to enjoy with his groomsmen at the reception. Chelsea rolled her eyes when they pulled up in front of the dodgy cigar shop on the outskirts of town. Jake flashed her a grin, making sure his dimples popped before he jumped out to pick up the goods. Chelsea waited in the car with the breeze ruffling through her hair through the open window. She thought back to the Chelsea from two months ago. Two months wasn't really a long time, but so much had changed. If she had told that version of her that in a couple of months, she would be sitting in the front seat of her high school love's car, while picking up cigars and flowers for her best friend's wedding, she would have laughed in her face.

After the quick detour, they finally arrived at the florist. The poor florist was flustered and waiting out the front for them when they pulled up, wearing a very apologetic look on her face. Jake insisted on carrying all the flowers out to the car, even when Chelsea argued she was perfectly capable. She rolled her eyes at him, such a gentleman.

"You've got wedding hair to protect," he said, winking as he stacked the flowers in the tray of the Ute.

Chelsea shook her head, laughing. "You've gotten cocky over the years. Plus, your reasoning doesn't make sense because I haven't had my hair done yet."

He slid into the driver's seat with a huge smirk. "Nah. You've just forgotten how charming I always was."

Chelsea laughed. "Delusional, more like it."

They took the long way back on instinct, winding past the cliffs and the coastline. Neither of them said anything for some time, Jake's country music playlist filling the comfortable silence. Chelsea couldn't help but steal glances at Jake as he drove with one hand lazily on the steering wheel and the other resting on the door. She tried to study the black ink that covered his arm without him catching her staring.

"What are you looking at, Chels?"

Chelsea startled, she obviously wasn't being as subtle as she thought. "Well... Your tattoos. It's different seeing you with them."

"Good different?"

Of course, it was a good difference. The man was hot either way, but the black ink somehow really topped it off.

"Yes, good different." She rolled her eyes at him. "Do they all mean something?"

He shrugged, "Some do. Some are just random. One day I'll explain them all to you if you're lucky." He said with a wink.

Chelsea laughed, "Wow, thanks!"

Jake flashed her a smirk. "You know, I didn't realise you still had my old hoodie."

Chelsea looked at him, mouth slightly open.

"The blue one."

Chelsea blinked, "Oh my god. I forgot that was yours. It's my favourite hoodie still."

Jake laughed, "Well, yeah, I gave it to you one night, and I don't think I ever saw it again. So, it's been yours longer than it was mine. Looks better on you anyway." He gave her a half smirk that made his dimple pop.

Chelsea smiled as she leaned her head back against the seat. She hadn't remembered that it was originally his hoodie until now. She had worn it throughout high school, and since then, it was always the one piece of clothing with which she couldn't part, despite it now being very worn.

After a moment, Jake glanced sideways at her. "You nervous for the big day?"

Chelsea shrugged. "It's not my wedding."

Jake gave her a lopsided smile. "True. But you are still allowed to feel things."

She didn't respond straight away, but her smile faltered slightly.

Sensing she didn't know what to say, Jake kept talking. "I'm just glad I get to be here for it, you know. I feel like I missed so much while I was travelling. It's kind of wild. Seeing all of us grown up. Married. Unmarried. Re… connected."

She gave him a look. "Reconnected?"

He laughed. "Don't make me regret saying that."

She smirked. "You are right. It is wild. But not as wild as the fact that Dean is actually settling down. I never thought I'd see the day."

Jake laughed. Like, really laughed. And the sound shot through Chelsea like an electric shock. God, she hadn't realised how much she had missed that sound.

"To be honest, neither did I."

Chelsea leaned back in her seat, letting the warm wind play with her hair, the sound of Jake's laugh replaying in her head.

But even as they bantered and joked, a flicker of unease brushed in her chest. He was saying all the right things, about being there, about caring, about staying.

But what if that wasn't enough?

What if she let herself fall again… and he walked away when things got real? It wasn't just her she had to think about anymore. She wasn't a sixteen-year-old girl anymore. She was a mother. She had two girls she had to think about. If she let Jake back in and he left again, he wouldn't just be leaving her. He would, in turn, be leaving them as well. The thought itself was enough to make her feel sick.

She turned toward the window, not wanting her thoughts to be shown across her face.

Jake drove on, humming along to the music.

He didn't seem to notice her thoughts drifting. But they were there, trailing behind her.

Twenty minutes later, they pulled into the driveway of Emily's parents' house after delivering the flowers to the brewery.

Jake cut the engine. "Delivery complete."

Chelsea smiled. "Thanks for the ride."

He shrugged. "Thanks for coming with me."

As she stepped out, their eyes met again, something passing between them.

"See you at the altar, Chels. I'll be the handsome one standing next to the groom who is crying his eyes out." Jake said with a wink.

Chelsea laughed and rolled her eyes at him as she shut the car door.

Oh god. She thought as she made her way up the path to the front door. *I am in trouble here.*

THIRTY NINE
Chelsea

Chelsea stood still as her reflection came into view. Her hair was in soft waves, framing her face and flowing down her back. Her makeup was natural but glowing, her skin flushed with nerves, excitement, and, of course, champagne.

Once Chelsea got back from the flower rescue mission, she jumped straight into hair and makeup with Emily and her sisters. They had a makeup artist there to do all the girls, and Emily's sister, Bec, is a hair stylist, so she did their hair. They spent the day drinking champagne and getting ready while dancing and singing to Emily's pre-wedding playlist. It had been exactly what Emily had wanted for the morning of her wedding, and now that they were all ready, the nerves were starting to kick in.

Chelsea took in her reflection in the mirror in front of her. The champagne-coloured bridesmaid dress hugged her in all the right places, falling just past her knee. She wore nude-coloured heels that made her legs look like they went on forever, and she finished the look with some gold earrings. She looked… like a version of herself she hadn't seen in years.

Whole. Soft. Present. Glowing.

Emily stepped beside her, already in her dress, her eyes shiny. "God, we look good."

Emily's wedding dress was a simple ivory satin slip dress that trailed behind her. She had a veil tucked into her low bun, finishing off her bridal look perfectly. She was an absolute vision.

Chelsea smiled, wrapping her arm around her friend's waist. "You're the bride. You're not allowed to get emotional before me." She paused before adding, "But you're right. We do look good."

Emily gave a watery laugh. "You've been my best friend for over half of my life. You're my something old, my something borrowed, and my emotional support all in one."

Chloe walked through the door at that moment, sipping a mimosa. "I guess that makes me the chaotic something new."

They all laughed as Emily's other bridesmaids finished getting into their dresses to join them for the pre-ceremony pictures.

"Alright, I am going to go and meet mum and the girls at the brewery… unless you need me to drive the getaway car, Em?" She said in a serious tone, but with a playful look on her face.

Emily laughed, "No, I think I will be okay. But if I look at you during the ceremony and mouth the word *'help,'* then you can." Emily tossed back playfully.

After the photographer snapped a few more pictures of the girls and they sorted out the finishing touches, Emily's mum called out that the cars were ready for them.

The other two bridesmaids were going in a car with Emily's mum, and Chelsea and Emily were going in a car driven by her dad.

As they made their way out of the house, Emily reached for Chelsea's hand. "I know everything's been a lot lately. But having you by my side today means more than I can explain."

Chelsea squeezed her hand. "You've been there for every version of me. I wouldn't miss this for anything."

The drive to the brewery was short, but Emily had the music cranking and a glass of champagne, looking like the epitome of a relaxed bride.

Chelsea, on the other hand, had her nerves buzzing loudly the closer they got to wedding time. She and Ryan had decided on a small, intimate elopement when they got married. Chelsea was pregnant with Lucy when they decided they wanted to get married. Both her and Ryan were not the type of people who liked being the centre of attention, so having a huge wedding with everyone watching them sounded like hell. Plus, they couldn't fathom spending so much money on one day when they were about to be young first-time parents. So, knowing she was about to walk out in front of all Emily and Dean's friends and family had her silently freaking out.

Guests were already gathering in the brewery garden when they arrived, slowly taking their seats positioned down the aisle, with flowers and greenery draping the arbour at the end. From where they were in the car, they couldn't see Dean or the grooms-men, but Chelsea spotted her daughters with her mum and sister, taking their seats close to the front with Emily's family.

The sunlight filtered down through the trees like golden rib-bons. The air warm with a light breeze. The weather this time of year could be temperamental. You never really knew when a tropical rainstorm would hit. But today there wasn't a cloud in the sky. It really was a perfect day for a wedding.

The bridal party got out of the cars and lined up, with Emily and her father behind them. Chelsea looked back behind her to give her best friend a quick smile before they started down the aisle.

"See ya when you are a wifey." She said with a wink.

A huge grin spread over Emily's face as the music began, slow and soft.

One by one, the bridesmaids made their way down the aisle to where Dean and his groomsmen were waiting.

Then it was suddenly Chelsea's turn.

She exhaled slowly, smoothed her dress, and began to walk.

She couldn't hear much over the noise of her heart thudding in her ears, and her own voice in her head repeatedly chanting *'Don't fall, don't fall."*

Her vision seemed to narrow.

She looked up at Dean, who already had tears falling down his cheeks. He gave her a soft smile.

Then she felt something —or someone, rather— pull her gaze to the right.

Jake.

Standing beside Dean, dressed in a tan coloured suit and open collar, hands clasped in front of him.

His eyes locked on Chelsea.

His mouth slightly hanging open as his eyes raked over Chelsea.

Then a slow grin spread across his face.

The moment stretched. Holding each other's gazes.

Chelsea walked on, her nerves suddenly settled, but still a flutter in her chest. She pulled her gaze from Jake to look at her daughters as she walked past them, poking her tongue out playfully, before looking back up and locking eyes once again with Jake.

A calmness took over her body as she made her way up the aisle.

FORTY
Jake

Jake had never believed people when they said that time could slow down. It had never made much sense to him.

Until now.

Standing beneath the soft arbour, draped in flowers and greenery, with Dean shifting nervously beside him as the music began to play, Jake felt everything drop into slow motion around him.

Sunlight filtered through the trees; the strum of the guitar echoed through the garden. He had noticed Lucy and Olivia sitting with Chelsea's mum and sister in the second row, excitedly looking back for their mum as the bridesmaids began to walk down the aisle.

And then he saw her.

Chelsea.

She stepped into view, a soft golden dress catching the light with every step, her long smooth hair draped behind her in soft waves, a tiny smile ghosting her lips.

He forgot how to breathe. Everything around him dropped

away. He had complete tunnel vision. She was all he could see. His heart, which was steady just moments before, now started hammering away in his chest.

Holy shit, he thought to himself.

She looked… not just beautiful. That wasn't the right word. It was never enough to describe her. But she looked like herself. Like the girl he remembered from all those years ago, but different. Softer. But stronger. Like someone who had carried the weight of the world. Like someone who had survived grief and heartbreak but had come out stronger than before.

She didn't look at him right away. Her eyes were focused straight ahead, he assumed, looking at Dean, but he couldn't take his eyes off her long enough to check. She seemed calm. Collected. But he could tell, in the way her hands were gripping her flowers in front of her, that she was feeling the nerves.

And then, as if something pulled her, her gaze flicked to him. Her lips twitched into a smile, her shoulders seeming to relax slightly.

And it hit him like a punch to the chest. There was something in her eyes that wasn't there before. A question, maybe. A longing.

Jake ripped his eyes from hers and travelled down her body and back again.

Incredible, he thought as he locked his eyes with hers again, a huge grin uncontrollably spreading across his face. Her toned golden legs looked extra-long thanks to the heels she had on. Her dress hugged her perfectly in all the right spots. She literally had taken his breath away, and he needed to remind himself to breathe again before he passed out. Dean would never forgive him if he did that and stole the attention from him on his big day.

Chelsea briefly looked away when she noticed her daughters in the second row and playfully stuck her tongue out at them.

Dean nudged him gently. "Wow."

Jake blinked, clearing his throat. "Yeah. Wow. I was not expecting that moment…"

Dean grinned, his eyes soft. "Yeah. I know."

Jake's eyes quickly returned to Chelsea as she hugged Dean before taking her place at the front. Her profile calm, hands holding her flowers in front of her. Gaze flicking between Jake and the aisle, where Emily was now making her way down.

He had seen Chelsea a few times now since she had moved home. He had seen her just this morning, but this... this was different. Something was shifting. Not just between them, but inside of him.

He didn't just want to wait anymore. Or chase her.

He wanted to show her that he could stay. That if she gave him the chance, he would stay. That she could trust him. That whatever happened next... he wouldn't disappear.

She was no longer just his past.

She was the clearest vision of his future, and there was no way he could ignore this feeling anymore.

~

The ceremony was a blur. Jake remembered snippets: Dean choking up halfway through his vows, Emily's grin the whole ceremony, and the sound of the breeze through the trees. But mostly, he remembered Chelsea. He did feel slightly guilty that he hadn't paid much attention to the actual wedding, but he was sure Dean would forgive him. There was no way he could concentrate on anything but Chelsea.

The way she stood beside Emily, her face quietly emotional. How she dabbed at her eyes when she thought no one was looking. How she kept glancing at Jake throughout the ceremony, a soft smile on her face. A look that said everything.

Once Emily and Dean had sealed the deal with a kiss, Jake held his arm out to Chelsea, and they followed the bride and groom back down the aisle, Chelsea's arm hooked in his. He had wanted to talk to her more than anything, but they were whisked off by the photographer for bridal party wedding pictures straight after the ceremony.

Now the reception was in full swing. Fairy lights twinkling above them, candles flickering on the wooden tables. The music drifted through the evening air while the sun cast a golden glow across the brewery garden as it slowly set.

Jake stood on the edge of the dance floor nursing a beer, chatting to a few old school friends, his eyes unconsciously drifting towards Chelsea.

They hadn't spoken much yet, a few comments here and there as they were getting their pictures taken with the bridal party. Since they had entered the reception, she had been busy dancing with Olivia and Lucy or catching up with her school friends, so he didn't interrupt her as much as he really wanted to. He noticed her a short time earlier, saying goodbye to her daughters as her mum loaded them into the car, taking them home to bed, he presumed. And since then, he had noticed her become even lighter. Letting her hair down, without the responsibilities she usually carried.

Chelsea was now standing near the bar with Emily and her sister, her dress catching in the breeze, her face flushed from the wine and dancing. She laughed at something Chloe said, the sound stirring something deep in Jake's chest. He hadn't heard her laugh like that in so long. He couldn't help but smile behind his beer as he watched her like a total creep.

The music shifted into a slow song Jake recognised from one of their favourite country singers. The MC got everyone's attention and announced it was time for the bride and groom to have their first dance. Everyone slowly formed a border around the dance floor as they watched Emily and Dean sway and twirl together across the wooden dance floor that had been set up on the lawn area of the brewery garden. Jake stood on one side of the dance floor, Chelsea on the other. He was trying to focus on his best mate and his new wife in the centre, but he couldn't stop his eyes from flicking to Chelsea.

The song slowly transitioned into the next slow song as the MC announced it was time for the family and bridal party to join the bride and groom on the dance floor. Before the MC had finished talking, Jake was already walking straight across the dance floor towards Chelsea. He stopped in front of her with his hand stretched out.

"Dance with me."

Chelsea blinked. "What?"

He gave her a lazy smile. "C'mon. We are the best man and maid of honour. Dance with me."

She laughed, hesitating for a second before placing her hand in his.

Jake led the way to the middle of the dance floor, not letting go of her hand until they stood facing each other. He moved his hands to lightly rest on her waist as she draped her arms lazily around his neck. The music wrapped around them, soft and golden.

The dance floor filled up around them, with the bridal party and families paired off, but Jake hardly noticed anyone around them. His whole focus on the girl in front of him. He leaned down so his mouth was close to her ear. "You look insane tonight, Chels. Insanely hot."

Chelsea let out a loud laugh, "You don't look so bad yourself."

Jake pulled back slightly so that he could see her face, both of them wearing matching grins. They continued to dance together, not saying much, just swaying together, her dress floating between them.

"You always were a good dancer," she murmured.

He smirked at her. "I always had a good dancing partner."

"Lies," she replied. "I just followed your lead when you would dance me around the bedroom or kitchen."

Jake chuckled, "True. You danced like you had two left feet."

Chelsea gave him a faux-shocked look before she laughed. "I really did, didn't I?"

Jake laughed. "Your parents must have thought I was such a weirdo, dancing you around the house."

She smiled back at him but seemed suddenly distracted, lost in her thoughts.

He leaned in, pulling her closer to him. "You, okay?" He asked, voice low.

She nodded, looking up at him. But her smile didn't quite reach her eyes.

More songs played. More laughter. Chelsea danced with her sister, then with Emily. Jake ended up in a ridiculous group dance with Dean and the groomsmen. Then he and Chelsea found their way back to dance together. Chelsea looked slightly flushed and tipsy, laughter spilling from her lips as he twirled her around the dance floor.

Everything felt light.

Felt right.

Until suddenly, it didn't.

Jake turned back to say something to Chelsea, but she wasn't there.

He scanned the crowd just in time to see her stepping off the dancefloor, slipping through the crowd.

Something in him twisted.

He followed without thinking.

FORTY ONE
High School: The Last Night
Chelsea

They stood under the porch light of her parents' house, the sounds of the party still echoing down the street from one of their classmates' houses. Music, laughter, car doors slamming shut. The end-of-school celebration was slowly wrapping up. They had graduated. Promises had been made. Futures planned.

But this moment didn't feel like a beginning at all.

It felt like quite the opposite.

An ending.

Chelsea was wearing a denim skirt and Jake's blue hoodie that she had claimed as her own years ago. The cool summer air was grazing against her bare legs.

Jake stood in front of her, one hand at his side, the other running through his hair. His hair was slightly tousled from the breeze and dancing. His eyes, usually so steady, looked uneasy now.

"I leave early tomorrow," he said quietly.

Chelsea nodded, arms wrapped tightly around herself. Throat thick. "I know."

"You're going to go to university. You'll be busy. New people. New everything."

She swallowed hard. "So will you."

He looked at her, really looked. And her chest cracked with the ache of it. She had always imagined they were forever. She knew that Jake had mentioned wanting to go and travel after school. That he wasn't ready to go to university or settle into a nine-to-five job. But she hadn't anticipated that it would really happen. That they would really end when school ended. That Jake would leave her to go travel and work overseas while she stayed. She never anticipated that they had an expiration date. But here it was.

"I don't want to hold you back, Chels." He said. "I don't want us resenting each other because we were too scared to grow."

Her voice trembled. "Who says we can't grow together?"

Jake stepped close, eyes full of something that looked a lot like grief. He put his hands on her waist, gripping her. "We could. But we might also break each other trying."

Silence.

Then, in a barely audible voice, she asked, "So this is really it? You aren't coming back?"

"I don't know when I'll be back. My uncle said the job is a six-month contract that might be extended. So it could be that long. Or more. Or less. But I don't want you to wait for me. I want you to go and live your life. Do everything you have always dreamt of. I don't know what my future will hold, or yours, but I think we both need to do this."

Chelsea didn't say anything. She just looked at him. She was hoping he would tell her this was all a joke. That he wasn't going anywhere. Or at least ask her to wait for him. She knew it wasn't fair for her to wait, but if he asked her to, she would. How could she ever love someone as much as she loved him? There was no way. This was something or someone she didn't think she would ever be able to move on from completely.

Jake cupped her face in his hands, thumb brushing her cheek as a single tear slid down. "You were the best part of my life so far. I will never stop loving you, Chelsea Quinn."

He kissed her, not softly. It was a kiss full of every memory, every I love you, every moment they thought they'd have more time. It was full of goodbyes.

When he pulled away, she was sobbing. Shaking. Feeling like she couldn't breathe. She looked up to find him almost mirroring her face. The tears he had not shown yet were now falling freely down his face.

"Please don't go," she whispered.

"I have to." He said with a shaky voice.

He stepped back. One step. Then another. Soaking in every last second looking at her. Before he turned around and walked down the front path, never once looking back.

Chelsea collapsed onto the porch steps once she lost sight of him. The cool night air wrapping around her as her world crashed down around her.

And there, on the same front porch where they had some of their best memories together, she sat with her heart shattered.

He was gone.

She was scared nothing would ever feel like it had before.

She sat there sobbing, heart shattered, until her parents found her and scooped her up to take her inside.

To begin putting their daughter back together.

FORTY TWO
Chelsea

She had been laughing just minutes ago. Jake's hand firmly in hers. Her body leaning close to his. Swaying back and forth together.

But then something sent her back twelve years ago. She wasn't sure if it was the alcohol. Or maybe it was the familiar smell. Or maybe it was just being this close to Jake again after all this time. Whatever it was, it brought the memory from twelve years ago flooding back to her mind. The memory gripping her like a vice.

She felt like she couldn't breathe and had to get off the dance floor and to some open air.

So, she ran.

She left Jake standing there.

Like he had left her all those years ago.

What if he did that again?

She was standing near the railing at the side of the brewery. The party continued behind her, while she tried to catch her breath.

She didn't hear Jake approach until he was right beside her.

"Chelsea- "

She flinched.

Jake paused, watching her carefully.

"Hey, you okay?" He said, hesitantly stepping closer.

She shook her head. "I thought I was."

He stepped forward, reaching out to touch her, but stopping himself before he made contact. He dropped his hand back down. "Talk to me."

She laughed, but it broke halfway out. She turned to face him. "This feels too right. That's the problem."

Jake frowned. "Is that… a bad thing?"

"It is when it reminds me of what it felt like last time."

Jake blinked. "Last time?"

She met his eyes, raw and wide open. "The night you left me. After the graduation party. When you said we'd be better off apart. I was just a kid, Jake, and I believed you. You kissed me like I was your entire world. And then you walked away from me."

Jake's expression cracked, pain flickering across his face. "Chels– "

"I don't think I ever really forgave you," she whispered. "Not really. Because I never got the chance to say anything I needed to. I fell apart after you left. My universe collapsed around me, and you just continued on as if I were nothing. So, I tried to bury my feelings. My pain. And to be honest, I thought I had done a good job of it. But being back here. Back with you…" She shook her head, "It's still all there. And now we are here again, and you are saying all the right things. And I want to believe you so badly… but I don't know if I can survive you walking away from me again."

Jake was quiet for a moment, wind brushing softly between them.

Then he said, "You have every right to feel that way. I screwed up. I thought I was doing the right thing back then. I let the noise around me win. I listened to everyone telling me to take the opportunity and leave. That we were young and that I needed to go and explore the world rather than settle down here. But I didn't realise the cost. And I'm not here to try and rewrite that. You don't deserve that. You deserve me to be better. And that's what I want to do. If you'll let me."

Chelsea's throat tightened. "It's not that simple."

"I know," he said gently. "I fucked up, Chels. I know that. I have had to live with that every day since. But you didn't fall apart alone. I did too. My entire world shattered around me when I left you that night. But I was too embarrassed to admit it to anyone, even to myself, in the beginning. And I knew if I turned back or reached out to you, I would have come straight back. I wouldn't have left."

He took a shaky breath before continuing, "And then the months started to pass by, and I didn't know how to come home. I thought about it every day. Then my six-month work contract finished, and I thought maybe travelling would help distract me. So, I tried that for a few months, but it didn't help. So, I came home. But when I came home, things were different. You had met Ryan and moved out of town. I was too late."

Her eyes stung. She had so much to say, but she had waited twelve years to hear what he had to say, so she didn't interrupt him.

"So, I left again. I didn't want to be in this town without you. I went travelling again and tried everything I could to show myself I was fine without you. I avoided coming home because everything here reminded me of you. I kept myself busy, and I really thought it had worked for a bit there. Until Dad called me, saying he needed to have surgery and needed help with the brewery," he waved his hand in the direction of the party. "So, I came back. And then you showed up. I worked out pretty quickly that it hadn't worked. I was right back where I started, just a decade older."

Chelsea sighed, looking away from Jake briefly.

He stepped closer to her. "I don't expect you to decide anything tonight. Or to even believe me right away. But I need you to know, I'm not eighteen anymore. And this time, I'm not walking away. Not unless you ask me to."

Chelsea felt it, deep in her ribs. The way his words cracked something open that she had fought so hard to keep sealed.

She looked back at him. "You say all the right things, Jake," she whispered, her voice shaking slightly. "You show up and say everything I have wanted to hear since that night. But what happens when real life hits again? Or the outside noise gets loud again? When the high wears off, and the mess creeps in? It's not just me I have to think about now."

"I stay," he replied instantly, like he'd been waiting to say it for years. "That's what's different now."

She shook her head, blinking fast. "You don't know what staying means. You've never had to do it. Not with me. You didn't have to raise babies when you felt like you were still a baby. You didn't have to patch up your shattered heartbreak while pretending to be fine. You didn't have to sit on the porch wondering why loving someone wasn't enough to make them stay."

Her voice broke on that last word.

Jake's jaw clenched, and he stepped forward, finally closing the space between them, "You're right. I didn't stay. I ran. I thought letting you go was what you deserved, that I would only hold you back. I hated myself for it. Every time I saw your name online, every time I heard a song that reminded me of you. I hated myself. Every single day. But I convinced myself that you were better off without me." His voice was low now, fierce. "That was a lie I told myself to sleep at night. To stay away."

Tears spilt from Chelsea's eyes, not the kind she could brush away or disguise, but she didn't care. She had always been comfortable around Jake; he had always seen all the versions of herself. "Then why now? Why come back and pull me apart again?"

"Because," he said, cupping her face in his hands. "I never stopped loving you. Not for one second. And I'd rather spend the rest of my life proving that than spend another day pretending I'm over you."

She stared at him, her breath shaky. Her tears were still falling, but now they were falling straight onto his hands that were still cupping her face.

Jake's voice softened as he stroked her cheek with his thumb, "I loved the girl you were back then, the girl who used to sneak out to the beach with me. Who shamelessly knew every word to every Justin Bieber song. Who fell asleep in my arms and said she couldn't imagine loving anyone else. But I think I love the woman you are now even more, Chels. You are fiercely strong. A fighter, with the kindest soul and a laugh that literally takes my breath away."

Chelsea couldn't breathe.

She didn't want to believe him.

But God, she really did.

Every wall she'd rebuilt, every bit of armour she'd worn, was cracking under the weight of his words.

"I hate that I still love you," she whispered. "I hate that after all this time, I still feel exactly the same as I did back then."

Jake's thumb continued brushing her cheek as his eyes searched her face. "I don't." He said. "I want this. I want everything with you."

"Me too." She said so quietly, she almost couldn't tell if she had said it out loud or not.

They stood in silence for a moment. Both searching each other's eyes with their own.

Chelsea felt like she was at war in her mind. She wanted this so badly. To give in to him and to herself. But she was scared. Scared of messing things up. This felt like the second chance they both wanted. But she knew she couldn't survive this if it didn't work.

Chelsea closed her eyes, lost in her thoughts. She pulled back slightly, trying to compose herself so that they could return to the party.

Jake tightened his hands gently on her face at the movement of her pulling back. Chelsea searched his face with her eyes. She noticed he was doing the same. Both desperately searching each other for some kind of sign on what to do next. She noticed he was breathing heavier now. His gaze dropped to her lips.

"Fuck it," he said, breathing heavily.

And then he pulled her to him and crushed his mouth to hers.

It wasn't soft.

It wasn't gentle.

It was years of ache. Regret. Love. Grief. Hope. Everything they'd buried, poured into one kiss that felt like an earth-shattering beginning.

Chelsea melted into him as one of his hands cradled her head and the other snaked around her body. She wrapped her arms around his neck, holding on like she was scared he would disappear right in front of her.

At some point, the kiss became more frantic. Jake moved his hands down her body to cup the backs of her legs before picking her up to set her on the fence post behind them. Not once breaking contact, the position allowed the kiss to deepen even more. Chelsea wrapped her legs around his waist, pulling him closer to her.

The kiss was messy. Teeth clashing, tongues exploring the mouths they once knew so well. Quiet groans getting caught in each other's breath.

But it lit her on fire. She felt an ache in her core that she hadn't felt in a while. Her body was screaming at her that she wanted more. Needed more.

The kiss wasn't going to fix everything.

But right now, they were remembering everything they had tried to forget.

She wasn't sure where to go from here, but she was sure that neither of them would ever be able to forget this.

FORTY THREE
Jake

Jake didn't know how long the kiss lasted. Time didn't seem to exist when her mouth was finally back on his. Her hands gripping his neck and roughly running through his hair. Her legs tightly wrapped around his body, like she couldn't let go. Like she had also been waiting years to have his body pressed against hers.

God only knew he had been waiting for this moment. Sure, he had thought about the moment they were reunited over the years, but it had always been a fantasy. Something that was never going to happen. But when they both ended up back in town at the same time again, the thoughts had turned into a little more than just a fantasy.

Jake didn't want to pull away. He didn't want this moment to end. But he was aware of the growing party behind them, and being the best man and maid of honour, it was only a matter of time before Dean and Emily came looking for them.

Chelsea, almost like she could read his mind, pulled back just enough for their foreheads to rest together, both of them breathless, chests heaving. Both of them still holding onto each other tightly.

Jake watched her eyes flutter open, slightly dazed and full of lust. He swore he could see the girl he loved in high school and the woman he was falling for now, all at once.

She exhaled, voice shaky. "Wow."

"Yeah. Wow." He could hear his voice was shaky. "So not over you by the way." He said with a smirk, his gaze dropped again to her lips as she took her bottom lip between her teeth, trying to stop the smile.

"What are we doing, Jake?" Chelsea said with a sigh, her arms still draped over his shoulders, fingers twirling in his hair at the base of his neck.

He let out a breathless laugh, still stunned by the weight of everything that had passed between them tonight. "Babe, we just had an amazing kiss."

Chelsea rolled her eyes at him, a smirk on her face. "I am well aware of that...but seriously. What are we doing?"

"I think... we're finally being honest with ourselves."

Chelsea didn't answer right away. Her hands slid down his chest and rested gently on his waist.

Jake looked at her then, really looked. His arms now loosely rested at her hips.

"Listen," he said quietly. "I know that kiss doesn't fix anything. Although it was incredible. It doesn't undo the years of pain. It doesn't fix everything you have gone through recently. But I meant what I said. I'm not here to relive our past. I'm here because I want a future with you. One that's real. Steady. Slow if it needs to be. Whatever you need."

Chelsea's lips parted like she might argue, but he stopped her with a small smile, pressing his index finger to her lips.

"You don't have to say anything yet. I know you're scared. I know this is big. And I know you have a lot going on. But I'm not walking away this time. You can believe that." He dropped his hand again.

She looked up at him, eyes big, cheeks flushed. Then she nodded softly.

They remained like that for a few moments longer in the cool air, the sounds of the music, laughter and clinking glasses filtering around them.

Chelsea finally exhaled and said, "You're right. That kiss was... "She shook her head.

"Yep. I know." Jake said with a grin.

He quickly dropped his lips to hers once more, like he wasn't able to stop himself, before he stepped back and lifted her off the wooden fence. He remained holding her around the waist for a moment, not wanting to let go of her. Not wanting this moment with just the two of them to be over yet.

He finally stepped back slightly and held out his hand to her. "Come on, if we don't go back soon, Dean is going to send everyone out to look for me. He made me promise I wouldn't leave the dance floor all night."

Chelsea laughed and looked at his hand. She then reached out and intertwined her fingers with his.

It was warm and familiar. It felt like home.

They walked back to the party, hand in hand under the soft glow of the fairy lights. He knew it wasn't perfect and that things would take time. But the air between them felt electric. Like something had been stirred up.

Jake finally felt like he was right where he belonged.

With nowhere else he would rather be than at his best friend's wedding, with the only girl he has ever loved.

FORTY FOUR
Chelsea

The next morning, Chelsea was awoken to the sound of a coffee machine roaring to life.

She lay perfectly still, trying to get her bearings of where she was waking up and what had happened last night.

Oh god, she thought. *The kiss.*

Her body instantly went up in temperature as she recalled the kiss and what effect Jake's words had on her. She didn't just feel hungover from the open bar and the free-flowing champagne; she felt like she had an emotional hangover.

Her head was pounding as she recalled the rest of the night.

Walking back to the dance floor hand in hand with Jake. Their friends noticed their hands intertwined together, but no one said anything. Just smiles on their faces and a few raised eyebrows. It was as if no one was surprised to see them together.

She had danced the rest of the night away under the stars and fairy lights with her best friend, Jake, her sister, and all of their high school friends. They danced and sang until the DJ announced it was the final song. They all formed a circle around the bride and groom and belted out the words to 'Horses' while

Dean and Emily danced in the middle. Jake had held Chelsea to his chest, standing behind her as they sang. She felt him kiss her head multiple times throughout the song while she clung to his arms that were wrapped tightly around her shoulders.

Then Dean announced he wanted the party to continue, so everyone jumped into the party buses that were there to take people home, and they headed back to Dean's parents' house. The party continued for a bit out on the back deck before people started slowly dropping off. Some went home, while others crashed somewhere in the house.

And that was where Chelsea realised, she was now. She vaguely remembered Dean and Jake dragging mattresses from the empty bedrooms out into the big lounge room of his parents' house. At the time, it seemed like a great idea for everyone to have a slumber party like they used to in high school. Although now Chelsea couldn't understand why Emily and Dean would want to spend their first night as a married couple, sleeping in a room with all of their friends. But she guessed that summed them up perfectly. They loved their people fiercely. That, and they wouldn't have wanted to miss out on any fun they had without them.

Something warm and strong tightened around Chelsea's waist.

Not something. An arm.

Jake's arm.

Chelsea tensed for a second. More flashbacks from the night before. Jake trying to be a gentleman and kiss her on the cheek goodnight before moving to the couch.

Chelsea still feeling buzzed from the alcohol, pulling him down to lie next to her.

Them staying awake whispering to each other until the early hours of the morning before they fell asleep, curled up together. She wanted to feel bad, but honestly, she felt great. Minus the hangover that was getting progressively worse the more time went on. But she felt right at home tucked in under Jake's arm.

Chelsea finally cracked her eyes open to look around the room. It was full of pillows and blankets, all the bodies tucked underneath were still. Her sister was on the bed mattress next to her, tucked in alongside Billy.

Chelsea smirked to herself and made a mental note to ask her sister what was going on with them. She noticed they were pretty close last night and hardly left each other's sides, so she suspected she had been seeing a bit of Billy since that night she first went home with him.

She looked around at the other beds occupied by the rest of their school friends. It really was just like they were back in high school.

A whisper coming from behind her caught her attention. "Chels."

She looked behind her, trying not to move too much. Not wanting to wake Jake.

She saw Emily standing in the doorway holding up a coffee cup to her.

Chelsea nodded to her best friend while she slowly turned over to try to untangle herself from Jake.

A soft groan came from him as she came to face him. She paused, waiting to see if he would fall back asleep.

Nope.

His eyes cracked open. A lopsided smile on his face as he drank her in.

"Hey."

She sighed. "Hey."

His warm arm tightened around her waist, pulling her closer to him.

They stayed like that for a moment. Soaking in the quiet moment together.

Chelsea was trying to ignore the ache she could feel as her body reacted to being so close to Jake again. Shirtless, mind you.

She was close to giving in to her body and letting her hands trail all over Jake's body when she heard Emily call out to her softly from the kitchen.

"Coffee," she whispered.

Jake nodded. A flash of disappointment on his face.

He leaned forward and gave her a quick kiss on her forehead. The moment fleeting, but intensely intimate. Going against everything she desperately wanted to do, she reluctantly dragged herself up and made her way to the kitchen.

"How are you up so early?" She asked as she followed Emily out to the back deck, coffee cups in hand.

Emily sat down on the outdoor lounge, "I think I was having too much fun on the dance floor that I actually didn't drink that much."

Chelsea sat beside her, curling her legs underneath her. "Ah, smart. I should have done that. My head is pounding."

"I can't believe it's all over."

Chelsea nodded. "I can't believe you are a married lady now," she said, nudging Emily's shoulder.

They sat together for a while, sipping their coffees, watching the sun creep higher in the morning sky while quietly debriefing on the wedding.

After a while, Chloe emerged from the house and joined them when Emily finally said what Chelsea could obviously see she had been dying to say.

"So, you and Jake seemed pretty close last night. And this morning." She said with a smirk.

Chelsea groaned and let her head fall backwards against the lounge.

"Yeah. I could hear a lot of whispering coming from the next bed over." Chloe added.

"I kind of freaked out at the wedding and left him on the dance floor. But he followed me, and we had a pretty deep conversation and then… he kissed me. Like really kissed me."

"About time," Emily said, finishing off her coffee.

Chelsea rolled her eyes. "It was… well, it was amazing. But I don't know. I am so scared. And I don't think I am ready for anything serious right now. I haven't even signed divorce papers yet."

"Just tell Jake that then," Chloe replied.

"I don't want to lose him again, though."

"Chels. Babe, that man is not going anywhere. He is obsessed with you." Emily said with a pointed look.

"She is right. I would love for a guy to look at me the way he looks at you."

Chelsea sighed again. It would be so easy for her to fall back into a familiar place with Jake. But it wasn't just her that she had to consider now. Lucy and Olivia were her main priority. They didn't know Jake. Was it fair to introduce someone new to them when they already had so much change happening? Was it fair to them? Or Ryan?

God, she had so much to consider, and her hangover was not helping.

She tuned back into the conversation between Emily and Chloe, which had shifted to Chloe and Billy.

"I don't think it will be anything serious. We are both just having fun. Bonus, that he knows what he is doing in the bedroom." Chloe said to Emily with a wink.

Chelsea laughed. A pang of jealousy hit her at how carefree her sister was able to be.

Chelsea had never really had that. She finished high school, had her heart broken, and pretty quickly fell into a serious relationship. Since then, she has had to worry about Ryan, Olivia, or Lucy. Putting herself and her wants and needs on the back burner. Jake's words from the night before had continued to replay in her mind. He was right, nothing needed to be decided right now, and they didn't know where they would end up, but she was beginning to think that maybe she owed it to herself to let loose a little. Maybe it was okay not to have everything exactly mapped out.

Maybe this was her time to really do what lit her on fire.

Follow her dreams.

Have fun.

They sat out there for a while longer, laughing, before everyone else started to wake up. Dean came and found Emily to sneak her back to his old bedroom. Chelsea assumed they wouldn't be seeing them again for a while. The others all tidied up the house for Dean's parents before slowly dispersing.

Chloe was out the front saying goodbye to Billy when Jake finally managed to corner Chelsea in the living room.

"Are you avoiding me?" He said playfully as he sat on the edge of the couch.

Chelsea shook her head as she turned to face him, "Would I ever do that?"

Jake laughed lightly as he gently tugged on her waist so that she was now standing between his legs. "I have to head back to the brewery to help clean up before the lunch shift. Do you need a lift home?"

"No, I think Chloe wanted to show me something in town on our way home," Chelsea said as she pressed her hands to his thighs. She surprised herself with how naturally the physical touch was with him.

Jake nodded, looking slightly disappointed but intrigued, his hands still resting gently on her waist. "Okay. Yeah. No worries," he paused. "When can I see you again?"

"I think I need to spend some time with the girls. Think things through. But soon, I promise."

Jake pulled her closer to him, wrapping his arms around her waist, resting his head against her stomach. "I'll be here. When you are ready."

Chelsea wrapped her arms around his shoulders and nodded, "Thanks, Jake. And thank you for last night. I had fun with you."

"Me too," he murmured against her t-shirt.

They lingered there, wrapped in each other's arms for a moment before Chelsea heard her sister calling out to her from the front of the house.

Chelsea sighed, "Guess that's my cue," she said as she reluctantly stepped back. "I'll see you soon, okay?"

Jake nodded. "Call or text me when you are ready. Same number," he said as he stood up and moved to walk her out of the house.

Chelsea was relieved that he hadn't changed his number so that she didn't have to do the awkward task of asking for his number again. She may have deleted it from her phone after they broke up because she couldn't trust herself not to call him and beg him to come back. But she was unable to delete his number from her brain. It was one of those weird things she was never able to forget.

Jake walked her out to her sister, who was waiting in her car. She quickly reached up to give him a quick kiss on his cheek before quickly turning to Chloe's car. When she got in, Chloe was smirking at her.

"What?"

Chloe continued smirking as she started the car, "Nothing, sis. Nothing at all."

Chelsea looked back at Jake briefly as they pulled out of the driveway. He was still standing in the same spot, like his feet were stuck to the floor, watching her drive away.

But this time it didn't feel like they were leaving each other. It felt like it could be the start of something.

Chelsea leaned her head back against the seat as they drove towards town.

"Where are you taking me, anyway?"

"You'll see."

Chelsea rolled her eyes as she took in the scenery flashing by them, the warm wind blowing through the open window.

For once, Chelsea didn't feel worried. She felt like she was heading in the right direction to take her life back.

FORTY FIVE
Chelsea

"What are we doing here, Chlo?" Chelsea asked her sister as she took in the building in front of her. They were standing in front of an empty shop located on the busy main street of Somerdale. One side of the street had small shops, cafes, and a few bars, and the crystal blue water and white sand were directly across the road. The main street was picturesque and always bustling with locals and tourists. The sound of laughter mixed with the salty air brought a wave of memories back to Chelsea. Walking up the main street with her friends, getting ice creams before wandering over to the beach to watch the sunsets. But now here she was standing on the sidewalk, looking into an empty shop with a huge 'For Lease" sign in the window.

"This is it." Chloe finally said, with a big grin.

"If by 'it' you mean the old antique shop that has now closed, then yes, this is it."

Chloe laughed. "Come on," she said as she pulled out some keys from her pocket and proceeded to unlock the door.

Chelsea grabbed her sister's arm in shock as she started walking through the front door. "Woah, what are you doing? Why do you have the keys to this place?"

"I walked past this place the other day when I came into town and saw it was up for rent. So, I talked the real estate guy into giving me the keys so we could have a look at it," Chloe casually said as they entered the empty shop. "He was a total creep, by the way."

"Okay… but that doesn't really answer my question."

Chloe looked around, smiling before turning to Chelsea, who had sceptically followed her into the empty space. "Because this is perfect. I thought it was from the outside, but inside is even better."

Chelsea looked around, just getting more confused by the second. The room they were standing in was sweet. It was very spacious with the original wooden floors and features. It had a lot of charm and huge storefront windows, which allowed the natural light to pour in, making the view of the beach across the road look like a live picture. But she still didn't understand what her sister wanted to do with a shop like this.

She turned back to Chloe, frowning as she spoke, "Are you okay? Are you really hungover or something? I don't get why you want to rent a shop?"

Chloe rolled her eyes. "Shut up, I am fine. And it's not for me. It's for you."

Chelsea blinked at her. "Me? I don't need a shop."

"What has been your biggest dream since you were a kid?"

"I don't know what marrying Justin Bieber has to do with this empty shop?"

Chloe let out a quick laugh. "Okay, your second biggest dream. What was that?"

Chelsea thought for a moment, "To open my own book and coffee shop."

Chloe smiled, "Ta-da!" She said with her arms in the air. "Here it is."

Chelsea almost choked on her own saliva. "What? You are crazy. I have hardly thought about that dream since I fell pregnant with Lucy."

That was a lie. She had thought about it multiple times over the years. Dreamt of what it would be like to go to work every day in a cosy little bookstore, with her two little girls growing up between the shelves of books. But it was always just that, a dream.

Chloe shrugged, "So think about it now. The rent is crazy cheap, and your house is about to settle. Use some of that money to get you started. Seems like the perfect time to think about it to me."

Chelsea shook her head, processing what her sister was suggesting. She was right, this was something she had always dreamt of doing, but she knew nothing about starting a business. "Chloe, it's not as easy as that. I don't know the first thing about starting and running a business."

"And you can't learn?" Chloe said playfully. "Look, you have friends who run their own businesses, Mum has a good understanding of accounting and running the books, and Jake basically runs his dad's business. All these people can help you. We can help you," she paused before continuing, "No offence, but you haven't worked properly in years. It will be hard to find a job that you enjoy, and that gives you the flexibility to work around the girls. You said you wanted to figure out your next step and take your life into your own hands. If this is what you seriously want, why can't you do this?"

Chelsea absorbed her sister's honest words as she slowly looked around the empty space. She couldn't help but start to imagine the cosy book shop vibe she could create here. Rows of books lining the walls, a small café area with the smell of delicious coffee and pastries filling the air. A reading nook for people to sit with their coffees and enjoy their new books. Space to hold book club meetings and a pre-owned book space where people can swap their books. She turned back to her sister, who was still watching her, a smile plastered to her face.

Chelsea felt herself start to smile, "You really think I could do it?"

Chloe nodded. "Without a doubt. So, can we go tell that creepy real estate agent we will take it?"

Chelsea laughed, "Maybe we will just tell him we are interested and let me sleep on it."

"Okay, deal."

They locked up the shop and walked out onto the busy footpath together, Chloe yapping about her plans with Billy this week.

Chelsea was trying to listen, but her thoughts kept wandering away from her sister's love life. She hadn't let herself thoroughly think about her dream of owning her own bookstore in years. It had always just felt like something that was out of reach. But seeing that empty space and having her sister remind her of her dream made Chelsea realise that this really could be her time. She wanted to set up a life for her and her girls. She wanted to create a place where people would enjoy spending their time. Where, even if she had to work, the girls could be there with her.

She felt slightly nauseous thinking about it.

Was she crazy?

Could she really do this?

She felt like maybe she could.

FORTY SIX
Chelsea

The days since the wedding weekend started to blend together. Chelsea had been busy helping the girls settle into their new school and homes. Setting new routines and getting used to switching between homes. She was proud of their resilience and how well they had adapted to their parents' separation. She and Ryan had agreed that the girls always came first. Which meant they were still occasionally doing things all together if they noticed the girls were needing some extra support. They had fallen into a respectful co-parent relationship, still checking in with each other, offering mutual support and being flexible. Chelsea wasn't sure how long it would last, and she expected there to be some teething problems eventually, but for now, everything was slowly working out.

Chelsea was now in the car, driving to Ryan's house to drop the girls off for the weekend. His shifts were slightly more predictable now since he had gotten the new spot at Watervale hospital, but it was hard to have a set co-parent schedule with shift work. They tried to keep it even, but due to his shifts, he sometimes wasn't able to see them for nearly a week. This had been the case the past week, so now Lucy and Olivia were heading to spend the next couple of days with their dad.

Chelsea looked back in the rear-view mirror at the girls singing their lungs out to the Taylor Swift song playing on the radio and smiled.

As they pulled onto Ryan's Street, Chelsea turned down the radio, as if the loud music affected her ability to see where she was going. They pulled into the driveway of Ryan's beachside unit as she said, "Okay, girls, remember if you need me, just ask Dad to call me. Doesn't matter what time or what I am doing."

"Yes, mum. Oh, I wonder if Dad got me some more rainbow ice-cream?" Olivia practically shouted.

Chelsea chuckled, pleased that having two separate houses clearly didn't seem to bother her youngest daughter. Her eldest daughter, on the other hand, looked more reserved in the back-seat.

"You okay, Luce?"

Lucy fiddled with her hands in the backseat, "Hm, yes. I just... sometimes I really miss you. I just wish we could all be together again."

Chelsea's heart cracked open. "I know it's hard. But mum and dad weren't happy living together anymore. And not because of you girls. Because of us. We are happier living separately, where we can really focus on you both."

"I guess..."

Chelsea unclipped her seatbelt and turned around in her seat to face her daughters. "You know we both love you so much. But I wasn't being the best mum to you both anymore when we were all together. I know it's tricky to understand right now, and someday you will probably understand it a bit better, but this was just something we had to do. For all of us."

Lucy nodded and thought for a moment before asking, "Can you come with us to Sara's birthday party on Sunday? I don't know many people from school yet, and I am a bit nervous."

Chelsea's face softened. They had agreed that because the girls were with him this weekend, Ryan would take Lucy to her classmate's birthday party. And to be honest, Chelsea hadn't really given it another thought until now. "Of course I can. I will check with Dad inside, but I'm sure I can meet you guys there, sound good?"

Lucy nodded eagerly. Chelsea relaxed slightly now that her daughter seemed happier. She knew the girls loved spending time with Ryan, so it never really worried her having to leave them with him. But on those few occasions where they were upset or unsettled before she left, Chelsea found herself worried the whole time she was away from them.

"Okay, let's go in and see Dad!" Chelsea said as she opened her door and got out of the car, the girls bundled out of the back seat behind her.

Ryan opened the door before the girls could even knock, seemingly just as eager to see the girls as they were to see him. The girls threw themselves into his arms, almost knocking him backwards. He muttered something to them about there being ice cream inside before they rushed past him, their giggles and footsteps echoing through the hallway.

Chelsea smiled to herself as she walked up to the front door, carrying the girls' overnight bags and the numerous stuffed toys they insisted they needed to bring.

"God, I have missed them this week," Ryan said as she got to the door and put down the bags.

"Well, don't worry, they have packed as if they will be here for months. And have a long list of things they want to do." She said as she stood back up.

Ryan laughed.

"Hey, keep an eye on Lucy. She seemed off in the car, asking why we couldn't all live together again. She also asked if I could come to the birthday party on the weekend with you guys. But I said I would talk to you."

Ryan nodded, "Yeah, of course. I will take her to the shops to pick out a present tomorrow, and we can meet you at the party on Sunday."

"Okay, thanks."

Ryan looked at her for a moment, "Did you see the email from the conveyancer?"

Chelsea shook her head, "No, I have been flat out all morning, I haven't had a chance."

"Well, the settlement has all gone through. Our house is officially sold."

Chelsea exhaled, "Oh… wow. That is…"

"Heavy?" Ryan finished for her.

"Yeah, something like that."

Ryan nodded. "Yep. So, I guess the money should be in our accounts soon." He paused before continuing, "What do you think you'll do with it? Look for a place?"

Chelsea thought for a second. She knew the house was going to sell eventually, but knowing it was actually sold now brought a wave of unexpected unease. Now, all of the decisions she had been putting off felt like they were pushing against her chest, making it hard to breathe. The settlement of the house brought a feeling of finality. But it also filled her with excitement, making her think that maybe her dreams were closer than she had thought.

"Actually, I have been playing with the idea of opening up my own bookstore and coffee shop," she finally said.

Ryan looked shocked, "No way! I had forgotten about that dream of yours," he said, rubbing his chin. "That's a great idea."

"Yeah, me too. But Chloe showed me an empty shop in town the other week. I wasn't sure if it was a good idea, but I am thinking of giving it a go. Plus, I think Mum still needs us at the house. It's a good distraction having us there, so I am in no rush to move out yet."

Ryan nodded. "That's good, Chels. You'll do amazing."

They smiled at each other for a moment before Olivia came running towards them.

"Come on, Dad, we need help opening the ice cream."

Chelsea followed them towards the kitchen to say goodbye to the girls before getting back into her car.

She checked her phone before heading back home. She had one unread message from Emily.

"Hey, babes. Dean and Jake have their first footy game of the season tomorrow. You are coming. 2 pm. Don't say no, I have something to talk to you about xxx."

Chelsea laughed to herself before typing out a quick reply telling Emily she would be there. It almost felt like they were back in high school. The boys back playing football for their local team. The girls going out every Saturday to watch them. Or check them out in their short shorts. She couldn't quite believe that Jake had agreed to play again for the local team. It seemed permanent. Like maybe he really wasn't going to leave again. Emily had mentioned that she and Dean were considering moving back to Somerdale, but as far as Chelsea was aware, nothing had been decided on. But Dean playing for the local football club was a good sign that maybe they would. Chelsea selfishly hoped it meant they would move back. The whole crew back together.

She smiled to herself as she put her phone down and put the car into reverse, pulling away from Ryan's house.

Completely lost in her own thoughts of bookstores, coffee shops, and football.

Completely lost in the thought of possibilities.

FORTY SEVEN
Chelsea

Chelsea sat on the end of her bed the next morning, stretching after a solid night's sleep without little feet kicking her in the back. When she had arrived back at the house without the girls, she noticed her mum sitting out the back, lost in her thoughts and pretty obviously full of grief. So, Chelsea cooked her some dinner, and they spent the evening sharing a bottle of wine and watching a movie with Crumpet propped between them. It had been exactly what they had both needed. Now she looked out the window, admiring the morning sunshine pouring through the glass. Summer was coming to an end now, with the mornings and evenings starting to cool down. But living in the tropics, it never really felt like winter with the hot and sticky days.

Chelsea padded down the hallway to the kitchen, the smell of fresh coffee guiding the way. She found her mum already pottering around the kitchen, brewing coffee and cooking pancakes.

"Mum, you know the girls aren't here, right? You don't have to cook them pancakes."

"Yes, I know," her mum responded, rolling her eyes as she

whisked the pancake batter. "But having those girls around more has made me feel younger, and you know what? I love pancakes. So, who says I can't have them for breakfast?"

"True that! I hope there is enough for me." Chelsea said as she made her way to the coffee machine.

"Course, darling."

They pottered around in the kitchen together, chatting and laughing. Chelsea caught herself looking at her mother in amazement. She had gone through the deepest of heartbreaks, losing her first and only love, and although there was an underlying sadness etched on her face, here she was, laughing and cooking pancakes.

They had just settled down at the kitchen table with steaming cups of coffee and plates overflowing with fluffy pancakes and maple syrup when Chloe entered the room.

"Good morning, my favourite people." She said as she plucked Chelsea's fork from her hand and stabbed a piece of her pancake.

"Wow, no worries, help yourself," Chelsea said as she watched her sister eat her breakfast.

"Someone seems very chirpy this morning." Their mum commented from across the table.

"Just a lovely morning, mother. Why wouldn't I be happy?"

"More like a lovely sleepover with Billy," Chelsea added, smirking at her sister.

Chloe scoffed and rolled her eyes. Their mum chuckled at the comment.

"Whatever, at least one of us is getting some," Chloe said with a wink as she made her way into the kitchen.

"Do I need to remind you that I am going through a divorce? That I am now a single mum of two? That I am trying to sort my life out?" Chelsea said as she forked some more pancake into her mouth before continuing, "When am I supposed to find time to *get some*?"

"No, you don't need to remind me, but I don't think it will be long before you are back there, considering how close you and Jakey boy were at Em's wedding." Chloe threw back at her, voice full of amusement.

"I wouldn't be so sure about that. I have hardly seen him or spoken to him since then. So, let's just blame that whole night... and the next morning, on the open bar."

Chloe huffed a laugh, "Sure, whatever you say."

Chelsea shook her head as she sipped on her coffee.

"Well, I guess you'll probably see him today at the football." Their mum said with a wink.

Chelsea groaned, "Oh god. Don't you start too."

"I'm not, I'm not. But you must admit, it will be nice to see those boys running around in those short football shorts again, won't it? They will fill them out even better now."

"Jesus, mum."

"She is right, they will look good. And you always had a thing for the footy boys, Chels."

Wrong. She had a thing for one footy boy only.

"Okay, this conversation is over. I am going to the football because Emily asked me to and to support our friends. That's it. So, get any hidden agendas out of your minds. Both of you."

Chloe laughed to herself as she pottered around the kitchen, putting some toast into the toaster and brewing a coffee.

Chelsea drew her attention back to her plate of pancakes as she listened to the coffee machine grinding the fresh coffee beans.

Although she played it down to her mum and sister, Chelsea couldn't ignore the buzz she felt through her body at the thought of seeing Jake later. It still confused her when she thought about what would happen next, or what she wanted to happen next, but she couldn't deny that she was excited to see him again.

Her mind started to drift to what Emily needed to talk to her about. She was absentmindedly picking at her food when her sister's voice cut through her thoughts.

"What's this?"

Chelsea looked up to where her sister was standing, holding a bunch of papers that Chelsea had forgotten to move.

Dammit, she thought to herself as she watched her sister reading the papers she had picked up from the kitchen bench.

"You're really doing it?" Her sister asked, voice laced with excitement.

Chelsea shrugged, "I don't know..."

"Well, it looks like you do know because you have filled out the lease agreement for the shop and signed it."

"You did? Oh gosh, Chelsea. That's amazing, darling." Her mum said excitedly before frowning, "Why didn't you tell me?"

Chelsea placed her mug back down on the table. "I don't know. It still doesn't feel real. And plus, it might not even work out. This could all be for nothing."

Her mum waved her off, "Don't be ridiculous. When have you ever failed at anything in your life? This is your dream, and it is exactly what this little town is missing." She reached across the table to grab Chelsea's hand, "and we will be right here supporting you. Even if it does all fall apart..."

"Which it won't!" Chloe interrupted, slightly glaring at her mum.

"Right, of course it won't. I was just saying I would support you either way."

Chelsea squeezed her mum's hand before standing up to take her plate and empty mug to the kitchen. "Well, thanks, guys. I appreciate the support. And if things actually look like they will work, then I will definitely be calling on you guys to help me get up and running."

"You know it, sister. As long as you are paying me." Chloe responded with a wink.

Chelsea stacked her dishes in the dishwasher before turning back to her sister, "Alright, I am going to go and get organised before I need to go meet Em. Will you be at the game later?"

Chloe nodded as she ate cereal straight out of the box, while waiting for her toast to pop. "As if I would miss out on an opportunity to see Billy out on the field. I just have some things to do beforehand, so I will meet you there later."

Chelsea laughed, "No worries. I'll be sure to keep the other girls away from your man until you get there." She said with a smirk.

"Not my man, Chels," Chloe said as she threw more cereal into her mouth.

"Sure. Whatever you say." Chelsea said as she kissed her mum on the cheek, "I will see you later, Mum. You're getting lunch with Em's mum today, aren't you?"

She nodded, "Yes, we are heading to the brewery for a wine and a platter," she paused, her face dropping slightly. "Wish the boys good luck for me. Your dad would be so proud watching Jake running around out there again. He never missed a game."

Chelsea felt her heart crack; the pain was visible on her mum's face. She hooked her arm around her mum's shoulder and gave her a squeeze, tears pricking at her eyes at the thought of her dad not being there on the sidelines, cheering loudly. "I know, Mum. But I don't think he would let anything stop him from being there. He will be there, just in a different way now."

Her mum sniffed, slowly nodding. Chelsea held her tighter for a moment, wishing she could take away the pain from her mum. It was easy to forget and get caught up in her own grief because her mum had been so strong since the funeral. But when she showed her emotions in moments like this, it broke Chelsea's heart, remembering that although she had lost her dad, her mum had lost the greatest love of her life.

They stayed like that for a bit before Chelsea's mum told her she would be okay and that she needed to go and get ready to meet Emily's mum. Chelsea hesitantly agreed once she realised the time and rushed out of the kitchen to get organised to meet Emily.

Less than an hour later, Chelsea parked her car at the familiar football oval. The oval was huge, with lush, green grass and tall white goal posts at each end. The oval was surrounded by fencing, where cars were parked around the boundary, ready to watch the game. On one side of the field, there were newly renovated club rooms with a bar and seating. Then, to the right of the club rooms, there was a small hill of grass where Chelsea, Emily and their friends had claimed as their spot in high school. This was where they spent most Saturdays, a picnic rug on the floor, snacks, and drinks in hand, chatting about God knows what and cheering on the boys. The spot had a good view of the whole oval and was conveniently located near the boys' change rooms, allowing them to exit right next to them after the game.

Chelsea got out of her car and made her way over to the hill, where she could see Emily had already snagged a spot and was sitting on a picnic rug with a small cooler bag next to her. Chelsea smiled to herself as she noticed all the young girls littered on the hill, presumably watching their friends or boyfriends play in the younger teams. It brought back a feeling of nostalgia, as she once sat in those exact spots, watching her high school love run around on the field. Her gaze drifted to the wall beside the exit of the change rooms, a wall she often perched on, waiting to see the boy she loved walk out in one piece after a rough game of football.

Her gaze drifted back to Emily as she heard her call out her name. She stood up and waved her over. Emily looked like she still had a post-wedding glow, with her hair shinier, her skin flawless, and her strapless maxi dress hugging her body in all the right places.

Chelsea smiled as she approached Emily, "Whoa, Em, getting married has somehow made you even hotter."

Emily pulled her in for a quick hug before standing back to look at her. "Like you can talk, look at you! Break up, glow up, or what?"

Chelsea scoffed. She had showered and gotten ready in record time. She had opted for a simple denim skirt and black tank top, letting her freshly washed hair fall naturally down her back. She had quickly whacked on her SPF and some mascara before running out the door. She definitely did not think she looked anywhere near as put together as her best friend did.

They plonked down on the picnic rug beside each other, "You

know I had to pretty much fight off some of those teenage girls to claim our usual spot." Emily said as she crossed her legs.

Chelsea laughed. "You know, we used to be those teenage girls. Plus, we haven't been out here in years, so it is probably their spot now."

"True. But still. It will always be our spot," she paused before continuing, "God, I can't believe they have really decided to play again. I thought we had passed this part of our lives. And their bodies aren't like they used to be 10 years ago."

Chelsea nudged Emily's shoulder with hers, "Are you nervous to watch your husband play?" she said with amusement.

Emily scrunched up her nose, "No, I know Dean can take all the young ones on still."

Chelsea laughed as they settled into a comfortable conversation, watching the younger team's game finish. Once the siren blasted to signal the end of the game, the girl's conversation was interrupted as Dean and Jake ran out onto the field with the rest of their team to warm up. Chelsea felt her breathing hitch as her gaze immediately found Jake. She had to admit Chloe and her mum were right; he did look good. His tan skin stood out against the team's black and white jersey and white shorts, which seemed even shorter than she remembered, hugging his strong legs perfectly. He had a big grin on his face as he kicked the red football to Dean, who darted in front of one of their other teammates. He looked like he was in his element, right back where he belonged. Chelsea dragged her gaze from Jake to look at the rest of the team and their opponents. There were a few familiar faces, but most of them seemed to be a lot younger than Jake and Dean. And although the boys had always had a natural talent for the sport, the younger ones would probably be a lot faster and their bodies more forgiving. This sport could be rough. Ruthless even. A shiver went through Chelsea's body at the thought of them getting injured and not being able to bounce back like they once could.

"God, maybe I need a drink to get through this game." She said as she looked back at Emily.

Emily laughed, "Good idea. I packed some in the cooler bag," she said as she passed the bag to Chelsea. "Help yourself."

Chelsea was thankful her friend had come prepared, but as she unzipped the cooler bag and opened the lid, she let out a loud gasp. "Emily... Oh. My. God. No way." She reached in to pull out what looked to be a pregnancy test. A positive one at that.

Chelsea blinked, looking at the test in her hand, not caring that Emily must have peed on the stick she was holding recently. She looked up to see Emily looking back at her, wearing a huge grin.

Chelsea pushed the bag aside, clambering across the rug to pull Emily into a hug. "Oh my gosh. When. How. What. Tell me everything! Oh my god, I am so happy for you." Chelsea all but squealed.

Emily laughed, trying to keep her balance while hugging her back, "It's so early. We only found out this week, and our doctor said we would only be a few weeks pregnant, but we must have been pregnant at the wedding and didn't know. I just had to tell you. I couldn't keep it in any longer."

Chelsea pulled back, smiling brightly. "I knew you had a glow about you when I saw you," she said as she picked up Emily's hand in hers. "I am so happy for you. How did Dean take it?"

Emily squeezed Chelsea's hand before sitting back on the rug, leaning back on her elbows. "God, Chels, he was so excited. More excited than me. We were hardly even trying. We had planned to travel a bit this year, work out where we wanted to land. Settle down, you know?" she exhaled, "But next minute we are looking at a stick I have peed on, and everything changed."

Chelsea nodded; she knew that feeling all too well.

"And when it went positive, Dean squealed. Like, really squealed," she laughed. "I don't think we both realised how much we wanted it until we saw those two little lines. And I know it's still early, and we will try to get some travel in before we have the baby, but I think we have decided we are going to move back here."

Chelsea's eyes widened, "Really? You'll move back here?"

Emily shrugged. "It just makes sense. Our families are here. You are here. We had the best childhoods growing up here, and that's exactly what we want for our future small people."

Chelsea couldn't hold back the grin that had spread across her face. Having her best friend living in the same town as her again hadn't happened since she had moved out of town with Ryan. She had always dreamed of living close to her and raising their kids together, but it always seemed like just that. A dream. But the reality of that happening now made her bubble with excitement.

"Ah, I can't believe I am finally going to be an Aunty."

Emily laughed, "At least Lucy will be almost old enough to babysit for us." She said with a wink.

Their conversation was interrupted when the siren went, signalling that the football game was about to start. The boys took their positions on the field, Dean's gaze quickly spotting Emily on the hill to give a quick smirk and thumbs up. Emily returned the gesture, a huge smile on her face. Chelsea pulled her gaze from the love birds to the man standing in the centre of the field, ready for the centre bounce. His gaze already on her, she instantly felt warmth spread through her body. She raised an eyebrow at him, a slight smirk on her face. A smile spread on Jake's face, making his dimples pop, before winking at her and returning his attention to the umpire who was about to start the game.

Chelsea's heart fluttered in her chest. It was the exact ritual he had always done before a game in high school. He would find her on the hill and give her a wink. It may have been small, but it brought back a massive rush of emotions she had tried so hard to hide away.

He hadn't forgotten.

The nerves Chelsea felt earlier, before she was distracted by Emily's news, quickly returned as the game began.

"God, you might not be able to drink Em, but I definitely still need one."

Emily huffed a laugh as she pulled out a can of premixed gin from the cooler bag she had prepared. She passed it over to Chelsea without taking her eyes off the football game.

Chelsea took the drink gratefully. As she cracked the can open and took a huge swig, she silently thanked her best friend for being prepared. Chelsea prayed the drink would help settle her nerves that were now swimming in her stomach.

He would be fine.

He had to be.

Because Chelsea felt that once this game had finished, things may never be the same again.

FORTY EIGHT
Chelsea

The game had been going great. The boys were dominating the field as if they had never stopped playing. The teams were an even match, with the scores never being more than a few points apart. Chelsea had finished off two cans of the gin Emily had packed for her, which had settled her nerves. She couldn't deny it was contagious watching the guys all play, clearly in their element and having the time of their lives. Chelsea had hardly watched any football games since she moved away. Occasionally, she watched some professional games, but mostly, she avoided them. Being back here, though, she very quickly fell back into the competitive mindset of watching people you know playing a game like this.

Chloe had arrived sometime around half-time and had already been yelling out things to the opposition about staying away from Billy. She had always been the loudest one on the sidelines of any sport, but if there was someone on the team who she had any connection with, it was best to stay out of her way.

They were now in the last quarter, with just 10 minutes left in the game. The guys were down two points and needed to get a goal or two to really seal the win. The game had turned rougher in the last quarter, both teams throwing themselves into trying to win their first game of the season. Literally throwing their bodies into it, into each other. The knocks got heavier, and there was a lot more pushing and shoving going on. Chelsea was thankful she had chosen to have those couple of drinks because Jake seemed to be the one the opposing team was really gunning for.

"God, they really want to take Jake out," Emily mumbled as Jake fought off another two players as he tried to get the ball down to their scoring end.

Chelsea felt the protectiveness rage bubbling inside of her as she watched the other team continuously knock him down. He managed to outrun them and kick the ball to Billy, who easily put it straight through the goal posts, putting them in front again. Chloe loudly cheered, wolf-whistling at Billy, who found her quickly in the crowd and pointed at her as he ran past, sporting a huge grin.

Chelsea glanced at the scoreboard and timer.

One minute and thirty seconds left of the game. She was getting anxious, needing the game to finish so that she could see Jake. Her feelings were quietly bubbling away under the surface, but she couldn't ignore the pull she was having to see him and speak to him. To tell him how she was feeling.

Both teams were fighting hard to get the ball down their end of the field. The other team wanting to score another goal to put them in front at the last minute, and our team trying to keep the ball away from them, just holding off until the final siren went.

As it reached the final ten seconds, everyone was on the edge of their seats, and the noise from the crowd was deafening. Louder than Chelsea had remembered for local country footy.

Just as the siren was about to go, Jake got tackled hard by a player twice his size, both smacking to the ground with incredible force. Chelsea gasped and jumped up as Jake went down, swearing she could almost hear the crunch of bones from her spot on the hill.

The whole crowd went silent, watching as the other player staggered back up, but Jake was still lying there, not moving.

The siren went to signal the end of the game; Somerdale had won, but no one celebrated. Dean ran over to Jake, joined by most of their teammates. The trainers and coach ran across the field from the sidelines to Jake's very still body lying on the grass. The away team all stood around, not knowing what to do.

"Please get up. Get up. Get up. Get up. Please." Chelsea whispered under her breath. Fighting against all of her instincts, which were screaming at her to run across the field to him.

Chloe and Emily stood beside her, all three of them holding their breath as the two trainers reached Jake. They knelt down beside him, with Dean, who had his hand on Jake's back, face etched with worry.

After what felt like a lifetime, Jake finally moved. It was slow, but he staggered up with Dean and the trainers taking most of his weight.

Chelsea let out the breath she had been holding in, collapsing back onto the rug as she watched Jake being walked off the field to the change rooms, flanked by Dean on one side and a trainer on the other, holding him up. She sat there for a moment, not saying anything, trying to get her breathing and heart rate back under control.

Chloe dropped down onto the rug beside her. "God. That was heavy."

Chelsea nodded, her heart still feeling like it was going to beat out of her chest.

"He got up. He will be okay. Dean has him." Emily said, trying to plaster on a smile even though Chelsea could see the concern etched all over her face.

"Billy just texted and said he is okay. Chels?" Chloe grabbed her hand, "He is okay."

Chelsea nodded again but knew she wouldn't believe it until she saw him, and he told her himself that he was okay. She felt overwhelmed with the adrenaline and emotions after watching him lying there, unmoving on the ground. Him slowly getting up after what felt like forever, and her not being able to run onto the field to be there for him and make sure he was okay, because, well, it was a football game with two teams of men who were double her size. And because he wasn't her boyfriend to check on. Something about that last reason really didn't sit well with her anymore. It didn't feel right. Something about the events of the past fifteen minutes put things into perspective. Her feelings and what she wanted were suddenly extremely clear.

Him.

It was him.

It had always been him.

She had been trying to convince herself that being back in Somerdale, back with her friends and her family, had clouded her judgement and she was just hanging onto the nostalgic feeling of the past. Hanging onto the thought that a dream could be a reality. But she had been kidding herself. This was real. And she needed to see him to tell him while she had the confidence to do so. She couldn't leave it any longer, or else she would lose her nerve. If she had learnt anything over the past few months, it was that life is short. She didn't want to waste another minute of Jake not knowing how she felt.

Emily's voice pulled her from her thoughts. "I told Dean we would meet them in the clubrooms. Let's go snag a table before all these young ones get in there." She said as she started packing up the rug.

Chelsea stood up, helping gather their things, but entirely on autopilot.

As they started walking towards the clubrooms, Chelsea stopped when they got to the wall next to the change rooms.

"I am going to wait here for Jake. I need to see him. I need to talk to him before we go in there." She said, pointing towards the clubrooms, the bar already filling up quickly.

"Do you want us to wait with you?" Chloe asked.

Chelsea shook her head. "No, you guys go get a table, and I will meet you in there. I just need to do this while I have the courage."

Emily and Chloe looked at each other and smiled before heading into the clubrooms. Chelsea stood, watching them disappear towards the bar. She let out a sharp breath before turning and walking over to the half wall near the exit of the change rooms. She lowered herself down so that she was sitting on the edge, her legs dangling over. This was almost exactly where she had sat after every one of Jake's games. It was like a ritual, something that started naturally and never stopped. Not until they had stopped being them.

Now sitting here again, looking over the empty football field with the noise increasing from the bar, she felt the same as she did all those years ago. Excited to see Jake after his game, but this time it was mixed with other emotions. Worry. Needing to know if he was okay, but the fact that an ambulance hadn't been called provided some comfort. And nervousness. What if he didn't feel the same? What if the space had made him realise being with her wasn't really what he wanted? What if he had realised that her baggage was way more than he could commit to?

She shook her head as if trying to shake the thoughts from her head physically. She didn't have time to change her mind now. The noise from the change rooms grew louder as some of the team started trickling out and heading towards the clubrooms and bar to celebrate their win.

The nerves in her stomach quickly grew as she scanned the guys walking out.

This was it.

FORTY NINE
Jake

Jake had just finished having the team's doctor check him over, clearing him from any concussions or broken bones. The doctor said he will be very bruised tomorrow, with perhaps a few bruised ribs after the big knock he took on the field. However, with a little bit of rest and taking it easy, he should be good to go.

Jake made his way over to the showers, where the rest of the team were showering and getting changed out of their football gear. Jake winced getting undressed. He was definitely going to be sore tomorrow. He stood under the warm water for a while, letting the water wash off the dirt and grass from his bruised body, as the change rooms emptied out. Once he finally stepped out of the shower and made his way to his gear bag, Dean came up beside him.

"Doc clear you?"

"Yeah, all good. Will be bruised tomorrow, but no concussion. Just a bit winded."

"Good man. Let's go get a bloody beer. We deserve it."

Jake nodded in agreement, quickly stepping into his shorts and pulling on a t-shirt. He gathered up his football gear and slung his bag over his shoulder before following Dean out.

He had his head down, lost in his own thoughts, when two long, tanned, and toned legs caught his eye. The familiar legs were dangling over the half wall, as they had done so many times before. His eyes travelled up the body they belonged to before settling on the familiar face that was smiling back at him. Jake's heart rate instantly rose when his eyes met the blue eyes already locked on him.

"Chels?" he said as he fell back from Dean, who was smirking at them as he continued towards the clubrooms. Jake made his way over to Chelsea, who was jumping down from the wall now. He stopped in front of her, steadying her as she landed on the ground.

"Hi." She said, holding onto his forearms.

"Hi."

"You're okay?" She asked, concern showing on her face as her eyes searched his whole body. He guessed she was searching for injuries.

He nodded, "Doctor cleared me. Just a bad knock. Winded myself."

Chelsea exhaled loudly, "Thank God. I was worried."

"You were?" Jake's eyebrows shot up.

Chelsea's gaze locked onto his, and she nodded. "Of course. I felt like I couldn't breathe when you were on the ground," she shook her head before continuing. "That guy almost knocked you out, but he also knocked some sense into me. Not physically, of course." She said as she tucked a piece of hair behind her ear.

Jake smirked; she was clearly flustered, but he knew better than to interrupt her. Plus, he was interested to see what she wanted to say to him and why it was making her so nervous.

Chelsea exhaled as her eyes searched his. "You know, I have been trying so hard to tell myself that being home again, being around you again, had rustled up the past for me. That everything I was feeling was just a mix of going through my separation and being back in my hometown, where I have only really ever been with you." She took another deep breath as she looked around them before locking her gaze back on his. "I really tried to push the feelings away. I wanted… I needed to let myself sit with my separation. I needed to let myself feel the feelings that come with the ending of a marriage. I needed to be with my girls and make sure they were okay. So, when I came back here and saw you…" she shook her head again. "I was almost angry at myself because it felt like the feelings I had for you had never left."

Jake's heart swelled and cracked all at once. The emotion on her face made it clear how much of an internal battle she had been having. He wanted to reach for her, to hold her and tell her it's okay, that she didn't have to say anything. But he knew he needed to let her speak. He knew she needed him to listen.

"I felt angry at myself because I had spent ten years with someone whom I did love and who I had made a life with, and then, within five minutes of seeing you, I felt like all of that was a lie. Like I had been in love with you the whole time. It felt like I had betrayed Ryan and lied to him the whole time…"

Jake couldn't help himself and had to interrupt, "Chels, no. That's not -"

Chelsea put her hand up to stop him, not in a rude way. More in a way of saying she needed to get this out in one go. "I know that's not true now. It would have been so easy to jump back into something with you as if no time had passed. But I knew I needed to grieve my marriage. I needed to do that on my own. With my girls. If I didn't do that then, then I would have ruined any chance of doing this."

Jake felt his heart rate increase; the nerves in his stomach suddenly felt like they would take over his whole body. He let his gear bag fall to the ground beside them. "What do you mean… 'this'?"

Chelsea looked at him for a moment before taking a step closer to him, "This. Us. Honestly, a couple of hours ago, I still wasn't entirely sure what I wanted… or what I needed. But then I saw you out there, and I was so proud. I was so proud watching you. And then you went down. And it took everything in me to stop myself from running straight through all of those huge football guys to get to you." She exhaled, taking another step closer and reaching out to take his hand. Jake threaded his fingers through hers, his heart hammering against his chest.

"I realised in that moment I had been trying to convince myself it wasn't real or that I was holding back because I thought it was the right thing to do. That it was too soon after my separation. But this is very real. And I am so tired of worrying about what the right thing to do is. I have spent the last ten years doing that, but I am done now."

Jake was holding his breath. He knew what she was saying, but he had been waiting so long to hear her say these things that he needed her to say the words. He wasn't sure he would believe it unless she said exactly what she meant.

"Chels, you are going to have to spell this out for me." He whispered, almost breathless.

Chelsea smiled at him and stepped closer again so that they were almost flush against each other, still gripping his hand in hers. "I want this. I want you. And if you still do, I want us." She exhaled loudly, looking up at him, waiting for him to say something.

Jake couldn't control the grin that spread across his face. He dropped her hand and brought his hands to cup her face. She instantly lifted hers to hold onto his forearms as his thumbs absentmindedly stroked her cheeks.

"Can I kiss you now?"

She had barely finished nodding when he finally crashed his lips to hers. He had been waiting to do this again since the night of the wedding. Waiting patiently for her to figure out what he already knew. That this was it. She was it for him. She always had been.

And God, was the wait worth it.

The kiss wasn't soft. It was frantic. Lips crashing. Teeth clashing. Years of unsaid words passing through them. But somehow it was the hottest kiss Jake had ever had. Nothing compared to this moment. Jake ignored the pain in his body from the football game as he dropped his hands from Chelsea's face to the backs of her legs and lifted her. Her legs hooked around his waist, her arms snaking around his neck, holding onto him like her life depended on it. God knows it felt like his whole life did depend on this kiss and this moment.

The kiss lit Jake's whole body on fire. He wanted to turn around and walk her to his car so they had the privacy to continue this moment, but he was so caught up in the kiss that he couldn't even bring himself to take a step.

Chelsea brought her hand up to run it through his hair. Jake groaned into her mouth. She smiled against his lips at his response, but he quickly moved his hand up to cup the back of her head so that he could deepen the kiss. Chelsea's breath hitched as Jake's tongue claimed hers. His body was quickly responding to finally having Chelsea flush against him when they were interrupted by shouting and cheering coming from behind him.

They paused, Chelsea, pulling back slightly to look over his shoulder.

"Finally!" He heard someone he was sure was Chloe shout out.

"Do we have an audience?" He said, his voice gruff.

Chelsea nodded, turning back to face him, "It seems our friends are happy for us." She smiled at him.

Jake leaned his forehead against hers, trying to catch his breath from possibly the best kiss he had ever had. He slowly lowered her to the ground, his body instantly missing the feeling of hers. He kept his hands on her waist, not ready to completely let go of her.

"Is this real? Are you sure this is what you want? Because I can wait if you aren't, but if you are sure, then I don't think I can hold back anymore."

Chelsea, who still had her arms wrapped around his neck, lifted herself on her toes to softly kiss the tip of his nose. "Please don't hold back. I was a little lost for a while there, but I think I just needed to find my way back to you. I am with you completely. I am done wasting any more time not with you."

Jake's heart again felt like it was going to beat out of his chest.

"About bloody time, baby." He said with a smirk as he pressed his lips to hers again. This time, the kiss was soft. Not as frantic as before. Like they had all the time in the world. Jake had to stop himself before getting carried away and physically picking her up again and walking her out of there.

"As much as I could stay right here forever, if we stay out here any longer, I think Dean will come over here and drag me inside."

Chelsea laughed.

"Do you have to go, or can you stay for a drink?"

Chelsea stepped back, untangling her arms from around his neck. "The girls are with Ryan for the weekend, so I am all yours."

Jake couldn't stop the schoolboy grin that spread across his face. "Let's go in for a couple of drinks and then escape as soon as we can." He said as he stepped forward, grabbing the back of her neck and pulling her to him again before pressing his lips to hers. He couldn't stop himself. He couldn't keep his hands off her, and he couldn't wait to have her all to himself for the whole night. They had a lot of lost time to make up for.

Chelsea laughed as he gently let go of her. "Deal." She replied as she laced her fingers through his, and they walked towards the clubrooms, where it seemed to be getting louder and rowdier.

Jake couldn't wipe the smile off his face. He hadn't expected the day to play out as it had. He did not expect to get taken out on the field during his first game back. He did not expect to walk out of the change rooms to find the love of his life sitting there anxiously waiting for him. And he definitely did not expect to be now walking into the clubrooms, hand in hand with said love of his life, after the hottest kiss of his life.

It felt like everything had fallen into place or was at least falling into place. He wasn't naive; he knew it wasn't necessarily going to be easy or smooth sailing. Chelsea had a lot at risk and to consider, but there was no doubt in his mind that this was exactly where he was supposed to be. Right here in this moment. With Chelsea.

This was it.

The start of the rest of his life.

Chelsea took a deep breath as she looked around the newly renovated space. The scent of paint still lingered slightly in the air, although the comforting aroma of fresh coffee and baked goods was already overrunning it.

She was standing in the middle of a book shop. Her book shop. Chelsea felt the grin take over as she took in the hard work around her. When she signed the lease for the shop six months ago, it was a blank canvas that ended up needing quite a bit of work. So, with the help of her family, friends, and Jake, she had transformed the empty shop into her dream bookstore, complete with a café.

When you entered the shop, you were met with a cosy café that had a cabinet filled with delicious baked goods from a local baker. There was a coffee machine on the counter, next to the till and jars that held cookies her mum baked. Each week, she planned to experiment with new flavours and offer them in the café for people to enjoy. Taking up the front space, there were tables and chairs, along with some comfortable lounges for people to sit and enjoy their coffees and new books. The huge windows that took up the whole front wall let in natural light and served as an incredible backdrop. The sun glistening off the turquoise water across the road. This space was planned with the hope of seconding as a space for book club meetings, where the coffee could be swapped out for a glass of wine. A place for friendships to be made and strengthened.

Once you made your way further into the shop, you were greeted with rows of shelves, lined with books that were sorted into genres. There was a table in the middle that was stacked with bestselling books for that month and new releases. Chelsea hoped that one day she could join the authors at that table. But that dream was for another day. Because today was the grand opening of her store, *Books & Brew*. Chelsea had enlisted the help of her family one night to help come up with the name for the shop. It ended up being her eldest daughter, Lucy, who came up with the winning name. Once she had said it while they were sitting around the kitchen table at their home, everyone looked at each other with huge grins, knowing it was the one.

Chelsea bent down to straighten a stack of novels on the table for what had to be the fifth time that morning, her heart hammering in her chest. Everything was clean and tidy, ready for the opening. Prepared for her friends and family, as well as the rest of Somerdale, to come and see her dream come to life.

A sound pulled Chelsea from her thoughts. The sound of a coffee machine grinding coffee. She turned to look towards the front of the store where the café was. She popped her hip and leaned against the table as she watched the man she was completely and utterly in love with work his magic on the coffee machine. She watched as he moved with ease, grinding the fresh beans and frothing the milk. And it was a bonus that he looked so good doing it. His tanned skin stood out against the casual white t-shirt he wore, paired with his blue jeans. His moustache and hair had really grown over the past few months, and when finished off with the signature backwards hat he was sporting, she had to admit he looked pretty damn hot.

Jake had been at the shop with her these past few months, painting walls, building furniture, listening to her crazy ideas, and bringing them to life rather than telling her she was insane.

They had spent countless hours here together, sometimes with others, but often on their own, blasting music, covered in paint. If she was honest, it was some of her favourite moments. She couldn't have done any of this without his support.

They had found out last week that Jake's dad was getting organised to retire. He had told Chelsea and Jake that he was planning to retire and, ideally, he would love for Jake to take over the business, but he understood if he didn't want that. Jake had always wanted to get away from the business and from Somerdale, but things had changed since then. Chelsea wasn't sure what he was going to do yet because they had been preoccupied with the new store opening, but once the dust had settled, she guessed Jake would make the decision. Chelsea knew that whatever he decided, she would support him just as he had supported her and her dream of opening up this store.

Chelsea smiled as she watched Jake in the store. Her store. She looked around again.

It's real. She thought. *This is mine.*

She looked back at Jake, who was now smirking at her as he made his way towards her, holding a coffee in one hand.

This is all really mine.

"Thought you could use this," he said, holding the coffee out to her. "Do you want a muffin or croissant, since I'm sure you have forgotten to eat breakfast this morning?"

Chelsea took the coffee from him with a laugh, "You know me too well. A muffin, please."

He nodded, with a smirk, making his dimples pop. "You ready?" He said, brushing a stray strand of hair away from her face.

She looked around at the space they had transformed, her chest swelling with pride mixed with a little bit of fear. "As I'll ever be."

Jake reached out and squeezed her free hand, "It's going to be great. I'm so proud of you." He said, his eyes soft.

Chelsea squeezed his hand back, "I couldn't have done any of this without you. There's no way I would have been able to do all those flat packs on my own."

Jake laughed. "That's what I'm here for."

At that moment, the bell above the front door jingled softly, they both looked over to see Chelsea's mum and Chloe stepping in. Her mum was holding a huge bunch of flowers, and her sister had a box full of what Chelsea suspected was champagne.

"I'll go warm your muffin up. You need to eat before this thing kicks off." He pulled her in for a quick hug, placing a kiss on the top of her head before he walked off in the direction of the café.

Chelsea watched him walk off, admiring the view, before her attention was drawn to her mum and sister approaching.

"Mum, what are those for?" Chelsea said, walking to meet them.

"For you. To say congratulations. This..." she said, waving her hand in the direction of the store, "is amazing. Your dad... he would be so proud." She took a breath, her eyes glossing over. "Oh god, I said I wasn't going to cry today," She sniffed. "I'm going to go put these flowers on the counter."

Chelsea huffed a laugh, "Thank you, Mum. They are beautiful, I love them. And you." She pulled her mum in for a one-armed hug.

"Okay, enough of that. No more crying today. Let's get this party started, shall we?" Chloe said teasingly as she held up the box of champagne.

Chelsea laughed, "Come on, let's go set this up over at the café."

~

An hour later, the store was bustling. Her mum fluttered about, chatting to neighbours, and making sure everyone's glasses or coffee cups were always full. Jake had been busy behind the coffee machine, fuelling those who didn't feel like drinking champagne before lunchtime. Chelsea had hardly spoken to him since he had cornered her and made her eat a muffin right before they opened the store doors to everyone. But their gazes kept finding each other across the busy room. Chloe hovered around Chelsea, keeping her distance but being right there to help when she needed. Now they had a moment just the two of them behind the counter after serving another lot of customers.

"I told you this would be great," Chloe whispered, pulling her into a side hug. "Dad would've loved this, Chels. He would be so damn proud of you."

Chelsea blinked back tears, nodding as she leaned into her sister. "I hope so."

The overhead doorbell jingled over the noise of people chatting around the store. Chelsea watched as her pregnant best friend and her husband walked through the door. Emily was stunning before, but pregnancy gave her a real glow. She had popped now and was finally over that stage where you couldn't tell if she was pregnant or had just had a big lunch.

"Sorry, we're late – someone insisted on stopping for fries on the way," Emily said as they approached Chelsea and Chloe. Chelsea rounded the counter to meet them.

Dean raised his hands, grinning. "Hey, don't look at me. She wanted them."

"Baby wanted them," Emily corrected with a laugh before pulling Chelsea into a tight hug. "This place looks insane, Chels. I'm so proud of you."

Chelsea hugged her back, giving her a gentle squeeze. She didn't want to squeeze her future niece or nephew too hard. Over Emily's shoulder, she noticed Ryan entering the shop, each of his hands holding a smaller hand. She smiled as she let go of Emily and waited for the girls to spot her. She vaguely noticed Emily squeeze her shoulder and mention that they were going over to see Jake and to have a look around, but Chelsea had her vision locked on the two girls walking over to her. Or rather, running over to her.

"Mum! I missed you!" Olivia said as she barrelled into Chelsea's arms.

Chelsea laughed, trying to keep her balance as she hugged her youngest daughter. "I missed you too! But we did see each other yesterday." She said with a wink as she looked down at Olivia.

Chelsea looked over at Lucy, who was looking around in awe at all the books. "So, what do you think, Luce?"

Lucy turned to look at her, a huge grin spreading across her face. "I think this might be my new favourite place."

Chelsea laughed, "I'm glad, because I am going to need your help around here." She reached out to pull her sister into a small group hug. "Grandma is around here somewhere; she mentioned something about apple juice in the fridge."

Lucy and Olivia squeezed their mum before they ran off down the aisles of books to find their grandmother.

Chelsea watched them run off before she turned back to Ryan. He was watching her with a small, gentle smile. He had the sleeves of his shirt rolled up and a relaxed vibe to him. It was new. But she assumed it could have something to do with the new woman he had mentioned to her. He had settled into his new job, and with that came new co-workers. Another doctor, in particular, he had really hit it off with. Ryan had pulled Chelsea aside a few weeks ago when she was dropping the girls off at his house to tell her that he had started seeing someone. Chelsea had given this situation some thought since they had separated, not knowing how she would feel when the time came. But surprisingly, she had felt genuinely happy for him. Chelsea had found someone who had turned her world upside down in the best way possible, so she could only hope Ryan would find that too.

Ryan stepped forward, "Congratulations, Chels," he said quietly. "You deserve it. All of this."

"Thanks, Ryan." She smiled.

He nodded toward the girls, "They're proud of you, too. We all are."

They both looked over to the girls who had now found Jake behind the café counter; she guessed they were convincing him to pour them some apple juice. Chelsea couldn't help but feel a flutter of unease as she watched them interact with Ryan standing beside her. Although this wasn't the first interaction with them all in the same room, it was still fresh, and she had never truly been able to read how Ryan felt in these moments.

After the night of the first football game, Chelsea and Jake decided to keep their new relationship just between them for the time being. This meant sticking to seeing each other only when Ryan or Chelsea's mum had the girls. She wanted to protect the girls since they had gone through so much change and grief over the past year. And they did have every intention of sticking to that, but this was Chelsea and Jake. There was nothing casual about them.

Chelsea had told Ryan about her and Jake shortly after the football game, before he found out through someone else. They had agreed to be open and honest with each other, and both wanted to meet their respective partners before being completely introduced to the girls. So that's what they did. About a month after that football game, Chelsea, Jake, and Ryan all met up for a quick coffee. It was awkward, and no one really knew how to act, but Jake and Ryan made small talk before Ryan received a call from work. Chelsea wasn't sure if it was a real call or just an excuse to get away quicker, but later that night, Ryan had called her and given her his blessing. He said he was happy for her and trusted her that he was a good guy to be around the girls. She was sure it wouldn't have been easy for him, but she was grateful that he was able to see how happy she was.

Then, before they knew it, Chelsea, Ryan, and Jake were all together celebrating Lucy's birthday. It was awkward to begin with, but having other family and friends there gave them all a buffer to maintain a polite distance. It was all still fresh, and she was sure the dynamic would change again once Ryan eventually brought someone else into the equation. For now, Chelsea was proud of how they were navigating this.

Ryan's voice cut through Chelsea's thoughts, "I will take the girls home after this, so you can celebrate and not worry about them while you are tidying up. And if you have time next week, I would like to chat with you about Renee from work. Things seem to be getting serious, but we can chat about that another time. Okay?"

Chelsea smiled, "Of course. Coffee next week."

"I know a new café, you'll love. Has books and everything." He said with a wink as he squeezed her arm and walked past her towards the girls and Jake.

Chelsea let out a laugh before she heard Chloe call out to her from behind the bookstore counter. She made her way over, smiling to herself.

~

The rest of the day stretched into a blur of laughter, new faces, old friends, and lots of sales. Locals bought coffee and browsed the shelves, many of them leaving with bags of books tucked under their arms. Jake floated around, switching between working behind the café counter and cleaning up empty coffee cups. Chelsea had hardly spoken to him since they had opened the doors earlier that day, but he was always close by. Small touches as he walked past, enough to keep her grounded.

By late afternoon, the last of the crowd had begun to thin. Chelsea stepped outside to take a minute for the first time all day. She leaned against the doorframe as the sun painted the town in a soft golden glow. Her body hummed with exhaustion, but her heart was full to the brim with gratitude.

Through the glass windows, she could see her mum laughing with Ryan and the girls at one of the tables, Dean fussing over Emily and her baby bump with Jake laughing beside them, and Chloe sharing a glass of champagne with Billy. Chloe and Billy had finally begun seeing each other exclusively in the past month, despite being together most weeks since that night at the beach. Chelsea smiled as she gazed back out over the beach, as she thought about all of her people in her shop behind her. The sight of them all in there together filled her with a fierce kind of love, a belonging she hadn't felt in years.

The door softly clicked open behind her. Jake slipped out, sliding one arm around her shoulders, pulling her to his chest. He then brought his other hand around her, holding a full glass of champagne.

"For you. You did it." He murmured against her hair.

Chelsea smiled, leaning back against him as she took the champagne glass from his hand.

"We did it," she corrected softly.

He chuckled against her, "I just made the coffee. This? This was all you, baby."

Chelsea tilted her head up at him, her heart twisting. For so long, she had been afraid. Afraid of wanting more, fearful of breaking again, afraid of what was next for her and her girls. But standing there looking up into Jake's steady gaze, she realised the fear was no longer loud. He had shown her, not only with his words but also with his actions, that he was really in this.

"You're really not going to run again, are you?" she asked quietly, but it came out more like a statement.

His brow furrowed slightly, his arm tightening around her. "What? Not a chance. You and the girls... you're it for me. Always have been."

Emotion swelled in her chest, sharp and sweet. She leaned her head back against his chest, bringing one of her hands to grip his arm that was tightly wrapped around her shoulders.

"So, what's next, Chels?"

Chelsea thought for a moment, realising for the first time she wasn't afraid of what would come next. She turned around to face him, "Next, we clean up and shut the shop. Then I am thinking we order pizza for dinner. And while we eat that, we should start looking for a place to live...together."

Jake's hand, which had been absentmindedly trailing up and down her arm, froze. "Really?"

Chelsea nodded, taking a sip of her champagne.

A huge grin took over Jake's face as he bent down, kissing her forehead softly before pulling back and cupping her face with his hands. "You have no idea how long I've been waiting to hear those words."

Chelsea laughed as Jake leaned down again and kissed her. She melted into the kiss, being sure not to spill her precious champagne in the process.

She couldn't believe where she was now compared to where she had been a year ago. A year ago, she was utterly lost, not knowing where or who she wanted to be. Now she was standing out the front of her very own store that was filled with all the people closest to her heart, both physically and in spirit, with the hottest guy ever. The guy who had known her and loved her since she was fourteen years old. The guy who she wanted to spend the rest of her life with.

Finally, Chelsea wasn't afraid of what came next.

She was ready for it.

THE END

ACKNOWLEDGEMENTS

Okay, wow! Thank you for getting to the end of my very first book (sorry, what??). I honestly cannot believe I have actually written and finished my first book. This was something I had always dreamt of doing after being an avid reader, but I just never managed to find the time, and to be honest, I didn't think I would be able to do it. I can't really remember the exact moment I decided to give it a real crack, but a story and characters came to me, so I just started writing. And well...here we are! There have been many moments throughout this journey where I have doubted myself, feeling as if I am crazy for thinking I could do this, but one thing I never doubted was this story. As a mother myself, Chelsea sang to me as someone who felt lost after having children, which I am sure many parents can attest to. I feel protective of these characters and this story, which makes putting this out into the world so much scarier! I had every intention of my first book being something light, funny and a little bit spicy (stay tuned!), but alas, I ended up writing something that often had me in tears or feeling overwhelmed with emotions.

Okay, enough about that for now. Time to thank the people I really could'nt have done this without.

Firstly, to my sister, Zigs. My proofreader, editor, and illustrater (wow, sorry. I probably should have paid you lol), thank you, thank you, thank you!! She was the first person to read the first draft of this book, because I knew she would give me honest feedback. She was there to bounce ideas off, and she even designed and illustrated the cover (what can't the girl do??). So, thank you, sis! I couldn't have done this without you, and I hope that going on this journey with me has given you the push to chase your own dreams. I promise the next book, I will pay you....

To my girls and husband. These three are my main driving forces (as well as the ones who drive me most crazy!). I felt lost after becoming a mother, but writing was something I always wanted to do. So, when I finally gave in and started this book, I often found myself sitting and writing with my eldest daughter beside me, writing her own story. I want to show them that they can do anything they put their mind to, and sometimes the scariest things are the most rewarding! So, thank you to you three for giving me the space and time to put this story on paper, finally.

Special shoutout to my parents for shaping me into who I am today and for always supporting me. I am sure my mum will finally be happy that I will let her read this after asking so many times when she could finally have a look! And Dad, I am sure he will never see this, but I appreciate you both!

And finally, to everyone who read this book (and hopefully loved it as much as I loved writing it), thank you!! Although I love this book enough, having you love it as well would be the cherry on top! I still find it surreal that this is actually out there, and people outside my circle can read my written words.

Ok, that's enough now. This is only the beginning of my journey, and I can't wait to share with you the next book!

Big love.
B xx

Bianca Lee Sharp

Bianca Lee Sharp is an Australian author who writes contemporary romance and women's fiction. When she's not writing, she is usually spending time with her family or escaping into the pages of a good book (she is a complete sucker for a good psychological thriller).

She believes the best stories come from everyday moments, a little bit of mess, and a lot of heart.